Intelligence

ALSO BY ROBERT NEWMAN

FICTION

The Trade Secret
The Fountain at the Centre of the World
Manners
Dependence Day

NON-FICTION

Neuropolis: A Brain Science Survival Guide
The Entirely Accurate Encyclopaedia of Evolution

Intelligence
Robert Newman

———

First published in Great Britain in 2026 by
SERPENT'S TAIL
an imprint of Profile Books Ltd
29 Cloth Fair
London EC1A 7JQ
www.serpentstail.com

Copyright © Rob Newman, 2026

1 3 5 7 9 10 8 6 4 2

Typeset in Tramuntana Text by MacGuru Ltd

Printed and bound in Great Britain by CPI Group (UK) Ltd, Croydon CR0 4YY

The moral right of the author has been asserted.

All rights reserved. Without limiting the rights under copyright reserved above, no part of this publication may be reproduced, stored or introduced into a retrieval system, or transmitted, in any form or by any means (electronic, mechanical, photocopying, recording or otherwise), without the prior written permission of both the copyright owner and the publisher of this book.

A CIP catalogue record for this book is available from the British Library.

Our product safety representative in the EU is BGC Sustainability & Compliance,
7 avenue du Général Leclerc, Paris, 75014, France https://baldwinglobalconsulting.com

ISBN 978 1 80522 661 1
eISBN 978 1 80522 663 5

Intelligence

1938

In at the Window

―

CLIMBING THROUGH A DIAMOND-LATTICE window sometime after midnight, Ida whispered to herself, not without surprise, 'I did it!' To scale the outside of All Souls was quite an achievement at any time, but to do so in the dead of night in a taffeta ball gown and while tipsy surely deserved an Oxford blue, a hero's welcome, a sweetheart's kiss.

She dropped from windowsill to floorboards and heard a cry in the dark. The nightstand light clicked on.

Glyn sat up in bed, hand on heart. 'How did you get up here?' he said.

'Little bit of wisteria work,' she said, 'a solid drainpipe and a gargoyle's snout.' Ida crossed the room, drank water straight from the tap and wiped her mouth with the back of her hand. 'I was practically Frenching that gargoyle. Can't believe I made it up to the fourth floor!'

'Actually, the third.'

'Fourth where I'm from. Only I do wish you still lived

out, so I could just knock on your front door and not have to risk my neck to see you.'

'I rather thought these ancient walls and gates would offer more protection.'

Ida stepped out of her ball gown. 'Think again.' She snuggled up to him under the sheets. Or tried to. When she kissed him, he didn't move his head towards her even a tiny bit. She had got more joy from the gargoyle.

'What's wrong?'

More nothing.

Waking at first light, she went through his closet for something to wear. From his cable-knit fisherman's jersey she eked a knee-length sweater dress. His woollen walking socks made a dandy pair of plaid stockings. She topped off the ensemble with his slouch hat. Sitting at his table, she read over his notes for a lecture he was preparing: 'On the difference between Epicurean and Stoic notions of ataraxia: the state of serene bliss'. She corrected a couple of misquotations, crossed out an elementary philosophical blunder and improved a translation – replacing 'serene bliss' and 'ecstatic peace' with 'heavenly joy'. That boy always went for transliteration over translation – but if you went and used a phrase that nobody ever spoke ('serene bliss'), then you lost the demotic feel of the original Greek.

When Glyn awoke, the fisherman's sweater achieved what the ball gown had not. An exciting start to the day, but she would have to watch him around trawler ships.

Out in the early morning Oxford mist, they walked to the market cafe, where they ate breakfast and drank large mugs of sweet, milky tea.

Glyn lowered his voice: 'I don't see you for days on end,

and then you climb in through the window when I'm asleep. I left a note under your door last week, and another in your pigeonhole. Not a word. Where've you been all this time?'

What to say? How to answer? She reviewed her misguided strategy. When Glyn had first introduced himself to her, she was flattered he should have come to her lecture, him being faculty and all. As they paced the quad, she told herself not to talk. *Listen. Don't gab.* But then he asked her to explain the title of her next lecture – 'The Influence of Lumberjacks on Plato' – and, well, that was a ten-minute answer right there. Even if she rushed it. When, after eight minutes, she dared to glance sideways, she was startled to find him still there! Still tagging along! And then she had a brainwave: why not ask him a question?

'So, uh,' she had said, 'what are you teaching?'

'Continental versus analytic philosophy,' he said.

'Ah, did you see Simone de Beauvoir's calamitous essay in the *Revue de Métaphysique*?'

'No, I only take it for the racing tips and the horoscope.'

'Any winners?'

'I bet big on Bad Faith in the three thirty at Kempton Park.'

'How did he do?'

'It was like he wasn't even trying.'

She had slipped her hand into his that same evening. But quickly won is quickly lost. She feared he would soon see through her, and that would be that. Early in their romance, therefore, she hit on a plan to postpone this inevitability: she would avoid him as much as possible. She found that, if she went a whole day without seeing him, the next day was a little easier, and so on, day after day. For a few months, this strategy seemed to be working, but now it appeared to have run out of road.

At the next table, two stallholders – fruit and veg, Glyn guessed, by the black earth under their fingernails – were discussing whether there would be another war.

'Well, I've decided to take a philosophical approach to the whole thing,' said one.

'How do you mean?' asked the other.

'I just refuse to think about it.'

Ida and Glyn's eyes met.

'Priceless,' he whispered.

'At last, a philosophical school I can believe in.'

As they ambled past the locked Botanic Garden, Glyn wondered whether his own refusal to think over his many doubts and fears about Ida was the only reason they were still together. He walked with her as far as All Souls, where he said, 'This afternoon, I shall talk for a whole hour on serene bliss.'

'You're welcome.'

As he watched her stride off, he let out a long breath and wondered whether the serene bliss (heavenly joy?) he now felt was the afterglow of her presence, or simple relief. Relief at getting himself back again. Whenever they parted, he felt he was sort of reassembling himself.

Reading her corrections to his lecture notes earlier that morning, he had seen that the elf made a better pair of shoes than the shoemaker. Each stroke of her pen had not just improved but saved his lecture. But the presumption irritated him – if she was so sure of the blunders in his work, why did she even bother with him?

Still, it had been sweet to walk hand in hand with her

in the fresh morning air, as the sun burnt through the mist. Glyn supposed he would ignore the warning signs that they were fundamentally ill-suited to each other and went days without seeing each other. Why spoil a good morning with the need to trace all the fault lines? Why rush to meet disaster? Let the costermonger's philosophical approach to war be his own approach to love. The Ostrich School would do for him. For now.

Idol of the Cave

THE STORAGE ROOM of the Pitt Rivers Museum was an odd combination of grand cast-iron pillars in amongst a cramped clutter of trays, boxes and shelves. Dr Dieter Wetzel sat at a workbench, his white gloves picking and pecking through chunks of broken mammoth tusk. The ivory rubble lay before him like a storm-damaged chess set. Some of the chunks were decorated with peculiar dots of ochre paint, many were carved and shaped. He was sure these fragments once formed a whole, but the question was, what? An idol? A utensil? A weapon? How do you reconstruct something when you don't know what it was to begin with? Where do you start?

Wetzel's method was to select pieces similar in shape or decoration. Not much of a method, he knew. After an hour of patient application, however, an order was emerging. His delight was intense. Never before had he felt so close to Upper Palaeolithic craftsmen. Never before had he experienced so strong a sense of receiving a twenty-thousand-year-old communiqué. Never before had he been so perfectly absorbed in his work.

So, when a kaleidoscope of gaudy lights flooded the workbench, he was vexed to the point of fury. Colourful rays stained his white cotton gloves and chunks of mammoth tusk, making his work impossible. Had sunlight struck a stained-glass window? Were students swivelling a spectrometer around?

He turned and was blinded by a multicoloured beam, full in the face. Shielding his eyes with a gloved hand, Wetzel made out a small woman holding a 35-mm colour projection slide up to the light. The source of the problem was wearing indigo denim jeans with shiny copper rivets like bad pennies. Over the thick denim she wore a thin cashmere jumper, subtly scarred by darning. It was uncanny how as tiny an object as that 35-mm Kodachrome, held at just the wrong position, should cast this large and catastrophic kaleidoscope. But how selfish of her not to notice. And how exasperating to be snapped out of his careful, painstaking, joyful work by one woman's ignorance.

Through gritted teeth, Wetzel said, 'Excuse me, please.'

She lowered the slide. 'Yes?'

Of course, the instant she lowered the slide, his gloves reverted to perfect whiteness and the tusk's ochre was restored. Now Wetzel had nothing to complain about but a five-second interruption.

Not wanting to look petty, he tried to rescue the situation: 'What's the slide?'

'Leg bone,' she said, and returned to her squinting.

'Whose?'

'Cro-Magnon,' she said, distractedly. She turned now and met his gaze, or rather looked through him, her mind preoccupied with what she'd been looking at. 'Yeah, and just left in the ground by the 1937 expedition like an old radish.'

He recognised her accent now. American. Of course. 'Was he a very important apeman?'

'Not an apeman at all. A Cro-Magnon, like I say, so, you know, a brain as big as yours or mine. Of equal intelligence.'

That 'yours or mine' was rather rich, thought Dieter. Her own skull was closer in size to the shrunken heads on display in the public galleries of the Pitt Rivers Museum.

'But you said this was a leg bone and not a skull,' he said.

'Yes. Take a look.' She passed him the slide. 'Now, what do you make of that mark on the femur?'

Covering one eye with a gloved hand, he squinted at the transparency. 'Calcite seam,' he said. 'Geological stain.'

'Get out of town!'

He lowered the slide. One was supposed to find this New World rudeness refreshing, and to be only too eager to shed one's fusty Old World values, such as good manners, decency and careful speech.

'I beg your pardon?'

'It's a fracture callus where a broken bone's mended,' she said. 'Absolutely extraordinary.'

'A broken leg is extraordinary?'

'Not that it broke, but that it healed, and that she lived for many years more, don't you see?'

'I'm afraid not.' He handed back the slide and click-clacked a finger through the ivory, hoping she would take the hint and leave. No such luck.

'It means she must have been cared for,' she said, 'which tells us something about Palaeolithic society, doesn't it?'

'Oh, no, no, no,' he said, holding up a white glove like a traffic policeman. 'No, no, that is too much, I'm afraid. Too much. From a tiny stain on a grubby bone, you deduce a caring society? That is far-fetched indeed. You would need to have the bones on a lab bench before you could establish even so modest a claim as the fracture callus, let alone your huge claim of Cro-Magnon altruism.'

'I know! I know! That's why I'm vexed y'all left her in the ground. I ask you, what sort of expedition leaves such a find as this behind?'

'The 1937 La Grotte Ardennes Expedition, that's who. And, given that we brought back perhaps the earliest human artworks ever discovered, I think we might be forgiven.'

'You mean this ivory bric-a-brac?'

'These pieces are part of a larger whole.'

'They look to me like those knucklebone dice used by the ancient Greeks. How do you know they're not supposed to be the size they are now?'

'Perhaps because I'm the acting professor of palaeoanthropology at Göttingen.'

'But not a professor of logic, I see.'

'No, palaeoanthropology, as I just told you.'

'You did indeed. You did indeed.'

'And as such I tell you,' he said in the voice of an adult scolding a child, 'that these pieces were once part of something much larger.'

'I think it might have been a mammoth.'

Dieter Wetzel's neck and face flushed hot. She was mocking him. Ridiculing his work. 'No, I mean a large figurative sculpture. You can see how these mammoth tusks have been carved and worked. If this all does in fact turn out to be figurative sculpture, then here we have a major landmark in world history.'

'This healed femur is a greater landmark,' she replied.

'That bone is a landmark?'

'It's evidence of love.'

'You must be one very hungry dog to look at that bone and see love.'

'And you must be very hungry for tenure,' she said, 'to look at these rummage-sale runes and see art. Where's the art in this boneyard rubble?'

Just when she thought they were on their way to a good old slanging match, he gave her an unexpectedly disarming smile and said, 'You tell me! I don't have a clue.'

'Really?'

'I don't suppose you would consider casting an eye over all this broken ivory? See if you can find any chunks that go together?'

'Oh no, not I,' she replied. 'I wouldn't know where to begin.'

'That could be a blessing in disguise,' he said. 'The innocent eye, don't you know?'

'But I don't even know what to look for.'

From a drawer he produced a fresh pair of white gloves. 'If you would,' he said, standing up and offering his place.

She pulled on the magician's gloves and wiggled her fingers at him. 'Just don't expect magic,' she said. She climbed on to the stool, placed her hands flat on the workbench either side of the fractured mammoth tusks and studied the problem. She understood now that these ivory chunks possessed a curious sense of latency. One second she was looking at boneyard rubble, and the next she couldn't tear her eyes away, mesmerised. She weighed a fragment in her hand. It sat in her palm, the thigh of a half-remembered china doll. She stirred a few ochre-stained chunks, looking for one shape in particular.

'What are you doing?'

'Hush, now.'

Dieter Wetzel watched as she rolled a silver dollar around the fingers of her white glove. Without looking, she flicked the coin at the ceiling. He looked up. The coin vanished in mid-air.

'Top pocket,' she muttered, staring at the ivory pieces.

'Pardon?'

'Top pocket.'

It took him a moment to understand her meaning and check the top pocket of his herringbone jacket, where he found her silver dollar.

Ida locked two tusk fragments together with a satisfying click. Her white gloves began to fly this way and that, fitting one piece to another. With each piece that locked into place, she was more certain which to pick up next, until she was cradling a seven-inch figurine of a woman with a lion's head. Like a midwife, she angled the statuette towards the proud father for inspection.

'*Ein Löwenmensch!*' cried Dieter. 'We found *ein Löwenmensch!*' In the joy of discovery, the haughty, snippy acting professor vanished like the dew, leaving instead a sweet and endearing boy, full of innocent delight. He put his face close to the figurine and whispered, 'Welcome to our world, little man!'

'Man? That's a woman, bud! *Eine Löwenfrau.*'

'But look at the mane,' he said. 'It's a male lion's head.'

'She's wearing a headdress, dummy.'

'It's clearly the head of a lion on the body of a man.'

'One day, you may save up enough money to see a naked

lady in the flesh, but till that day comes, just take it from me, won't you? That there's a woman. In fact, I'd hazard a guess she's the medicine woman.'

'A witch doctor? Why do you say that?'

'Kiowa medicine women wear wolf heads.'

'Kiowa? Where's this?'

'North-west Texas. Wolf heads and buffalo heads, too.'

'Ah, but does a medicine woman wear a *male* buffalo head?'

'If it's powerful medicine. If it does the trick. Sure.'

'May I?'

The ivory chunks chinked, wobbled and settled as she handed him the lion lady. The proud father cradled the idol of the cave in his arms. With extreme care, he laid the lion-headed statuette on the workbench and began to number its fragments.

Ida crossed the lab and switched on the projector. It hummed and she could smell the dust on its surface toasting.

'For God's sake,' he said. 'How can you be going back to your mouldy old bones only moments after we have reconstructed this absolutely historic treasure?'

'*Naturwissenschaft über Kulturwissenschaft*,' she said. Natural science over cultural studies.

'Unbelievable.'

She sorted through a little pile of slides and slotted a promising one into the projector. A cave in the Ardennes sprang on to an Oxford wall. She focused the beam, sharpening the image. Around the Last Glacial Maximum, a subterranean river wound through La Grotte Ardennes. That river was long gone, leaving in its wake a cave wall plastered in calcite crust. This crust was patchy, exposing cap rock here and there. On a strip of exposed cap rock, on the wall behind the Cro-Magnon bones, there swirled a constellation of brown spots. Squinting through the 35-mm slide, she'd taken those spots for blotches of damp. But now it dawned on her that this pattern of dots was made by human hands.

And then she experienced something extraordinary, a sudden shift that made her head spin. With one of those gestalt flips in which rabbit ears become a duck bill, or two white noses one black candlestick, the abstract pattern of dots revealed themselves to be a spotted hyena. Once seen, the hyena could not be unseen. How could she ever have thought it anything else? With its ass-dragging, cringing gait and crest of fur on its sloping back, it could *only* be a hyena. The hyena's head was hidden by calcite, but the rest of the body broke cover.

'Look!' she cried. 'A hyena! The Ice Age cave hyena!'

'If the rest of the painting is to scale,' he said, 'then what's hidden under the calcite will be a mural the size of *The Last Supper*.'

'Should have chiselled that wall when you had the chance!'

'Oh, what a find we left behind!'

'Now you know how I feel about that femur.'

'This painted hyena might persuade Göttingen to fund a return expedition to the Ardennes. To discover both the cave painting and the *Löwenmensch* within minutes of each other! Oh, my! Oh, my! Does nothing escape you? I must offer you my sincere thanks, Miss … ?'

'Ida Marshall.'

He peeled off a white glove and extended his hand. 'Wetzel. Dr Wetzel. Dr Dieter Wetzel.'

'Pleased to meet you, Dieter!'

'Do you know, I think this may also be my first conversation with anyone since I arrived in Oxford, Miss Marshall.'

'Well, then you must come along to my rooms at Somerville tonight. It's an informal discussion group and the presence of an outsider might make even philosophers behave in a civil fashion.'

The Rule of Law

―

IDA'S ROOMS ON F STAIRCASE, Somerville College, were bent out of shape by a curving wall, shared with a spiral staircase and a folly tower. The party wall bulged into the living room and the ceilings sloped along different planes. Merry said it was like being on the wrong side of a novelty cake mould. From the living room's sunken floor, six steps led up to a little landing, with only four balusters in the short balustrade, like a demonstration model in a joinery class.

Gathered in F7 that evening were Glyn, Merry, Austin, Shaya, Vernon Alwynne and Ida's guest, Dieter Wetzel.

'Should we,' asked Glyn, sitting on the third step, 'close the gates of a level crossing, trapping two people in the way of a speeding train, if by so doing we save twenty people stuck on the track further down the line?'

Merry was perched on the arm of F7's tatty armchair, repairing Ida's crown plait, which was unravelling on one side of her head. She was keen to maintain this corona braid for fear that Ida would revert to the distressing pigtails she sometimes wore. While Merry fixed Ida's hair, she grew vexed by the breezy way in which Glyn said, 'It's the same principle as in the ticking time-bomb situation.'

'How does that one go, again?' asked Vernon Alwynne from the deckchair.

'The prisoner knows the deactivation code on the time bomb. If he tells us the code, we can switch it off ourselves. So, the question is, should we torture this prisoner *now*, so as to achieve fewer deaths in the *future*?'

Slotting the last hair grip into Ida's crown plait, Merry said, 'But, Glyn, all these actions you're considering are against the law.'

'I imagine they are. But sometimes one must break the law in the cause of justice.'

'Well, that's big of you,' she said, 'but what strikes me is that you don't mention the law *at all*. Isn't this a rather serious omission?'

'What do you mean?'

Merry stood up to refill her glass from the bottle of Malbec on the mantelpiece and said, 'The fact that law-breaking is involved changes the nature of a question. For example, if you say to me, "Merry, please will you help me push this car back to my house?" that is a very different question from, "Merry, please will you help me push this car that I like the look of back to my house?" But you fail even to *mention* the law.'

Austin barked a laugh and banged the table. Balding, bright eyed, bespectacled and lean as a whippet, the twenty-nine-year-old-year-old John Langshaw Austin was Oxford's leading philosopher.

'You misunderstand the nature of these proceedings, Merry,' said Glyn. 'This is not a planning meeting.'

'No, Glyn, she's got you there,' said Shaya, dropping the needle of Ida's record player on Toscanini's new recording of *La Traviata*.

'Come on, Ida,' said Glyn, 'you're a Wild West sort of a girl. Please tell Merry that sometimes these ugly realities have to be grasped. Tell her that's the value of thought experiments.'

'Well, honey,' said Ida, 'I find the phrase "thought experiment" a tad exalted for what you've been up to this last half hour. In all your highfalutin realpolitik, I hear nothing but the pirate code.'

'What on earth do you mean? I simply don't understand you.'

'Yes, I don't understand you, either,' said Alwynne. 'Not a word!'

It was a curious feature of Oxford philosophy that the less you understood what someone said, the cleverer you were. Failure to understand a single word meant you were a genius. The ultimate put-down was to say, 'I don't know what you mean,' or, 'I don't understand you.' Merry and Ida often puzzled over why this should be so. How did it come about that it was your fault when your interlocutor didn't understand, and not his? Surely it wasn't the same in other subjects. Would Gottlob Frege say, 'Differential calculus? Nope. You lost me. Not a clue.' Would Marie Curie say, 'Atomic number? What's that when it's at home?' Merry wondered whether studied incomprehension was a prerequisite for careers in the Colonial Office, where purblindness to the crimes of empire was essential, or for a career in banking, where appeals to the human costs of foreclosing a mom-and-pop store had to look not just jejune but so far off the mark as to be incomprehensible. Maybe. But there was something else too, she thought: an imputation that you had strayed so far from ordinary human concerns as to be operating on a level that only dogs could hear but not proper, decent men. Something like that. Merry never felt she completely penetrated the mystery of why incomprehension became glamorous, but, for whatever reason, both Glyn Gower and Vernon Alwynne looked decidedly chuffed with themselves when they said they simply didn't understand Ida, not a word.

'Standpoint,' said Ida. 'Standpoint.'

'I'm none the wiser,' said Glyn.

'Me neither,' said Alwynne.

'All your thought experiments,' said Ida, 'take the standpoint of powerful people for whom the law holds no fear, deciding the fates of powerless people, for whom the law offers no protection. It's the pirate code, m'hearties, pure and simple.'

'No, no, no,' said Vernon Alwynne. 'You're failing to grasp the nettle here, my dear.' His drinker's flush and tight blond curls gave him the look, Ida once said, of the painting Shirley Temple keeps in her attic. Merry thought he looked more like a Toby jug. 'Look at it this way,' Vernon Alwynne now explained. 'If by pushing a large man into the path of an oncoming train, I thereby save the lives of dozens of folk further down the line, then, you see, I have a moral duty to shove this chap off the platform. Same with trapping the people in the level crossing when the express is due. Sacrificed for the greater good and all that.'

'About these extra-judicial killings on the railway network,' said Austin. 'It seems to me that these killings have a suppressed premise, which is that we live in a World Without Law. But you haven't thought this through,

Alwynne, for, in a World Without Law, the train driver need obey no speed limits, no signals, need not be sober nor even know how to drive a train. And in this libertarian paradise, I submit, nobody is boarding any trains anyway, nor even going near one.'

'No, Austin, with respect, I'm afraid that's a non sequitur,' said the oblivious Alwynne, not hearing the click of level-crossing gates behind him, nor the train track's subtle didgeridoo as the express approached. 'Because, you see, when one law is repealed, it simply does not follow that every other law in the statute book has to be changed as well. Even after the repeal of homicide laws, it's perfectly likely that transport rules and regulations would still apply.'

Austin knocked out his pipe on the table. Merry always compared the knocking of his dottle to a railway wheel-tapper detecting a crack with his hammer. In tutorials, Austin's thoughtful tap-tap-tapping of his pipe was all that was needed for the wheels to come off whatever foolish argument you were hoping to advance.

'What sort of regime,' asked Austin, 'decriminalises murder but remains a stickler for train regulations? Who's in charge, here? It seems to me, Alwynne, that you're far too hopeful of an Oswald Moseley landslide victory at the next election.'

Alwynne flushed right up to the centre parting of his curly blond hair while everybody laughed.

Feeling sorry for him, Merry shifted the pressure back on to Glyn, saying, 'Unlike in the dreamland of your thought experiment, Glyn, in our world the rule of law obtains. In our world, there is a law against murder, which means that it will *never, ever* be your decision who to kill.'

And it was at this moment that Ida's German guest Dieter Wetzel spoke.

'What about during a war?' he asked.

'Well, now,' Ida told her guest, 'that takes us into a different area of law.'

'But not of philosophy, I think,' said Wetzel. 'So, let me ask you – all of you – the following question: if you could prevent a world war between our two nations by killing one person, would you do it?'

'Can it be Alwynne?' said Ida.

'You are using humour to avoid answering the question,' said Wetzel. 'This tactic is well known, but not well respected.'

Merry was impressed by the confidence with which he, a palaeo-archaeologist, stood up to explicate things to some of the leading lights of Oxford philosophy. But she was also a little troubled by his curious mixture of energy and stillness, which put her in mind of an electric whip.

Wetzel looked around the room and said, 'I see I have set the cat among the pigeons.'

'No, I'm with you, Wetzel,' said Glyn. 'I can't believe the rest of you believe that we must sacrifice hundreds of thousands on the altar of a point of principle.'

To which Merry replied, 'But who gave you, Glyn Gower, or you, Vernon Alwynne, or, with the greatest respect, you, Herr Doktor Dieter Wetzel, the power over life and death?'

1940

The Interpretations of Wembley

WALKING IN THE EARLY EVENING from Wembley station to work, Merry saw smoke from an allotment bonfire rise vertically into a cloudless sky. If the skies over Mecklenburg or the Baltic littoral were anything like this, she would find a rich haul of reconnaissance photographs awaiting her. Imagining the crystal-clear definition of the latest aerial photographs of north-eastern Germany, she quickened her pace over the broken glass and debris littering Beresford Road since last night's bombing raid. What she loved most about her job was how she became attuned to far-off places. Was it like this, she wondered, for fishermen? Did a Dorset fisherman sniff the wind and deduce weather conditions in Wight, Sole and Fastnet? Certainly it must be like this for migratory birds, as they attended to whatever cues from the earth's magnetic fields sent them from a chimney pot in Tenby to a courtyard in Tunis.

Lorries thundered by on the North Circular as she entered through the double doors of a white two-storey building, under large black letters: *AIRCRAFT OPERATING*

CO. LTD – INCORPORATING AEROFILMS. She wiped her feet on the mat, stamping the broken glass from her shoes, and climbed the stairs.

Here, in this little white suburban factory, Merry studied aerial reconnaissance photographs using a novel technique called 3D spectrometry. This involved placing two aerial photographs of the same location, taken a second apart by a speeding aeroplane, side by side under a stereoscope, a little three-inch-high platform with two inset magnifying lenses. If the two photos, known as 'covers', were arranged just so under the stereo, then quite magically a three-dimensional image sprang into being when looking through the lenses, which had the effect of throwing into relief all kinds of details lost in the plan view. Shadows became shapes, dimensions and angles.

There had been talk of evacuating the Photographic Interpretation Unit away from Wembley's bomb-worthy goods yards, railway sidings and light industry. But other civil and military departments had already requisitioned the most suitable country piles within a thirty-mile radius of London, and so here they stayed. As a stopgap measure until a move, sandbags surrounded the squat white building, but for some reason – lack of sand? Jute? Men? – the sandbags stopped halfway up the wall. Merry's desk was on the first floor, above the sandbags, which let her enjoy natural light through her east-facing window when dawn broke at the end of her shift. Like Mimi in *La Bohème*, in her little white room looking over rooftops and the sky, the first sun was hers – *il primo sole è mio*. But she hoped that, unlike Mimi, she would not pay for this privilege with her life, should a bomb drop near her un-sandbagged, east-facing desk.

She hung up her coat and rolled her shirt cuffs over the sleeves of her tweed houndstooth jacket. Merry's first task at the start of each night shift was to review the day shift's work before sending it out to Joint Intelligence. Top of the pile, the day shift had left a shouty note: *New Baltic Oil Silo! For Urgent Attn. Bomber Command!*

If the enemy were indeed building new oil infrastructure on the Baltic, that would offer a fresh clue as to their strategic thinking, as well as providing an early warning of where the next build-up of forces would occur. But that was still no reason to use capitals and exclamation marks. The note was paper-clipped to a pair of black-and-white covers. She placed her stereoscope over the five-by-five-inch photographs. Beneath the glass, she could see the disc of the putative oil silo. With both hands, she fidgeted with each photo, trying to coax what she privately called 'the pop' or 'the lunge'. This was her term for the moment when the covers suddenly became three-dimensional, like when the foreground blur in Holbein's *The Ambassadors* turns into a skull when looked at from the right angle. Often, when it came, she instinctively jerked back her head as the image lunged at her. But, at the start of this night shift, the 3D effect just wouldn't come. Try as she might, Merry couldn't coax the pop or lunge into being. This sometimes happened. The 3D effect could be elusive. The trick she'd learnt was to get into a certain receptive frame of mind, to allow the hidden perspective to come to her. Was she trying too hard to summon the image? Was she imposing her own assumptions? But then it occurred to her – and here, perhaps, a philosophical training helped – that the problem was not the perceiver but the percept, not perception but reality. The problem was not inside her, but outside in the world.

For, if this were indeed an oil silo, where were the service roads for the oil-tanker lorries? Where was the trackway flattened by workers' boots? (Grass trampled by boots or vehicles showed up lighter than undisturbed grass. She loved this fact for its timelessness. Skills that a Pleistocene hunter might have possessed while she looked down upon open savannah from a treetop canopy, Merry possessed still. Except her search was done through a stereoscope placed upon two overlapping photographs taken one second apart by a speeding plane.)

She noticed a strange bump on the circumference of the alleged oil silo and thought it might be a clue to help explain why the oil silo stayed stubbornly flat and 2D. From a side drawer she carefully extracted a small velvet purse. She pulled its ribbon drawstring and lifted out a clothier's loupe, stumpy as a jeweller's glass. This powerful magnifier was designed for counting the number of threads in a weave. She had bought it with her own cash from her family's South Molton Street tailor. She set the loupe on one of the two photographs, over where she had seen that inexplicable bump on the circumference of the supposed oil silo. She put her eye to the loupe. To her delight, the bump resolved itself into the perfect silhouette of a goat. On a long tether, the old goat had been mowing the grass round and round, day after day, describing a perfect circle that grew and grew until it was visible from the air, the size and shape of an oil silo.

Merry chuckled at the day shift's howler. She was happy to have spared not just the innocent goat but also the crew of whichever Wellington or Lancaster bomber would have been unlucky enough to have been sent on this fool's errand. Indeed, such was the inaccuracy of RAF bombing raids, she may well have saved the lives of anyone living within a fifty-mile radius of that goat. She crossed out the day shift's melodramatic *New Baltic Oil Silo! For Urgent Attn. Bomber Command!* In its place, she wrote, *Old Nanny Goat! No Bombing Needed!* She paper-clipped the note to the cover and placed it on the day shift's desk.

She reviewed the rest of the day shift's work, forwarding some discoveries to the Central Interpretation Unit and filing the rest in one of the overstuffed ring binders lining the shelves that ran the length of all four walls.

Some of the binders were labelled by infrastructure, which gave them pleasingly Auden-esque titles such as 'The Interpretations of Shipyards', or 'Aerial Masts and Other Decoys', or – and this was her personal favourite – 'Possible Communications Transmitters'. Less Auden, this one, more Wittgenstein, with its focus on possible communications only. Whereof one cannot speak, thereof one must be silent. *Wovon man nicht sprechen kann, darüber muss man schweigen.* Merry had always thought this to be a very Cambridge way of telling one to shut one's cakehole. She'd been present when Elizabeth Anscombe brought Wittgenstein to Oxford to speak at (perform for?) the Jowett Society. Having seen him in the flesh, Merry could no longer hear the phrase 'thereof one must be silent' without seeing his arms irritably chopping down anything anybody said if it deviated in the slightest from what he would have said himself.

The day shift's work squared away, Merry was at last able to get down to studying the fresh covers from her own designated area, the German north-eastern Baltic municipalities. The five-inch-square photos on her desk came from Spitfires and de Havilland Mosquitoes which had flown over Mecklenburg around noon, before returning to RAF Benson or RAF Heston, where 'First Phase' PIs, or Photographic Interpreters, had printed the negatives and dispatched them by train or motorcycle to Wembley and Merry's 'Third Phase' analysis.

When she placed her stereoscope over the first covers, she saw that, just as she'd hoped, the cloudless skies of north-west London had indeed spent the early morning floating over north-east Germany. She stared through the lenses of her spectroscope at a three-dimensional Baltic morning as bright and clear as if she were looking through a glass-bottomed boat at Mediterranean shallows. The edges of buildings were pencil sharp, the shadows well defined. When she looked up from her stereoscope, it was a shock to see how dark the night was outside her first-floor window. Not just ordinarily dark, but the new primordial darkness of the blackout.

It was around midnight when she came upon an odd coastal structure that looked like a ski jump. But is there skiing by the shore? One suspected not. If not a ski jump, she wondered, could it be a rollercoaster or amusement park ride of some sort? A giant slide? But this spit of land with its cluster of small villages was no Blackpool or Coney Island.

She went to the basement to have the covers reproduced, then sent them, along with map references, to the Central Interpretation Unit at the Air Ministry and filled out a formal request slip for an RAF sortie. In her card index, she jotted down the words: *Peenemünde: odd ski-jump structure. Poss. rocket launcher (?) Sortie requested.*

Had she known then the significance this structure was one day to have, both personally and militarily, even she might have used capitals and exclamation marks.

F Staircase Break-up

―――

'IT'S NOT ABOUT MERRY, for the umpteenth time,' said Glyn. 'It's about the sixty miles from Oxford to London. It's about my being there and your being here. I just wish there were two of me.'

'You'd both be in love with Merry,' said Ida.

'You're too much for me.'

'I'm half her size.'

'It's not about her,' said Glyn. 'Why won't you listen?'

'If you've fallen in love with her,' she said, 'I can't say I blame you. I love her too.'

'I know you do,' he said.

'And, if all the graffiti around town is to be believed, fourth base with Merry is really something.'

'That's beneath you,' he said.

'As once, in a happy hour, were you.'

'For God's sake, Ida.'

She was worried that he had kept his coat on. She used to like this cream shorty mac, which made him look like

Charles Boyer, the French movie star. This evening, she hated it.

He usually threw his coat over the banister before perching on the third step up to the inner room, but not today. Shunning the tatty salvage armchair and the faded stripy deckchair, he stood there like a bailiff, both hands thrust in the pockets of the mac.

'Are the two of you spending a lot of time together?' she asked.

'Not in the sense you mean,' he said. 'Our war work throws us together.'

'Sounds sexy.'

'Merry and I both work in intelligence, so we meet up and talk shop. That's all.'

'Are you dating?'

'Merry is far too loyal a friend of yours ever to tolerate my two-timing you.'

'Ah, so that's why you're here.'

'What do you mean?'

'You've come to get a pass.'

'Quite apart from anything else,' said Glyn, 'you're off to France on sabbatical, so where does that leave me and you?'

'Well, I've decided not to go to France after all.'

'Why ever not?'

'I was thinking that we could live together in London, while I look for war work myself.'

'But why not go to France?'

'Don't you know there's a war on?'

'A phoney war.'

'So far.'

'Shouldn't be too risky,' he said. 'France has the

impregnable Maginot Line after all. Imperial are still flying to Paris.'

The way he was packing her off was so cold. Scalding tears pricked her eyes and began to roll down her cheeks.

'Every word you say is so cut-and-dried,' she sobbed. 'I didn't see this coming.' She wanted him to put an arm around her shoulder. But, at the same time, she didn't, because it wouldn't be a loving arm, it would be a cold, stiff, formal arm, a consoling anglepoise. So, she knuckled her eyes and said, 'I didn't know I'd lost you for good. I thought you were just having one of your cold snaps.'

'*My* cold snaps,' he cried. '*My* cold snaps? You've got a nerve! You're the one who disappears for weeks at a time with no explanation.'

'I didn't want you to get sick and tired of me.'

'I'm sick and tired of waiting for you, sick and tired of thinking you've dropped me every time you vanish. I feel like a glass that cracks under cold, then hot, then cold water. I spend whole days listening to Billie Holiday records, mourning your loss, only for you to come in through the window, like we've been playing hide-and-seek. I'm sorry, Ida, but I just can't take it any more.'

And then he was out through both doors, and she was alone.

Back in his All Souls rooms, Glyn was elated no longer to be holding on to what he couldn't keep. He rejoiced to be free to begin the next part of his life. Outside his fifteenth-century diamond-pane window, a waxing moon was completing itself. He set out his best stationery and uncapped his Mont Blanc fountain pen. He had a letter to write.

The point of the letter was to tell Merry he was now single, but he knew he'd best be careful not to let it read that way, not to let slip any trace of jubilation, like a wine ring staining a letter of condolence. So, he chose a middle course: cut up about the split, while maintaining a manful sense of proportion.

Among the privations of war, it would be unseemly for me to bewail lost love – especially when one thinks of the sufferings of the North Atlantic convoys torpedoed in the night.

He folded the letter and addressed the envelope to Merry's Soho flat in Denman Alley. The moon emerged from behind a cloud and spangled his room with diamonds of light, which crossed the wooden floor like golden footprints, one after the other, through the window and straight to the sink. The shadow of the gargoyle entered the room. He experienced a moment of utter tranquillity.

Among the privations of war ... He didn't quite recognise this voice as his own. But perhaps that was because, with Merry, he was becoming a new and different man. If he and Merry should become lovers, theirs would be a more grown-up affair.

He went round his two rooms, closing each and every catch on each and every fifteenth-century diamond-lattice window.

Snakehips Swing

IN THE CAFÉ DE PARIS, off Piccadilly Circus, Ken 'Snakehips' Johnson, band leader of the West Indian Dance Orchestra, stepped up to the microphone.

'Ladies and gentlemen, please welcome tonight's guest star, the one and only Al Bowlly!'

Al Bowlly's slow swing version of an old Shakespearean song had become an unlikely hit. The floor filled with dancers as he crooned:

'It was a lover and his lass,
With a hey and ho and a hey nonny no,
That over green cornfields did pass
In springtime, the springtime.
The only pretty ring time ...'

Glyn marvelled at how effortlessly Merry glided over the dance floor. Her dance steps flowed as smoothly as the silver satin of her heart-stopping sleeveless dress. Under his palm, he could feel the satin slide over the fall of her back and the bumps of her spine. He leant closer to inhale the scent of her hair, her neck.

She wore silver, he wore a white tuxedo to show her he knew how things were done in London. But he didn't, and he'd blundered. Every other man was wearing a black jacket. The only man in a white tuxedo, apart from Glyn, was Ken 'Snakehips' Johnson.

Al Bowlly left the stage to tremendous applause. The West Indian Dance Orchestra struck up with 'Snakehips Swing'. A single spot followed Ken as he sashayed off the stage, down the steps and on to the dance floor, passing through the dancers to cut in on Merry and Glyn. Ken began dancing cheek to cheek not with Merry, but with Glyn, dancing him all the way back to the stage. Holding Glyn's hand, Ken stepped up to the microphone and pointed at the rival white tuxedo.

'A pretender to the throne!' With elaborate ceremony, he presented his conductor's baton to Glyn, then turned him to face the swing band, who were vamping the intro to 'Tuxedo Junction'. 'Swing it, boy! Let's see what you've got!'

Well, how hard could it be? Glyn grinned and began waving the baton up and down in time to the beat: da-da-DA, da-da-DA, da-da-DA. In response, the swing band played a crazy drunken cacophony that drew gales of laughter from the audience. The trombone blew one tempo, the cornet another, while the saxophone wailed a whole other tune altogether.

'No! No! Nooooo!' Ken cried, and demonstrated a regular 4/4 tempo by moving his hand like a papal blessing.

When Glyn copied this with the baton, the West Indian Dance Orchestra mercilessly played the 'Dead March' from *Saul*.

'You're killing business!' Ken wailed into the microphone. 'Return my baton, puh-llleeeeze!'

He led the audience in a round of applause for Glyn, who bowed and left the stage to find Merry.

'I'm afraid that may have been my fault,' she told him at their table. 'I taught Ken when he was reading law at UCL.'

'But you're a philosophy fellow, not a lawyer.'

'Philosophy of law. I'm probably the reason he packed it in at the end of the first year to study dance.'

'Where's he from?'

'Marlow. But who'd pay coin of the realm to see the Buckinghamshire Dance Orchestra?'

'That's almost as exotic as Wembley,' said Glyn. 'How's life with your head bent over a stereoscope?'

Merry looked at him with her eyes crossed. 'I don't think it's affecting me too much, do you? How's work with you?'

As the conversation turned to intelligence work, they spoke in lowered voices, with their heads almost touching. Every now and then, one of them would glance around to check that nobody was listening. It was all rather excitingly like two people conducting an illicit affair, Glyn thought. Secret lovers, not secret operatives.

'I've been studying B-Dienst communications all week,' he said.

'B-Dienst?'

'German naval codebreakers. The *Beobachtungsdienst*.'

'Observation service,' she translated.

'Yes, and I believe the B-Dienst have broken the Royal Naval Administrative Code.'

'What makes you think that?'

'The sheer tonnage of ships sunk off Norway.'

'How often does the navy change their codes?'

'They don't,' said Glyn.

'But have you told the Admiralty their code may be broken?'

'Only fifty million times! They just don't believe me.'

'How very galling,' said Merry.

They held their tongues while a cocktail waitress set their G & Ts down on the white linen tablecloth and changed their ashtray. The instant she left, their heads drew close again. Glyn kept forgetting that this was not because of romance, but because of the Official Secrets Act. Was this distinction becoming as hazy for her as it was for him?

Perhaps he was about to find out, for tonight he was going to make a confession. Though it was a confession about work, not love, if she had feelings for him, it might bind them closer together. Half his reason for confessing was to show Merry how much he trusted her, so it was, in a topsy-turvy way, also a declaration of love. And he wanted her to admire how brave and principled he was, too.

'Yesterday morning,' he began, 'I was supposed to pass information about the positions of merchant ships to Royal Naval Intelligence, but I just couldn't let all those boys drown in the North Atlantic.'

'You withheld intelligence from the navy?'

'Yes, but also from the U-boats and the Kriegsmarine.'

'Oh, Glyn! What have you done?'

'Saved lives, that's what I've done! Stopped German torpedoes sinking our merchant ships, that's what I've done! I'm surprised you can't see that.'

'Off your own bat?'

'Nobody else at MI14 knows what I did, if that's what you mean.'

'So, you did it on a whim?'

'Not on a whim! Why do you say "whim"? My God,

Merry! What could be less whimsical than life or death? Hundreds of sailors would be dead but for me.'

'Says who? You don't know that. All you know is one tiny corner of a vast and complex intelligence picture, and yet you arrogate to yourself all the power of a Sea Lord.'

'What if one corner of the picture is all I need to make a solid inference?' Glyn asked.

'That's called a guess,' said Merry, the ordinary-language philosopher. 'You guess the code is cracked, but you don't know. Guesswork is often wrong. Inference is the word we use when we base our decisions on evidence, but you have no evidence that the codes are cracked, so far as I can see. Just a hunch.'

'My evidence is all the merchant ships being sunk. I'd call that ten thousand tons of solid evidence.'

'But evidence of what? Most people would conclude this to be evidence that German U-boat crews are learning on the job and getting good at what they do. What most people wouldn't do is commit an act of treason.'

'What do you mean by "treason"?'

'To aid and abet the Kriegsmarine by depriving the Royal Navy of intelligence information sounds like treason to me. You're going to end up in jail, Glyn Gower.'

'How can it be treason to save British sailors?'

'But what if *more* merchant seamen perish, thanks to you?'

'That's conjecture about the future, but a fact about the present is that, when I keep a ship's course secret, I save many sailors' lives. Can't you see that?'

'Dear God, Glyn, it sounds like you plan to do it again.'

'If I have to.'

'If I have to! If I have to! Hark at the hero's lonely vigil!

Hark at Mussolini, guided by his divine afflatus. If I have to! But it's not your decision to take, Glyn. And never will be!'

'We're not on F Staircase now, Merry. This is not abstract philosophy. There are real-world consequences here.'

Glyn's crass remark so angered Merry that she did not trust herself to speak for several minutes. She quivered with rage.

Eventually, she allowed herself to say, 'You sound like a travelling salesman in a hotel bar.'

'And you sound like a snob.'

'If ever there were an instance of philosophy *not* being abstract it is right now, because the crime you just committed stems *precisely* from the very philosophy you were spouting that night in Ida's rooms on F Staircase. All your heroic grasping of nettles! All your brave confronting of ugly realities the rest of us run from!'

'Merry, you're attracting attention.'

'You were a fool to suppress intelligence, and you were a fool to finish with Ida.' She lifted and slammed the glass ashtray on the table.

Glyn held up his hands in a placatory gesture, desperate for her to calm down and not make a scene. 'All right,' he said. 'Please, don't storm out.'

'I'm not leaving, Glyn. You are. Goodnight.'

He left his cigarettes behind. Player's Navy Cut. Merry tapped one out and lit it at the candle. She knew exactly the night he'd been referring to when he said, 'We're not on F Staircase now.' Their discussion of justifiable homicide, back in Ida's rooms, now seemed uncannily prescient. It seemed to Merry that a line ran straight as a train track between the tosh Glyn had trotted out that night and the crime he'd just confessed to her. No doubt Glyn would argue that he was refusing to sacrifice one human life for the sake of a greater good. But the point he'd missed in Ida's rooms on F Staircase was the same point he failed to grasp here tonight in the West End. Was lawlessness the way to defeat tyranny? Or was it tyranny's triumph?

She stirred the ice in her G & T. She wouldn't snitch on him herself, but surely it was only a matter of time before someone else at MI14 found out what he'd done and the military police clapped him in jail.

'Sent him home to change his jacket, have you?' asked Ken Johnson, sliding into the banquette beside her.

'We fought.'

'What about?'

'Work.'

'Oxford work or London work?'

'Bit of both. Glyn made a bad decision. Oh, and he's just jilted Ida, would you believe?'

'You do realise Glyn is sweet on you, don't you?'

'In an unflattering sort of a way.'

'What do you mean?'

'He feels Ida swamped him like an electrical storm, overstimulated him, oversaturated his senses, and so I'm the dry land – altogether less exciting, but safe, predictable, English. The vicar's wife after the actress.'

'You're so wrong. The boy is counter-jumping. He sees in you the glamour of the truly posh. You can stop him making the social faux pas. And feeling déclassé.'

'That's no basis for love, is it?'

'Of course not, but I sometimes think there's a reason why people make a run of bad decisions.'

'Which is ... ?'

'It's because they're in a process of change.'

'That makes it sound positive, but I think he is just being foolish.'

'Well, that foolish boy is making one bad decision after another.'

'Yes,' said Merry. 'He's already got the white jacket.'

'What's that supposed to mean?'

'I fear his next move will be to abandon a promising academic career, date a man twice his age and become the poor man's Cab Calloway.'

'Back in the knife box, Merry Havoc. At least my man doesn't show up to a swing dance dressed as Hermann Göring.'

Merry threw back her head and laughed her oink of a laugh. Ken pulled a face of fastidious recoil and stood up to go.

Just before he reached the dance floor, he turned and said, 'Come backstage after the show, Lady Havoc, and I'll chaperone you back to Denman Alley. Blackout's been intense lately.'

'That's extraordinarily thoughtful of you, Kenrick. Thank you.'

'Oh, and I have champagne in the dressing-room sink.'

'I'll bring a ladle.'

The Peter Robinson Department Store

―

IDA STOOD IN DAMP SHOES outside the Peter Robinson department store in central London, utterly confused. On this cold and slushy morning, she had come all the way from Oxford to Oxford Circus, only to arrive at completely the wrong address. No way was this the HQ of MI14.

The previous day, a Somerville porter had handed her an envelope embossed with a lion, a unicorn and the legend *Military Intelligence German Army Section (MI14)*. On a stiff index card, Mr Glyn Gower had summoned her to 252–262 Regent Street at eleven o'clock.

Was this the moment when Ida's life would enlarge? The moment when she would enter the exciting intelligence world that had already snapped up friends and colleagues? Could she forget about going to France altogether?

In her excitement, she had caught a much too early train, walked all the way from Marylebone and still arrived at 252–262 Regent Street with a whole hour to spare. Only this couldn't be the place. Twice she circumnavigated the enormous building, crunching through the filthy, days-old snow, but failed both times to find any sort of ministerial-looking door. And now she was back outside the main entrance of Peter Robinson. She must have scribbled the address down wrong, thereby proving at a stroke how perfectly unsuited she was for intelligence work.

Humiliated and bewildered, Ida entered the department store – at least it would be warm inside. She hesitated at a glassy crossroads of tall perfume display counters. From a high stool, a saleswoman in blue and yellow eyeshadow and scarlet lipstick peered down at her through a mist of atomiser, like a parrot in the steaming clouds of a tropical rainforest.

'You look lost, ducks,' said Blue Macaw lady, slowly blinking large cyan eyelids.

'Well, there're just so many different perfumes to choose from!'

Blue Macaw chuckled. 'If you're looking for the secret agents, love, they're on the top floor.'

Ida gave such a startled look that Blue Macaw squawked with delight.

'Much obliged to you, ma'am,' Ida said, with a smile.

She rode the elevator to the seventh floor, where a commissionaire led her through a clickety-clack turnstile into an open-plan office which sprawled over the entire floor. He pointed to a line of people queuing to speak to someone seated at a desk.

'You'll find Mr Gower somewhere under that lot.'

She joined the back of the queue. A queue! As if Glyn were eight ounces of sugar, two ounces of butter and four rashers of bacon!

Brown sticky-tape criss-crossed the window to protect against flying glass from bomb blasts. The brown-paper diamond lattice looked like a theatrical set-build of his old All Souls College room for a low-budget production called *Glyn and Ida*. Would it be a farce? A musical comedy?

One hour later, she was still queuing, but furious, and *Glyn and Ida* was a bitter Ibsen play. Why tell her to come at eleven just to queue for an hour? Was he trying to impress her? To remind her of his importance? To rub her nose in her insignificance? Or, worse still, maybe he wasn't trying to impress her at all. Maybe he simply attached no importance to her time. Perhaps he gave no more thought to her than the Ministry of Supply gave to her ration book. And now here she was standing in line for her Glyn Gower ration.

When Ida finally reached the front of the queue, she was startled by how haggard Glyn looked. Instantly, she forgave him the wait. He wasn't being high and mighty. The boy was all ends up. The job was running him ragged. His face lit up to see her standing there. She guessed he was pleased to be reminded of a time when he was less beat.

'It's so very good to see you, Ida.'

'Glyn. How does my old beau?'

'Dog-tired. We need more staff.'

Good God, was he about to offer her a job? Was he about to recruit her into the secret service this instant? She held her breath as he slid a card file towards himself. He flicked through the box index for a long time. Was he searching for the card with her new job title? Frogwoman, codebreaker, assassin, saboteur – whatever it was, she'd do it!

Glyn plucked out the typewritten card he was looking for and swivelled his chair to face her. 'Ah! Here it is! Here's what I wanted to ask you about. There's a Dr Dieter Wetzel attached to the staff of General von Manstein, head of Army Group South, and I was wondering whether he might be the same Dr Dieter Wetzel you brought to F Staircase that time. So, I wanted to ask, are you still in touch with him?'

'Jesus Christ, Glyn! Goddammit! For *this* you summon me all the way to London?'

'Please keep your voice down, Ida.'

'You couldn't have left a note at the porter's lodge for me to call you on the telephone?'

'I'm afraid not.'

'Why ever not?'

'German intelligence might be listening in.'

'To the Somerville porters? Get a grip, man!'

'No, I mean listening in to this place, to MI14.'

'You never heard of a call box?'

'Ida, please! Lower your voice! This is all open plan.'

'A call box, Glyn! A moment's thought. Then I wouldn't have had to traipse all the way from Oxford for one question.'

'Please don't shout. Excuse me one moment.' He stood up, found an empty office chair and trundled it towards her. 'Please, take a seat, Ida. Forgive me – I really should have offered you one sooner. You've been standing a long time, and your shoes are wet.'

'Thank you, Glyn.' She sat down and took off her gloves.

'Let me fetch you a hot drink,' he said.

'That would be most welcome.'

He returned a few minutes later, holding a cup of tea with a ginger biscuit perched on the saucer. 'Here you are, Ida.'

'Why, thank you, Glyn,' said the mollified Southern lady, pleased to have the basic proprieties observed at last.

Munching her cookie, she asked, 'You get a discount here, Glyn?'

'Beg pardon?'

'You know, do you get a cut rate on purchases from Peter Robinson, since you work here? Cufflinks, crockery, perfume for a lady – all that kinda stuff?'

'Alas, no.'

'Now, Glyn,' said Ida, 'is it likely the Nazis would have bugged a West End department store on the off chance that it would one day be a nest of secret agents?'

'What if I told you that we now intercept almost all radio communications of the Abwehr?'

'Of the what-where?'

'The Abwehr. German military intelligence. Thanks to radio intercepts, we eavesdrop on the Abwehr every single day. Would you believe that, yesterday, I was even listening to their codebreakers as they were struggling to crack our codes?'

She tilted her head to one side, engrossed by this idea. 'So, you're saying that what the Germans think are two-way radios are really three-way?'

'Precisely. And that's my point. For all we know, the same could be true of these telephones.'

Ida picked up the receiver of his desk telephone and spoke in a deep and manly RP accent: 'Hullo. May I speak to the Nazis, please? England, here. We absolutely *adore* your union-busting and your swish new highways, and we would like to surrender. We'd like to invite you to do the same over here, diary permitting. Toodle-pip.' She hung up.

'Since you're here, now,' he said, 'you may as well let me ask you a few questions.' He scuttled his seat forwards until they were knee to knee.

She cut him a look. 'If you're after my cookie, you can roll right back, cos I ain't sharing.' She placed her wet shoe on the seat between his legs and shunted his chair back.

Glyn sailed back a few yards, then scuttled up to her again. 'There is, as I say, a Dr Dieter Wetzel working as an attaché for General Erich von Manstein, who is chief of staff at Army Group South.'

'Your army or theirs?'

'Theirs. Now, Manstein is in charge of what the Germans have named *Aufmarschanweisung, Nummer Vier, Fall Gelb*, which means—'

'Deployment Instructions, Number Four, Case Yellow.' Was it possible that Glyn had forgotten she spoke excellent German? Surely, he must remember so central a fact. If he'd forgotten that, what else had he forgotten about her?

'*Entschuldigen*,' he said, 'I wasn't sure you spoke German.'

He *had* forgotten! Which meant he'd also forgotten that time in the hay barn when she recited Rilke's 'Der Panther' from memory. And if he'd forgotten the recital, had he also forgotten what else happened in that barn?

'Oh, I do believe I speak rather better German than you, Glyn. The way you pronounce *Auf-MARSCHAN-weisung* sounds like you're talking about Our Martian Invasion.'

He threw back his head and laughed. 'Our Martian Invasion!' he barked. 'Ha! Ha! Our Martian Invasion! Ha-ha-ha!'

Heads turned across the open plan, for he was laughing a little too loudly. With a stab of care, Ida realised that overwork and too much responsibility had rendered him half hysterical.

'So, Glyn, what do you want to know about the imminent Martian invasion?'

'What can you tell me about Wetzel from your famous memory?'

That was more like it. Whatever else he'd forgotten about her, he still remembered that.

'Twenty-seven going on forty. Acting professor of palaeoanthropology at Göttingen. When I met him in the Pitt Rivers in thirty-eight, he'd just returned from an archaeological dig in the Ardennes. Rather an important dig, too. Discovered some of the earliest ever figurative sculptures. Last I heard, he was going back to Göttingen to raise funds for a return trip to La Grotte Ardennes.'

'Would you be so good as to ferret out a forwarding address for him from the Pitt Rivers, or the anthropology faculty office – because, you see, I was thinking you might enter into correspondence with Dieter Wetzel. Become pen pals.'

'Pen pals.'

'You'd be amazed how useful personal letters often prove to be. Even a postmark might reveal Manstein's latest HQ. Could you perhaps start off by writing to Dieter Wetzel as one bone-collector to another, sharing journal articles about the Palaeolithic or what have you?'

'Won't that seem odd when we're at war?'

'Think of Russell and Wittgenstein in the last war,' said Glyn, 'swapping letters across the battle lines. You could write to each other like they did. Sometimes academic, sometimes personal letters.'

'No, thank you, Glyn.'

'Pardon me?'

'No way I'm gonna write him.'

'But, Ida, this Wetzel is the private secretary of General Manstein himself! You are in a unique position to glean vital intelligence about German military planning. How can you possibly say no?'

'There's no point me contacting him.'

'Why ever not?'

'You know very well that, when a man gets seconded to important military work, he has no time for a girl he once knew on F Staircase.'

'Oh, for crying out loud!'

'Besides which, I'm fixing to go to France.'

'France? Don't you know there's a war on?'

'A phoney war. Plus, there's the impregnable Maginot Line.'

'We've been here before, haven't we?'

More people were queuing to see him.

'So long, Glyn,' she said, standing up.

'Goodbye, Ida.'

She lifted his chin towards her, ran her fingers through his quiff and stroked the back of his head down to the collar of his shirt.

'Don't work too hard, old beau. You can't win the war on your own.'

Walking up Regent Street, Ida wished she hadn't held Glyn's chin like that. She hadn't missed his touch until she'd touched him. Now, she'd gone and reminded her body how wrong it was that they were no longer on touching terms. Had she reminded his?

The Oval

―

AT THE OVAL, a six-thousand-strong crowd was watching the All England Women's Hockey Association – white shirts, grey pinafores – trounce the United States Field Hockey Association – blue shirts, blue pinafores.

The hosts led the visitors 4–0, when the USA won a short corner. The corner ball came towards Ida, who trapped it with a nice clean clack on the edge of the shooting circle. She looked up. Two enormous English defenders were charging her down. Ida feinted left, then reverse swept the ball to her right, wrong-footing both Englishwomen. This earned her a yard of space. Enough for a scoop shot. She set her stick's heel under the ball and slid her leading hand down the shaft. She looked at the goal, bent her knees and scooped the ball high into the air. The English goalie flailed, and the ball struck the top corner of the net. It was to be the USA's only goal of the game. Final score: 5–1.

In the locker room, Ida banged the mud off her boots, before dropping them into the canvas satchel that more usually carried her palaeontology kit – palaeontology having been the subject of her first degree at the University of Texas at Austin.

After graduating summa cum laude in palaeontology, Ida had won an overseas scholarship to read philosophy, politics and economics at Somerville College, Oxford. Her fellow Somervillians were sniffy about the University of Texas. Did she major in rodeo or whittling? Ida countered that the University of Texas had been awarding degrees to women since 1883, whereas Oxford only started to do so in 1920, and, of course, Cambridge still did not. What shut them up good and proper was when the philosophy faculty awarded her a junior fellowship before she even completed her degree.

There was only one other philosopher to whom that singular honour was given, and her name was Merry – from Medora. Medora Danes. Tall and blonde, with twinkly brown eyes, she wore timeless tailored suits of grey wool or houndstooth tweed, well cut to her slender frame. Over sherry in the Somerville senior common room, they discovered that, starting from vastly different worlds, they had both converged on the same *Weltanschauung*, as if Truth were a clearing in the forest into which each had stumbled at the same time, there to look up and lock eyes with the other. Both shared, for instance, what was then a deeply unfashionable attachment to moral philosophy.

Ida adored how the tall Englishwoman weighed her words, tipping her head this way or that as she tried to get things 'just so' or 'just right'. Though the phrase 'cut-glass accent' was pejorative, intended to suggest a cold, self-conscious formality, it seemed to Ida that it worked as an honorific to describe Merry's bright precision of speech and her crystal-clear articulation.

Both had been warned off higher education by their families, but for different reasons. Merry because it was not the sort of thing that well-bred ladies did, and Ida because it was the sort of thing that only well-bred ladies did.

To be the only Southern lady among Oxford philosophy fellows was one thing, but to be the only one on the US field hockey team was another, and it made her feel lonesome. She listened to her teammates discuss getting home before U-boats controlled the Atlantic and made return impossible. The Yankees were all sharing plans for what they'd do when they got back to the US. This one would be working in the same office as that one. These two would be living just a block away from those three. To hear them talk, you'd think the United States was a small market town.

She belted her mackintosh over her navy-blue USA kit and bid them bon voyage. She walked to Oval Underground station and rode the escalator down to the welcome smuts and rattle of the Northern Line. Was it odd that she never for a moment considered going home? Odd or not, she couldn't imagine leaving. She'd found her place in the world, the only place where error was in retreat. As the Tube train rocked her towards a lunch date with Merry, her gaze rested on butt-ends wedged in the grooved wooden floor. Some were shaken loose by the rattling train, others weren't going anywhere. She'd wedged herself into the slats of England's wooden floor and was staying put, thank you very much. If the world would let her.

She emerged from Goodge Street station into brilliant Bloomsbury sunshine. Swinging her satchel, she walked up Gower Street, past sumptuous Portland stone buildings, singing, 'So long, it's been good to know yuh'.

Halfway up Gower Street, her way was blocked by a man in a camel overcoat, spreading his arms wide across the sidewalk to usher military top-brass and senior mandarins into the back of a waiting two-tone Rolls-Royce. Ida thought she recognised a couple of cabinet ministers, but was hazy on the names. Hore-Belisha? Halifax? When the man in the camel coat turned to permit ordinary pedestrians to use the sidewalk once more, she found herself face to face with Vernon Alwynne.

'Ah, it's the American girl from F Staircase! How the devil are you?' He spun round to open the car door for another panjandrum, touching two fingers of his black leather gloves to his forehead.

So, she thought, he had secured himself a job as a chauffeur. She never suspected him capable of such humility, and felt bad for all the ribbing they had given him back in Oxford.

But then he grinned at her and said, 'Been roped into MI3, for my sins! Must dash. Meeting with the PM.' And, with that, he climbed not into the front, but the back of the car, slamming the door shut.

Moments later, the Rolls-Royce glided away, driven by someone other than Vernon Alwynne.

'Why should I be tutoring sophomores,' said Ida, 'when a knucklehead like Alwynne is right at the heart of things?'

'You're not the first person to have her day ruined by bumping into Vernon Alwynne,' said Merry. They were eating fish-paste sandwiches at a small table in a busy Lyons teahouse.

'Seems the war has enlarged everyone's life but mine,' said Ida. 'Glyn's got his cloak-and-dagger job. You've got yours. Austin's got his. And now here's Vernon Alwynne, of all people, hugger-mugger with the high muckamucks who are actually directing the course of the war!'

'Well, I'd hardly describe my job in a suburban factory on the North Circular as cloak-and-dagger. Plus, I still tutor in Oxford once a week.'

'But you're in the war, Merry. You're doing war work. I'm still playing hockey, like a schoolgirl. Still lugging set texts around Oxford. Still teaching conchies and 4-Fs.'

'4-Fs?'

'Men who fail the draft.'

'Give me the lame, the sick and the Quakers over rugger-buggers and hearties any day of the week.'

'One day a week.'

'On top of which, you have this extraordinary influx of refugee scholars from Vienna and Berlin, plus a far higher proportion of women students than ever before. I doubt the Oxford intake has ever been stronger.'

'I was gonna defer my sabbatical, but now I feel I'll *burst* if I don't go to France. I've just got to do *something*.'

'Yes, but what will you actually do in France?'

'Two years ago, in the Pitt Rivers, I saw a healed femur on a slide, which seemed to me to be evidence of prehistoric moral obligations. I want to wield this femur as evidence that moral obligations are an endowment of our natural history.'

'As opposed to being a late add-on to our essentially savage and beastly selves?'

'Exactly.'

'Well, these large questions hang in the air like barrage balloons just now, don't they? You know: if the Germans have gone ape, are we called upon to go temporarily ape ourselves in order to defeat them?'

'Yes, and I've been thinking about that night on F Staircase – Glyn and Alwynne talking about extra-judicial killings.'

'How peculiar. I've been thinking about that night myself.'

'Lurking under that whole debate was the idea of the inner savage, the Mr Hyde, the apeman within. But we were social before we were even human.'

'When a man thinks he is at his most primal and elemental,' said Merry, 'he is often at his most modern and contrived and affected.'

'Yes, and there's a great point Dewey makes ...'

Ida paused. Her friend was the only colleague not to roll eyes at Dewey's name. The American Confucius was seen as terribly old hat and detached from the truly exciting currents of modern analytical thought. Still, she checked Merry's expression and waited for her to say, 'Go on.'

'Well, in the 1880s, Dewey says—'

At that moment, the Nippy in her black-and-white cap came and asked Merry if she wanted a second pot of tea, and then added, 'Cake for your daughter?'

'We're colleagues, actually,' said Merry, in her oil-on-troubled-water voice.

The Nippy laid a hand on Ida's shoulder. 'Oh, I'm so sorry, love,' she said. 'Really, I am. Only it's your pinafore, you see. It's the spit of my old school uniform. That's what threw me. That and the pigtails.'

'No cake, thank you,' said Merry.

'And the hockey stick,' said the Nippy. 'Oh, and the satchel, too.'

'Just the bill, please,' said Merry.

'And you being such a small thing. Still, no harm done, eh?' The Nippy left the bill and whirled away.

Merry poured the last of the tea. 'I'll be mother.'

Ida finger-shredded her plaits, roughly, angrily. 'The irony is that, when we met, I was a graduate and you were just out of school.'

'Haggard crone though now I be,' said Merry. 'Where were we? Yes, we were discussing the topicality of some twenty-thousand-year-old bones. I believe your trip to La Grotte Ardennes would make a fine sabbatical project. Let me investigate the bursaries. While you may be the digger-upper of bones, I'm your girl for excavating research grants. Oxford is positively seamed with them. Untold grants and bursaries lie beneath its streets. One just has to know where to dig. I'll drop you a line by the end of the week. Now, let's go and get a drink at the Sun.'

'If they'll serve me, in this get-up.'

They stepped out, arm in arm. Merry wore high-waister trousers with two vertical rows of three buttons at the front, a short tweed bolero jacket and a grey cotton blouse.

'Why were you thinking about that night on F Staircase?' Ida asked her.

'Something Glyn told me.'

'Can you tell me?'

'Forgive me.'

'Loose lips sink ships? I envy your cloak-and-dagger talk with Glyn. Its intimacy.'

'Ken thinks Glyn dotes on me.' Merry turned her eyes to Ida's with an open expression, ingenuous, inviting her to talk about a subject she knew they should have exposed to daylight long before.

'I think he's in love with you,' said Ida.

'I know you do, but you're wrong. When I was his shoulder to cry on, he used to complain that you oversaturated his senses. He compared himself to Stendhal suffering *fièvre de Florence* – you know, his famous fainting fits brought on by overstimulation from all Florence's beauty. Glyn hopes a romance with me will finally get you out of his system. You were his Florence. I'm his Eastbourne. Nobody ever suffered a *fièvre d'Eastbourne*. Stendhal would be quite safe from overstimulated nerve endings and synapses on that cold English shore.'

Merry pushed open the door of the Sun Tavern on Drury Lane. They perched on high stools by the window, with their frothy halves, far from the other drinkers.

'When I say I envy your intimate talk about the intelligence world,' said Ida, 'I mean I envy him, not you, dum-dum. I envy him getting to talk to you about those things. I just hate there being something I can't talk about with you. I cannot abide there being one single thing off limits between us; it's as dismaying as barbed wire across a sandy beach on a sunny day.'

'Not pebbly, like Eastbourne?'

'No, sandy and posh, like Aldeburgh.'

'Yes, as I passed a building site earlier today, someone called me a "hoity-toity beach", if I heard correctly.'

Ida threw back her head and laughed. Merry did disingenuousness very well.

'You know, there is actually very little I'm not allowed to tell you about my work, Ida. It's just the topical nitty-gritty I must keep mum about. But I can tell you everything else.'

'I'm listening.'

Merry flicked and caught a *Be Like Dad – Keep Mum* beer mat a few times as she thought where to begin.

'When I first started at Wembley, my job was quite different from what I do now. My first week in the job, I had to go to Bomber Command HQ, in a stately home somewhere, with a series of enlarged photographs which showed that not a single bomb had landed on its intended target.'

'What was the target?'

'A chemical refinery on the German island of Sylt. Bomber Command thought the raid was a tremendous success. Direct hit on a chemical refinery! Immense flames spotted by the aircrews! Front-page headline: *God bless the RAF!* Imagine their joy when I broke the news that they had bombed some hay ricks. Not only that, but they had in fact bombed the wrong country. Not Sylt, but a Danish island instead.'

'They weren't even German hay ricks!'

'When I handed them my report, complete with time-stamped photos of the still-standing chemical refinery, do you know what the wing commander did? He wrote the words *I refuse to accept this report* on the front page and handed it back.'

'He sounds like those clerics who refused to look through Galileo's telescope at Jupiter.'

'Exactly so,' said Merry.

'Talking of cosmology, did you know that Kepler's mother was the landlady of a pub called the Sun? Kepler grew up in the pub, so his whole world had always revolved around the Sun! How could he *not* believe in heliocentrism?'

'Not to have done so would have shown a want of filial piety!'

'That boy's mama raised him right!'

A few days later, back at Somerville, Ida found an envelope addressed in Merry's handwriting under her F Staircase door. Inside F7, she kicked off her shoes and socks and hung her feet over the arm of her tatty armchair, toasting her toes over the two-bar electric fire, while she read Merry's letter.

Dearest Ida,

Emboldened by that Nippy to act in loco parentis, I filled out the application forms myself rather than sending them to you. Would you believe that I've somehow managed to secure not one but two bursaries?!

The larger of the two was bequeathed in the roaring twenties by a St Hilda's alumna from Pennsylvania and is earmarked for Oxford Americans who wish to travel around Europe. The other grant is for Oxonians researching French antiquities. Strictly speaking, your prehistoric is not, of course, your antiquity, but I persuaded them you were interested in how Classical antiquity viewed the prehistoric. To wit, did you know that, in 35 BC, Horace argued that prehistoric humans were at each other's throats until they learnt Latin!

'When human beings first crawled on earth,' says Horace, 'they fought for acorns and lurking places with their nails and fists, then with clubs, and so on from weapon to weapon until they discovered language, by which to make sounds and express feelings. From that moment they began to give up war and to frame laws.' (One suspects Neville Chamberlain believed much the same Horatian whimsy at Munich.)

Together, the two funds add up to a whopping £35 sterling! Enough that you may not only enjoy a comfortable sabbatical, my love, but also purchase a small-to-middling aircraft carrier.

Leastways, I trust that this thirty-five nicker will enable you to obtain the best French acorns and lurking places without resorting to fisticuffs or cudgels. Ditto escargots and Veuve Clicquot.

Your doting and ever-loving mama,

Merry xxx

The Border Guard at Aachen

THE BORDER GUARD AT AACHEN, Johannes 'Hanno' Sterkenberg, was growing suspicious of Dr Dieter Wetzel. The particulars were all convincing enough, but his story didn't hang together.

Dr Dieter Wetzel's travel pass was issued by the office of General von Manstein. He had a return ticket for the day after tomorrow, and was using his leave of absence to take part in an archaeological expedition. But Hanno was troubled by the lack of a date stamp on the travel pass. If there was nothing to say that Wetzel had leave for *these specific days*, then there was nothing to say he had leave for *this specific purpose* either. And the stated purpose nagged at Hanno, too. By the time Wetzel got to the Ardennes, he would only have a couple of hours to get busy with his trowel if he was going to catch his return train. Was an archaeological dig something you could do in an afternoon?

Now, all this would have made Hanno Sterkenberg suspicious at the best of times, but it so happened that Dr

Dieter Wetzel had chosen the very worst time to confront him. One hour earlier, Hanno's boss had broken the news that the position of border guard was no longer a protected occupation.

'What does that mean, sir?'

'It means, Sterkenberg, you can expect to be called up any day.'

Hanno was stunned.

'But border security is more important than ever, sir.'

'Yes, it is, Sterkenberg. But you forget one thing. This war will shift the Reich's western border from Aachen to Nantes, to Cherbourg, to Liverpool, Glasgow and the Irish Sea. So, expect to be called up any day!'

A call-up would leave Hanno's young family destitute. How would his wife and children fend for themselves? Who would support his aged parents, his father having lost both legs in the last war? Active service would no doubt maim Hanno himself and leave him clanking a begging tin in Aachen town centre, wearing a service medal on a hand-me-down coat, with an empty sleeve.

'Passport, please.' Hanno glanced from the passport photo to the man himself. Wetzel was still the fresh-faced college boy who had sat for this photo. Of course he was. Easy life. For men like him, life was always easy. Always the cushy posting to Koblenz. Always the soft landing. Never the call-up.

The passport showed that Wetzel was born in the very same month of the very same year as Hanno himself. What were the odds they would die within a month of each other? Wetzel would outlive him by decades, thanks to his protected occupation on a general's staff.

The Wetzels of the world always put their good fortune

down to their superior brains. Well, thought Hanno, for once in your life, Dr Dieter Wetzel, you find yourself on the level playing field you have so far avoided. Oh, you may have risen high enough to be safe from conscription, but you're not safe from me. You're not yet safe from a man who has been condemned to die this very morning, even though he does his job better than you do yours. If there is to be no justice in the wider world, there can still be justice right here in the little office of the border guard at Aachen.

'Come this way, please.' Hanno led him out of the queue and into the office. No doubt Wetzel thought he was being whisked past the hoi polloi.

They faced each other across a broad and cluttered desk. 'Where will you be staying in Charleville-Mézières, Herr Doktor?'

'At the Hôtel Saint-Michel.'

'Do you have a booking confirmation I can see? Just a formality, but they're asking us to be much stricter about these protocols lately, as you can imagine.'

Wetzel produced the letter from the hotel confirming his booking.

'Just the one night?'

'Yes,' said Wetzel, tapping his heel impatiently.

'You must be a very fast digger.'

'Pardon?'

'Well, if you're going to catch your return train, you'll only have a couple of hours to fit in your archaeology.'

'It's a site I've visited before.'

'Roman?'

'Older.'

'But doesn't that mean you have to dig deeper? Which must take longer, I would have thought.'

'It doesn't really work like that.'

'No? Well, you're the professor.'

'It's a cave. La Grotte Ardennes.'

'A cave in the Ardennes. I see, sir.'

With all the alacrity of a monk illuminating a manuscript, Hanno copied out the hotel's address and phone number. While he was about it, he also copied out the address of Manstein's HQ at the Altstadt Hotel in Koblenz. The slower Hanno went, the more he knew he was on to something. If all was above board, why wasn't Wetzel losing his rag? Why wasn't he demanding to know if all this was really necessary? Waving General Manstein's signature under his nose?

'You were in England until 1938, Herr Doktor.'

'That's correct.'

'Do you like it there?'

'Oxford is pretty enough, but I was very glad to come home.'

Was Dieter Wetzel crossing the border to sell military secrets to the French? Or to his friends in England? Or was it just possible that General von Manstein, chief of Army Group South, would send his personal attaché on a secret mission behind enemy lines? Hanno decided to test whether Wetzel was secret-agent material with a little experiment.

'Well, everything seems to be in order,' he said, stamping the passport and travel pass. Hanno opened the side door that led directly on to the train platform, and said, 'Come this way, Herr Doktor; it's much quicker.'

'Thank you very much,' he replied, and stepped through. 'Good day.'

A secret agent would remember to ask for their passport

and travel papers back, but Wetzel walked a good twenty metres along the platform before Hanno called out, 'Oh, Herr Doktor!'

Wetzel turned on his heel, angry at last. 'But what now?'

Hanno smiled and wagged the forgotten passport and travel pass in the air. Wetzel trotted back, gushing with relief and gratitude. Just as he reached for his papers, Hanno snatched them back, and, with a level of sanctimony that would have sent an honest man insane, he instructed Wetzel to take care not to let so important a document fall into the hands of the French. Instead of being outraged at the condescension, Wetzel did indeed promise to be more careful in future. Hanno relinquished the documents and watched him disappear down the platform.

Now, why would a general's attaché allow himself to be patronised like that by the lowly border guard at Aachen?

Hanno put in a call to the Altstadt Hotel in Koblenz and asked to speak to an adjutant on Manstein's staff.

'Who shall I say is calling?'

'This is Herr Johannes Sterkenberg, from Aachen Border Control. I have urgent information about Dr Dieter Wetzel, attaché to General von Manstein. Dr Wetzel is absent without leave, and has crossed the border into France, where he is on his way to the Ardennes.'

'Who did you say was calling?'

'Herr Johannes Sterkenberg, from Aachen Border Control.'

If they remembered his name and position, he might receive a commendation for alerting them to this danger. Perhaps there would even be a vacancy in Koblenz. A protected occupation in Manstein's office.

This could be Hanno's passport out of the passport office.

Charleville-Mézières

IN THE TOWN OF CHARLEVILLE-MÉZIÈRES, outside a concrete box of a garage, Ida inspected a row of motorcycles for hire. A short young grease monkey, with thick black hair like Charlie Chaplin, emerged from the garage. He suggested a scarlet two-stroke moped with pedal ignition and hairdryer engine, but instead she walked straight towards a sturdy Peugeot 350 cc, with art deco chrome pipes, triangular saddle and a scuffed brown leather pannier.

'How much to hire this per day, please?'
'Is it for you?'
'How much?'
'It's very heavy.'
'How much?'

With a shoulder shrug that said, *It's your funeral*, they agreed a price.

She detached the brown pannier and crossed the cobbled market square back to the Hôtel Saint-Michel. From the kitchens, she collected the bag lunch they'd prepared for her and went upstairs to her suite.

Inside the Blériot Suite, she sat on the corner of her bed, snipping at the stitches of a suede elbow patch on a cashmere cardigan. She slid out three hundred francs, then stitched the patch closed again, over a cushion of seven hundred folded francs still in the elbow. She packed the bag lunch and a clean change of clothes in the pannier and slung her canvas palaeontology kit over her shoulder.

Back at the garage, she was met by the bossman, or so she took him to be on account of the shirt and tie he wore under his green overalls, and his being in his mid-thirties, when the other mechanics were her own age, or a little younger. Bossman expressed grave reservations about letting her hire so large a machine, wanted to know if she'd ever ridden such a big beast before, and accepted three hundred francs up front.

The baby of the motor pool, the pretty little Chaplin, handed her a nearly new cream-coloured helmet with padded leather earflaps and goggles. She put on the helmet and clipped the pannier on to the rack.

The whole motor pool of five men in green overalls gathered at the apron of the garage to watch the Big Beast Little Lady Show. They got what they came for when she couldn't get the kick-start to work. Again and again she kicked, over and over the engine turned, but still the spark would not ignite the gas. The more she failed, the more the grease monkeys enjoyed the show. She knew how this show was supposed to end. The grand finale would come when she gave up her Big Beast hubris and settled for the Two-Stroke Pedal Moped of Defeat. But she wasn't licked yet. At the risk of flooding the engine, she twisted the throttle wide open and jumped with both feet on to the kick-start. At last, the Peugeot flamed and growled into life.

'*C'est ça le truc!*' said the bossman in his shirt and tie.

She revved the engine so her voice could not be heard, and, smiling sweetly, said, 'Oh, now you fucking tell me!'

Sitting astride the purring bike, she buckled the earflaps under her chin, waved to the oily rags and glided out of the garage, waiting a good twenty yards before lifting her heels on to the rests, just like back home on Highway 207.

A few minutes later, the oily rags were loafing in the sunshine, smoking and chatting, when they heard the *pok-pok-pokety-pok-pok* of a Peugeot 350 in distress. That was the sound its engine made when an inexperienced rider was on the verge of stalling it. They stood up and craned their necks, waiting for her to reappear.

She came round the corner, standing on the saddle and steering with the sole of her shoe. Passing within a yard of them, she called out, 'Am I going the right way for the D1?'

Too stunned to speak, Bossman slowly pointed in the direction she was going. She seat-dropped on to the saddle and tootled slowly out of town.

She took the exit for the D1 and rode alongside the Meuse river. With nary another car on the highway, she couldn't resist pouring on the coal. She clicked up into top gear and sped down the highway to Nouzonville, where she turned on to the D22. Unlike the English, the cocksure French were not taking their road signs down for anybody.

Tall Thistles and an Old Map

THE ARDENNES WAS NOT THE DENSE, impenetrable wodge it appeared on the map, but patchy and varied. One minute she was riding through tunnels of mixed deciduous and coniferous trees, where she had to drop her speed way down and lift the goggles from her eyes to see in the sudden dark, and the next minute the forest was thinned to a roadside line of poplars and cypresses, with meadows and cereal crops stretching beyond, and the sunlight was blinding.

As the great forest enclosed her again, she lifted her goggles on to the top of her helmet and searched for the turning for the Grotte Ardennes. According to the map, she should soon come to some kind of path at the border of a meadow.

One kilometre later, she slowed at a bumpy, grassy fire track leading into the forest. Beside the track was a meadow with a solitary field maple and, in its middle, a stand of tall purple thistles. If she lost her bearings in the wood, the meadow would be easy to find. She drove a little way down the track, then killed the engine and wheeled the motorcycle across the meadow. In the engineless silence, she listened to the wheels squelch juicy yellow gentians and snap the stalks of goat's rue. She entered the thicket of towering thistles, more fluff than prickle, and pulled the motorcycle on to its stand. She liked the thought of hiding the motorcycle in plain sight. The uninviting thistles offered protection the way the anemone shelters the clownfish, making an excellently cool and shady enclave.

Stuck to her head with sweat, the crash helmet made a sucking sound when she lifted it off. She scratched her itchy scalp and finger-combed her damp hair. She unfolded the *Service Géographique de l'Armée* map and spread it on the hot hob of the fuel tank.

Rubber-stamped *Property of the Pitt Rivers Museum*, the map was infested with ink and pencil annotations from the original expedition to La Grotte Ardennes. Ida puzzled her way through a confusion of symbols, arrows and squiggles, all in different handwriting. One especially cryptic symbol stumped her until she realised it was a food stain. More helpful was a sharp pencil drawing showing the entry to the cave through a hole in the ground. It seemed you went in through a ceiling hatch and down a rope.

Ida slung her palaeontology kitbag back over her shoulder, unhooked the pannier from the rack and left the tall thistles' shade for the meadow's bright sunshine. She startled a green woodpecker, which flew up. She loved its headlong, clumsy flight, like a bird blown in a storm, never sure what will happen next. The woodpecker bowled itself along and then rose up into a tall larch.

She stepped into the cool of the forest and inhaled its

musky, earthy humus smell. How she loved forests! Here she was in the Forest of Arden, where Shakespeare set *As You Like It*, his best stab at an MGM musical, with five songs, including the showstopper 'It Was a Lover and His Lass'. Here was where headstrong Rosalind disguised herself as the shepherd Ganymede, and Celia as Aliena. Here, Orlando nailed his love poems to the tree trunks.

> *And therefore take the present time,*
> *With a hey, and a ho, and a hey nonny no,*
> *For love is crownèd with the prime,*
> *In spring time, the only pretty ring time.*

And here, blue and yellow chickadees – which the British call blue tits, she remembered – flitted through the branches.

> *When birds do sing, hey ding a ding, ding.*
> *Sweet lovers love the spring.*

A pair of red squirrels froze when they saw her, then dashed across the fallen needles to spiral up a lodgepole pine. Something shiny on the forest floor snagged her attention. Squatting down, she scraped away leaf litter and pine needles, expecting to uncover a jewel beetle. Instead, she found a shell fragment from the Great War beside a peel of tin helmet, a rusty brim. She pocketed the jagged metal shard.

Thinking she was still about fifty yards short of the cave entrance, she tripped over a length of rope looped around the base of tree. She followed the rope into a glade, where it disappeared down a hole in the ground. Beside the hole lay a blue steel manhole cover, straight out of main street. Was there an expedition down in the cave already? Or who knew what illicit local trade? Local criminals stashing contraband? A crypto-fascist cell stockpiling weapons and swastikas? She hid the pannier behind the pine, crept to the entrance again and stood irresolute above the manhole. The woodpecker's sempiternal drilling, the chickadees' busy flitting, the scent of the pine – all these things combined to allay her fears a little, but not enough to make her go down the manhole to join person or persons unknown.

But then she heard a plaintive, but pitch-perfect whistling. A tune she knew. A Bizet song.

> *Je crois entendre encore*
> *Caché sous les palmiers*
> *Sa voix tendre et sonore*

She sat on the edge of the manhole, dangling her legs, and put on her head torch and canvas work gloves. She cast one last look around the forest, then took hold of the rope and inched her way down, as silent as a snake. She wanted to see them before they saw her.

On the cave floor sat a road mender's safety lamp with a glowing yellow eye and a hook grip like a question mark. Shadow giants zoomed up the walls and over the cave ceiling with sudden bursts of energy. It took Ida a moment to realise that all these leaping shadows were cast by just one man walking among multiple light sources.

'*Bonjour, monsieur,*' she called out.

A man shrieked in shock. Oddly, her mind went back to Glyn abed in All Souls, surprised by her coming through the window, shrieking in the same way.

'*Desolée, monsieur,*' she said.

'*Ne vous en faites pas,*' came a young man's voice in accented French. Not a native speaker. The beam of his head torch grew as he walked towards her. '*Êtes-vous une collègue archéologue, mademoiselle?*'

'*Paléontologiste.*'

'*Française?*'

'*Américaine.*'

'But I know you, don't I? From Oxford? Ada? Ida?'

'Would you be so kind as to turn your torch away, *monsieur*? You're blinding me.'

He removed the forage cap to which his torch was attached. She saw him now.

'Ah, the *Löwenmensch* guy himself! Dr Dieter Wetzel. Have you come for that wall?'

The Cave

DIETER WETZEL LED HER DEEPER into the cave, to where he had hammered a dozen climber's pitons into the wall, marking out a rectangle three metres wide by two metres high.

'I have chiselled to a finger's depth all round the rectangle, at which depth one hits solid cap rock.'

Even though he was speaking in the first person, she kept looking over his shoulder and into the reaches of the cave for other members of the expedition team. Her last doubt that this was, in fact, a solo mission, was quashed by the rather desperate improvisation he now described.

'I'm afraid I had to steal a few iron railings from a churchyard in Charleville—'

'You did what? Why?'

By way of explanation, he showed her where he had hammered the black iron spars into the wall, their points converging somewhere behind the crust, like spatchcock chicken skewers. Her guts sank at this reckless pile-driving of church railings. How careless he seemed to be of the cave paintings he was trying to expose! She felt dread and disgust, for he was almost guaranteed to destroy what he had come to uncover by so clunky a method.

'The outer crust is soft as plaster of Paris, and I think we can prise it off with these metal rods. Your arrival here is actually a godsend, for I drove them in too far to pull out on my own and I shall need another pair of hands to lever away the calcite crust.'

He handed her two ropes of climber's twine, the other ends of which were knotted around the iron levers that lay behind the mural.

They wrapped the ends of twine around their gloves, turned their backs to the wall and walked forward like mules, until the rope tautened. On a count of three, they heaved. The cave wall creaked, louder and louder. Fearing the whole cave was about to collapse on their heads, Ida stopped pulling.

'Again,' said Wetzel. 'One, two, three!'

Once more, they hauled away, each leaning their whole bodyweight against the straining ropes. Abruptly, the calcite crust snapped cleanly from the cap rock. They staggered forwards. Wetzel lost his footing and went sprawling to the floor. Behind her, Ida heard the crust shatter on the ground, sending up a calcite cloud, which rapidly filled the cave.

She heard him cough. She unwound the rope from around her gloves and wiped the sweat from her forehead with her shirtsleeve. The clay dust made a solid cylinder of her head-torch beam. Calcified light. She stood still, breathing heavily, waiting for the dust to settle.

She saw colour before shape. Scarlet, blue, brown and

ochre. Then bold, black charcoal strokes became visible. The outlines of animals, plants, a long river. Here and there, clumps of calcite still clung to the cap rock, but a scene emerged. The river was the centrepiece of the mural.

A swimming stag's eyes were wide with fear, as the river swept him toward hyenas on the riverbank. Oblivious to this drama, a shaggy brown mammoth placidly dipped her hairy trunk to drink from the shallows, while her calf suckled. In the foreground, a grey-blue rhino skulked.

Ida was intrigued by the rhino's six horns, each horn long and sweeping. Dieter Wetzel broke in on her thoughts with an observation not about the mural, but about themselves.

'We are the first to see this in twenty thousand years,' he whispered.

'What do you make of the rhino?'

'A lost species of six-horned rhino?' Dieter ventured.

'Or do these repeated upstrokes record an artist's hesitation or uncertainty about what those horns actually looked like when he saw them?'

'Or perhaps they record a disagreement between teacher and pupil over the correct way to draw a rhinoceros?'

'Or was the painter trying to capture movement?' she suggested.

'*Zweck sein selbst ist jegliches Tier*,' said Dieter.

'Goethe,' she said. 'Each animal is an end in itself. Yes, you're right, that is just what the painters are trying to capture.'

Her eye strayed to an ornamental border of geometric patterns, but then, with a lurch, she saw that they were supposed to be people: a row of seven identical stick figures, arms out by their sides, each with one leg raised. She was affronted by how crudely they were drawn, with none of the quiddity or scrupulousness that had gone into the animals. Instead, they were as uniform as a chain of paper dolls.

'People,' she said.

'Where?'

'There.'

'Incredible,' he whispered. 'Are they a marching army, do you think?'

His whispering was giving her the creeps. She wished he'd knock it off. They were the only ones there, after all.

'Dancers,' she said, in the pointedly loud and secular voice of a dissenting minister in a Catholic cathedral.

'My God, can you believe these painters mastered the art of perspective so well?' Still with the whisper.

'I don't see any perspective,' she said.

'There. Look. That row of faraway people.'

'No, Wetzel, I think you'll find those are children.'

'But what makes you say that?'

'If they were in the distance, how could they be holding hands with the big people?'

To her dismay, he put his face in his hands and wept.

'Oh, if only the world had seen this before the war,' he cried.

She patted his shoulder. 'Better late than never,' she told him, adopting his whisper.

'My camera,' he said. 'I must fetch my Leica.' He snatched up the works lamp by its hook and set off with the urgency of a newspaper photographer to where he'd stowed his photographic equipment by the cave entrance. Returning with tripod and camera, he was all business. No more tears. No more sacred hush and whisper. No more pussyfooting on hallowed ground. Perhaps his wobble was just that – a wobble.

She sighed with relief. 'Well, I'm gonna hunt up that Pleistocene femur that's lying somewhere in the dirt of this cave.'

Ida shouldered her canvas satchel and entered the deeper reaches of the cave, searching for the partial remains of a woman who lived and died long before that mural was even painted, probably before paint and painting were even invented.

She came to a reef of dry, sandy soil. Beyond it, the ceiling tapered down to the floor. If the femur wasn't here, it was nowhere.

Wetzel began photographing the mural. Each time a flash bulb popped, subterranean sheet lightning illuminated the cave for an instant.

She trod slowly and carefully, anxious not to crush any prehistoric remains underfoot. In a flash of light, a bone appeared and disappeared like a ghost-train skeleton. She angled her head torch. A ridge of bone stuck out from the sandy soil. She knew it at once for the femur she had first seen on that Kodachrome slide in the Pitt Rivers before the war. From her satchel she took out a soft badger brush and a dental pick. She knelt and brushed dirt and detritus from the half-buried femur and iliac girdle. Brushing revealed what she had come all this way to find. There it was: an indisputable fracture callus, the infilling of new bone subsequent to a break, clear evidence that the broken leg was not the death of this prehistoric woman. This fracture callus proved that people looked after her until she was back on her feet. Here was evidence of a society that protected and cared for a woman no longer able to fend for herself.

Ida wondered how she broke her leg. Did she slip on the

ice? Fall from a tree? Did an enemy warlord whack her with his cudgel? Or a mastodon toss her with his tusks? Or did she find herself trapped in the cave with a lunatic? The joy of discovery expelled her fear. She had found what she came for.

Using a steel dental probe, Ida scored a groove around the outside of the fossilised bones. Scraping away with the probe, she sang to herself a snatch of Rocco's let's-get-digging song from *Fidelio*:

> '*Nur hurtig fort, nur frisch gegraben!*
> *Es währt nicht lang, er kommt herein.*'
> (Come on, let's dig this grave
> It won't be long before he gets here!)

She was singing very quietly, but the cave acoustics betrayed her by means of a natural geological version of the Whispering Arch at St Louis station.

From his end of the cave, Wetzel sang Leonora's response, and in an unexpectedly pitch-perfect soprano:

> '*Ich helfe schon, sorgt euch nicht.*
> *Ich will mir alle Mühe geben.*'
> (I'll help you, have no fear.
> I'll do my utmost.)

Ida chuckled to herself and went back to her buried bones, careful not to sing again now she knew that the cave acoustics gave him access even to her murmurings. She bit her lip, realising that even that chuckle would not have escaped him. But the resumption of singing was a good sign. He had returned to the happy opera buff she had heard singing Bizet through the blue manhole cover when she dropped into the cave.

She worked a pointed four-inch trowel under the femur and along its length to lift bone from soil. Mineralisation over millennia had fused the bones into one solid spar. When she slipped her hands under it, femur, pelvis and iliac girdle came away in a single unit. She sat back on her heels, holding this long, bony sceptre in both hands.

Instead of camera pops and whirs, there now came a hammer-and-tongs 'Anvil Chorus' from Wetzel's end. Surely he couldn't have finished photographing the mural already? Why was he hammering the wall? Was he hoping to find yet more wall art? Carrying the mineralised bone in both hands, Ida went to investigate. What she saw so appalled her that her knees sagged and threatened to give way. She steadied herself with her hand on the cave wall.

Chunks of mural were missing. Cave art that had survived twenty thousand years undisturbed had lasted less than an hour with Dieter Wetzel. The chisel rang loud and shrill as he hacked into cap rock, trying to gouge the mural from the wall. She wanted to scream at him to stop, but she was alone in a cave with a man with a hammer, so she just watched him desecrate one of the wonders of the world.

Using the claw of the hammer, Wetzel tried to prise out the section with the swimming deer, river and riverbank, levering it away from the wall. The whole thing came away as one. But he only carried the slab a few paces before it disintegrated in his canvas gloves and fell in chunks of rubble to the floor.

'*Scheiße!*' Wetzel's shout echoed around the cave.

From the ground, he picked up the stag's head and wrapped it in cheesecloth, laying the bundle inside a long leather holdall. He became aware of her watching him.

'You don't approve,' he said.

'What's the stag's head without the river?' Ida asked him. 'Without the hyenas waiting for him on the riverbank? Now, it's just the stag's head from any old English pub sign or Bavarian Gasthaus!'

Wetzel picked up a triangular chunk of cave wall on which could still be seen most of the head of one of the riverbank hyenas. 'Here's your hyena,' he said, and held it up.

'I just don't understand,' said Ida. 'Not half an hour ago this Upper Palaeolithic art reduced you to tears, now here you are destroying it for ever.'

'I am saving it from the war.'

'It survived the last one all right.'

'Modern French artillery can turn a hill into a valley with a single shell! The Luftwaffe has bunker-buster bombs that can turn all this to mist!'

'But what makes you think a battle will be fought here?'

He froze. Their eyes met.

Her next words came out before she could stop them: 'Because you know your general's plan.'

The silence in the cave deepened, broken only by the sound of cave water dripping into a puddle. He turned the hyena fragment this way and that.

Ida stepped closer and said, 'You've seen the map.'

'I don't know what you are talking about.' He turned away from her.

'This is your route to France,' she said, pulling his shoulder back so he was forced to face her.

He looked at her hand on his shoulder. Then looked into her eyes. 'No,' he said, coldly now. 'You are in error.'

'Your tanks are coming through these woods.'

He struck the side of her head with the hyena chunk. She fell back against the wall. Hot blood drenched one side of her face. She stared at the blood-dripping rock in his hand. She tried to form words but could not seem to speak. She raised her arm. He hammered the rock against her head again. Her eyes rolled back in their sockets, and everything went black.

A Swan's Egg

SHE OPENS HER EYES. She is lying on her side on the cave floor. Her wrists are bound behind her back, and her ankles trussed together with a coil of rope.

At the end of her nose is a swan's egg, grey and oval and steel. A grenade.

At the grenade's base is a steel ring. Tied to the ring is a length of climber's twine. Swivelling her eyes in their sockets, she follows the twine as it snakes along the cave floor for a few yards, then rises to a piton banged into the wall at about head height.

She jolts at a bang. But it is only her captor banging a box lid shut. By rolling her shoulders back, she squirms several inches from the grenade, wincing with the pain of movement. Her wince cracks the dried blood matting her hair to her cheek. She studies the piton pegged halfway between the grenade and the cave exit. This piton is the fulcrum that will let him detonate the swan's egg from a distance. When he has packed the last slab of mural, and lugged the last bag from the cave, then he will pull the climber's twine on his way out, like switching off the bathroom light. Methodical Dieter Wetzel.

She moans in dismay. Her moan summons the minotaur, who comes crunching through gravel and splashing through puddles. Avoiding the grenade, he lifts her into a sitting position, which shoots stalactites of pain through her head. He props her against the wall and squats down in front of her.

'This one grenade,' he says, 'will save a million lives. Maybe more. You do see the logic, don't you?'

She tries to speak. Her jaw moves like an orangutan stripping a leaf. The low rattle that comes out of her mouth sounds like her nanna after her stroke.

'You brain me ... with a rock ... then ask me to ... see logic.'

'My point is very simple. If all goes to plan, the war will be over before it's begun. But if I let you betray the Manstein Plan, the death toll will be in the millions. Another Somme, Mons, Passchendaele. Trench slaughter. Right where we sit. In Oxford, you philosophers justified sacrificing one life to save a dozen. But to save millions? Well, there's no debate, is there?'

She works her orangutan jaw, trying to bring sensation back to her mouth. 'Let me go, please ...'

'If I do, you will make me the man who lost the war.'

It is hard work to shape her mouth to form each syllable. 'I won't say a word ... America's not at war ... It's not our dance ... More Germans in America than Germany ... Let the neutrals go ... You can let me go.'

'I think not.'

'No, I have a ticket ... Dieppe to New York ... White Star Liner ... Six weeks at sea ... In six weeks, you're in Paris.'

'You will have to be very brave for me, *meine Kleine*. Do you think you can do that?'

He lays her down on her side again. The grenade is once more at the end of her nose.

'No!'

'Now that the grenade is primed,' Wetzel informs her, 'the slightest wobble will set it off. Should I scuff it with my foot, or accidentally kick gravel on to the grenade, we'll both be blown to bits. To lift it but a millimetre would be the last thing I do.'

He very carefully steps round the metal ovoid.

Her heart thumps against the earth so loudly she fears the vibrations it radiates under the dirt will be enough to set off the grenade. She hears his footsteps receding. Each step he takes fills her with dread, each takes him closer to where he can safely tug the string that pulls the pin. His boots crunch past the halfway piton, the fulcrum. He's out of the kill range now. The next sound she hears might be her last. The steel ring softly tinkling from the grenade. Then the explosion.

Instead, she hears him hauling a bag of wall art up to the surface. She has until he winches the last bag or box up out of the cave.

At the other end of the cave, by the dangling blue rope, Dieter remembers how he was singing before she came in.

> *Je crois entendre encore*
> *Caché sous les palmiers*
> *Sa voix tendre et sonore.*

And now she has put him in this impossible situation.

Now, she has made him – or is about to make him – a murderer. A murderer! She has put him in a murderous situation. But one does not judge a man for killing; one judges him for how many factors must be aligned before he kills. The moral question is about necessity. It's the situation, not the man. An impossible situation, bad luck, bad timing, and war. And he lacks the easy alibi of an enemy depersonalised by uniform and distance. He has no such conventional cover to blur the moral boundary. He slams the lid shut on another wooden box and then stows it in the bag.

Ida stares unblinkingly at the grenade as she very slowly worms and coils herself into a tuck, pressing her knees hard against her chest. Fearing the grenade's slightest wobble, she delicately loops her bound wrists under her boots to bring her hands out in front of her. Resting her weight on her knuckles she hauls herself up on to her knees. Pain spikes her skull. She slides her index and middle finger into her tab pocket to tweezer out the Great War shell fragment. Clamping the metal shell between her teeth, she starts to hack its jagged edge against the twine binding her wrists, sawing it to and fro. She tastes blood. She is sawing more lip than rope. She rejigs the ancient munition between her teeth and bites down hard, jerking back her head to drag the serrated metal over the fraying rope. The pain of jolting her head is excruciating, but she can smell the rope fray. So, once more, she stiffens her neck and jerks back her head. Abruptly, the twine snaps in two and her hands come free. She spits out the shell. It lands beside the grenade. She freezes. An inch to the right and that shard from the last war would have pinged on to the grenade from this one, blowing Ida to pieces. She unlaces her left boot with the trepidation of a bomb-disposal expert, as if the laces were wires. She slips her foot from the boot; once down to her sock, it is easy to slide the tether from her ankle. She puts her boot back on and searches for a fissure into which she might spelunk to shelter from the bomb blast. But the cap rock is solid all the way down. From the ruined mural, a mammoth's eye meets her own.

On the gravel beside her lies the mineralised bone she had excavated. Using it as a crutch, she climbs to her feet. Now, she will at least die standing. Holding the bone in both hands sets off a muscle memory. There is something familiar about its heft that she cannot place. Familiar, and somehow connected to an expertise she once possessed.

On the day she first met Wetzel – in the Pitt Rivers, 1938 – it was only when weighing a fragment of mammoth tusk on her palm that its heft and weight reminded her of a china doll from infancy. That was the moment when she knew the fragments formed a female figurine. In the same way, it is only now she holds the bone in her hands that her muscles understand. Her mind catches up with her body: what she is holding has the shape and heft of a hockey stick.

Her vision swims, she sways, then faints for an instant. Instinctively, she jabs the bone into the ground to stop herself from collapsing. This jerks her back to consciousness. She feels sweat covering her face. The cave is a blur. She blinks and blinks until the cave comes back into focus, like the slide-projected image in the Pitt Rivers, years ago. She sucks down a deep, deep breath and trusts herself to stand without the mineralised bone for balance.

Gripping the femur with both hands, she slots the smooth pelvic girdle under the grenade. If she fails to tuck enough bone under it, her flick shot won't fly. She holds her breath until the pelvis is lying right under the base of the grenade and readies herself for a scoop shot.

Just then, Wetzel disappears behind a bend in the cave. Is he going? Is he done?

'Please don't leave me here!'

Silence. Only her own voice echoing.

She tries again: 'Where's the sweet boy who sang *Fidelio*?'

Again, silence.

She whimpers in fear of the coming detonation. 'You will feel bad about this all your life!'

And then, at last, he speaks: 'This is anguish for me,' he says, his voice ragged, choked.

She tightens her grip on the femur.

Wetzel emerges from behind the bend, head torch like a midnight train. 'I wish there were another way.'

She flexes her knees and flicks.

The grenade flies, trailing its twine like a kite tail. The twine snags on the fulcrum, tugging out the steel ring. No twine, no ring, the grenade glides free.

The cave turns inside out and upside down. The blast wave knocks Ida on to her back, burying her under earth, calcite, gravel and rockfall.

Sky Miner

COUGHING, SPLUTTERING AND CHEWING DIRT, she crawled towards daylight, a bone in her hand, the satchel strap tangled on her ankle. As she drew near, she saw the light for what it was: the burning wreckage of the road mender's lamp. A dead end. Not the cave exit. There was no cave exit. The explosion had sealed her in. Her fingertips flinched from something wet – gobbets of Wetzel?

She used the thigh bone to dig at the soil above her head. Each time she gouged earth with bone, her arm muscles scorched ever more painfully. She let out a wild yell and stabbed upwards with the femur. A shelf of earth swamped her. Sudden daylight flooded the cave. She hauled herself out into the air and rolled on to her back. Hot sun beat down on her face.

She had mined the sky, excavated present from past, unearthed the Holocene from the Pleistocene. There was no sound in this new epoch, save the ringing in her ears. Smoke and dust rose from the cave in a single straight column. Climbing to her feet unleashed a pain so intense that she clung to a pine trunk with her eyes screwed tight for several seconds. She felt her way round the tree, as if hanging on to a swaying mast in a storm, but tripped over an object and went sprawling. Lying among beech husks and pine needles, she recognised the object for her pannier. This was where she had stashed it.

Pannier in hand, satchel on back, she reeled from tree to tree like a drugstore pinball, staggering from one to the next. Searching for the meadow where she'd stowed her motorcycle, she arrived instead at bright, sparkling water that jabbed the back of her eyes.

She slumped at the foot of an alder tree, staring at the river. The adrenalin left her body and she found herself hardly able to move her fingers to unbutton her blouse. Each movement was separate and slow. She leant forward. Stretched her hands out to her boots. Stopped. Took off one boot. Rested. Then the other. When she stood up, she felt as precarious as a circus elephant on a tumbrel. To spare herself from bending once more, she dragged off her socks by standing on her own toes and kicked off her trousers.

Ida stumbled to a shallow bank, where anglers had left Y-shaped sticks in the mud and scattered cigarette butts. Cold water itemised each cut and bruise on her body as she waded into the river. She let herself sink under the heavy weeds, down to the silty riverbed, and came up gasping with the cold. Climbing from the river, long green tresses of river weeds fell to the small of her back. She tossed this headdress on to the dry grass. Warm liquid cascaded over one side of her face. Blood. She folded her blouse into a wad and pressed it hard against the wound to staunch the flow.

Goosebumped and naked, she was trembling. At first, she thought it was the cold, but after the sun had warmed her, the trembling continued. Perhaps she was in shock, only it didn't exactly feel like that either. Then she realised: she was trembling with rage. She wanted to dig him up and kill him again, and this time see him blown apart.

She sat on the sunny riverbank, still deaf, glancing over her shoulder occasionally to check nobody was behind her. When she looked back at the river, she saw a pair of brown eyes staring straight at her. An otter peered from the entrance to her holt, raised her head and sniffed. Judging the amphibious human to be harmless, the otter sow led her pups out towards the riverbank. Was this the same stretch of river, wondered Ida, where cave painters had seen the suckling mammoth, the swimming deer, the rhino and the hyena? Long free of hyenas and other predators an otter might fear, this riverbank would soon be inundated with panzer tanks.

She inspected the wad she'd been pressing against her temple. Staring at the blood-soaked fold of fabric, it took her a moment to recall that the wad used to be her blouse. This failure of her famous memory troubled her. How much of her summa-cum-laude smarts did Wetzel destroy with his hyena chunk of cave wall? To test what was left, she resolved to parse the word *panzer* to within an inch of its life.

Panzer. Panther. Rilke wrote his poem 'Der Panther' about a captured panther in the Ménagerie du Jardin des Plantes, pacing round and round his cage. She used to know this poem off by heart. How did it go again?

Sein Blick ist something something *von der Stäbe*
so müd geworden, dass er tum-ti-tum,

Tada-da-da-da.
Und hinter tausend Stäben keine Welt.
Sublime.

Start again. Panther. In 1938, in Czechoslovakia, palaeontologists discovered a complete fossil of the European Ice Age panther, *Pantherea pardus spelaea*. Later that same year, panzer tanks overran that whole country. And now those panzers would soon come crashing through this very forest, where she was suddenly cold and ravenous.

From the pannier, she unpacked her change of clothes and her bag lunch. She changed into blue jeans and a green cashmere jersey. She crunched into her ham, olive, artichoke, egg, tomato and cheese baguette. Nothing ever tasted so delicious since the invention of agriculture.

When she clicked her fingers beside her ear, she heard a muffled click. She popped the swing-top bottle of Bière de Meuse. Heard that better.

Though hearing and memory seemed to be on the way back, she'd left her pathfinding instincts down in the cave among the rubble: having set out for the motorcycle meadow, she'd ended up here by the river. She unfolded the army map again, looking for the way back to the meadow. Her attention glommed instead on to *La Ligne Maginot*, represented on the map by a cross-stitch pattern running the length of France's borders with Germany and Luxembourg.

She recalled a Pathé news reel about the Maginot Line. The greatest defensive structure ever made, said the voice-over, its concrete was reinforced with more than 50 million tons of steel, and it boasted its own underground railway, observation turrets, air con and artillery.

With a buttery finger, Ida traced the Maginot Line to where it stopped just inside Belgium. If they'd continued that pretty cross-stitch all the way to the sea, they'd have closed out the Hun till kingdom come. But now the Germans needed only to penetrate a quarter inch into Belgium to bypass the Maginot Line completely. Once in Belgium, the panzers could do a handbrake turn, then kitty-corner through the Ardennes Forest into France, before bursting from the trees on Highway D22 and putting pedal to the metal all the way to Paris. Hunkered in their impregnable Maginot bunker, meanwhile, the first any French soldiers would know about it would be Radio Paris playing the Horst-Wessel Song on rotation.

Ida folded the map and climbed to her feet. No stalactites through the brain this time. Instead, a new sound penetrated the tinnitus in her ears. At first, she thought this was just a new pitch of ringing, but then she recognised the sound for the sweet, high-pitched song of the chickadee. She was back in the world, in the only pretty ring time, when birds do sing, hey ding a ding, ding. She chugged the last of her beer and chucked her empty bottle into a gap between trees.

Tank stopper.

Little Green Men

IDA HOBBLED ACROSS A GREEN CORNFIELD, stumbling and falling, the whole field swaying. She reached a row of poplars lining a road, climbed down the grass bank, but tripped and slammed hard on her back in the metalled road – resisting the urge to close her eyes and drop away into unconsciousness and oblivion. She flung out an arm and dragged her pannier over the dusty, crumbly tarmac towards her. Rolling over on to her tummy, she crawled by degrees to the bank, one elbow after the other, one knee after the other, hauling herself up to her feet by the green tree roots as if she were still climbing out of the Meuse river.

As she tottered along the road, the clouds parted. It hurt to tip her head away and so her eyes stung and watered in the direct sunlight until she came to a bend in the lane and a high bank full of shadow. After the bend, she saw again the meadow with its lonely maple and its tall purple thistles. Sunlight glinted off the chrome pipes of her ride, a heliograph flashing the Big Beast's welcome from its lair inside the thistle thicket.

Coming now at the meadow from the opposite direction, she also saw for the first time Wetzel's van, a grey Citroën with corrugated panels and Betty Boop gig lamps. The getaway vehicle. If it had been him and not her who came out of the cave alive, Wetzel would now be driving this hire van back to the Reich, loaded with its sorry chunks of Upper Palaeolithic mural, each hardly bigger than the broken mammoth tusks with which he'd been toying that first time in the Pitt Rivers. Before the war. Before he went to work on Manstein's staff. The sun went in behind the clouds and a breeze stirred the maple and the meadow grasses. It struck her that, if she had proof of Wetzel's official role as Manstein's attaché, her warning about the invasion would stand a better chance of being believed when she got to the British embassy in Paris. If she could find his ID papers in the Citroën's glove compartment ... She quickened her step.

Coming closer, she saw that behind the van was a parked car, brown and cream like a wingtip shoe. A flicker of movement made her freeze. Two men emerged from the trees. She dropped to her belly among yellow bracken.

Each man carried one of the long holdalls that Wetzel had loaded with boxes of chiselled-out cave wall. They dumped the booty in the back of the van. The stockier of the two men opened the trunk of the brown and cream car, then came waddling back into view lugging a bulky radio transmitter, which he carried to the solitary field maple.

A few minutes later, Ida saw the taller man slowly turning round, calling: '*Aber wo bist du?*'

'*Hier drüben, Lothar.*'

Lothar joined Radio Man by the field maple. He trained a spyglass on the surrounding fields and roads. Ida slammed her face into the stalks and soil. When, after a full minute, she dared raise her chin from the earth and inch apart the bracken, Lothar was scanning the horizon.

She was confused. What could he be searching for? For Dieter Wetzel's killer? No, that could not be. After all, if Herr General Manstein sent this goon squad to arrest Wetzel for being AWOL, they must have found the collapsed cave entrance and assumed the impatient tomb robber accidentally blew himself up with his own dynamite, greedy for another cave chamber full of treasure. So what else were they looking for? Was Lothar simply checking that no inquisitive farm workers or field hands were around to draw the same inference from the field radio as she'd done, viz. that these two men were German secret agents?

If they were from the Abwehr, then they'd got what they came for: Dieter Wetzel, Dead or Alive. Mission accomplished. Soon, they would be on their way. So, if she just lay hidden in the bracken until they drove off, she would be sure to outlive the ringing in her ears.

A shaft of sunlight warmed the back of her hand. Clouds pulled apart and revealed the sun. Fifty yards away, the chrome pipes flashed their treacherous heliograph. She saw Lothar jerk his spyglass to the pink and pale purple patch where her ride was parked. Her heart sank through the soil as she watched him nudge Radio Man, who swiped off his headphones and got to his feet, reaching for a buckled gun case. It would take a few seconds, she calculated, for him to get that pistol out of its case.

She sprinted across the meadow, zigzagging like a hare,

her terror stronger than her pain. A clod of earth jumped up and struck her face. A pistol shot. She dived headlong into the purple thistles.

From way back by where the vehicles were parked, she heard Lothar call out to Radio Man to keep his head down. Then came a volley of shots from an automatic rifle. Bullets zipped past her. She lay flat until the magazine emptied, then rolled the motorcycle off its stand. She hopped on to the kick-start with both feet. The engine wheezed, but didn't start. She tried again. Spindles span uselessly. Then stopped.

A pistol shot. Closer, this time. She looked over her shoulder. Through the thistle heads, she saw Radio Man firing while walking. That was an inaccurate way to shoot. She risked rising from her cringe and standing straight.

She twisted the inert throttle all the way and jumped on to the kick-start as hard as she could. The engine roared, then backfired with a sound like gunshots. Radio Man threw himself to the ground. She revved the engine and ran alongside the motorcycle, before taking a flying leap into the saddle.

She skidded into the road with a long broadside, the wheels chucking up sods of earth and meadow grass. Bullets ricocheted off the tarmac in a fluid volley – the rifle again. She wobbled and straightened up, then flattened her torso against the gas tank, her head on the handlebars, and poured on the coal. She counted three more shots before a blind corner's high grassy bank took her out of range. Sitting back in the saddle, she twisted round to check that no bullets had punctured the gas tank, and whimpered with relief to see no oil trail in the road.

After a few miles, Ida stopped on the brow of a hill, where

a high metal signpost offered her and history a choice of fates: Reims and Paris, or Sedan and Bastogne. Which way to go? Right now, she was the only person outside of German high command who knew the Manstein Plan. So, should she ride straight to Paris? Or head for the first town from which she could cable the British embassy? But why would they believe she knew the Germans' order of battle? Why would anyone? Glyn might, but MI14 were not in the phone book, and he never saw fit to give her the number for his London bachelor apartment in case she spoiled his fun.

The hornet buzz of a distant speeding car arose from the valley, mingling with the ringing in her ears. She looked down on the brown car and the grey van. Here come the Abwehr. The what-where. She heard Glyn's voice in her head, the last time they met:

Thanks to radio intercepts, we eavesdrop on the Abwehr every single day. Would you believe that, yesterday, I was even listening to their codebreakers as they were struggling to crack our codes?'

Now, she knew which way to go. Now, she knew just what to do.

'I'm not going to tell MI14,' she said out loud, to the grey and brown vehicles toiling down below. 'You are!'

She took the cream leather helmet from the handlebars. It was painful to put on, but would make her return to civilisation less sensational by hiding her gashed and bloodstained noggin. She let the ear flaps hang loose and rode on, keeping her speed to 5 km/h.

For her plan to work, she needed the goon squad close, but not too close. Close enough to follow her all the way to Charleville-Mézières and L'Hôtel Saint-Michel, but not close enough to shoot out her tyres on the highway.

For want of wing mirrors, she twisted at the waist to look behind her. At last, the brown and cream car rounded the bend, close enough for her to make out the model. A Renault Juvaquatre. The Betty Boop Citroën followed right behind. She sped up and let them chase.

Ahead, a fingerpost read *Charleville-Mézières 10 km*. This was a different road from the D22 she'd rode in on, but had the advantage of signposting to her pursuers exactly where she was going. She made sure the Renault saw her take the turning before she dropped off the highway. Now, she could go hell for leather and leave them behind. Except she couldn't, for she found herself in a narrow, rutted lane with a Mohawk of mud and grass. The front axle bucked in protest at the bumps and potholes. Just when her plan called for some speed, for ten klicks of slick blacktop to let her lose the Abwehr, this muddy lane slowed her down to John Deere pace. Leaning into a corner, she skidded on farmer's slurry and only just righted the machine in time.

When she reached Charleville-Mézières, she parked outside the Saint-Michel, unhooked the pannier and strode into the lobby. The receptionist handed her the key to the Blériot Suite. Thanks to the helmet, he didn't slow her down with questions such as, *What happened to your skull?* and *Would you like me to go and look for the rest of it?*

Once inside the suite, she made straight for the complementary block pad on the table. Pressing down extra hard with the sharp pencil, she printed the following words:

MARTIANS LAND JUPITER'S ICY MOON & ALIEN SHELTER. ONLY PRETTY RING TIME. O2 PUMPS NO DEFENCE.

She tore off the top sheet, then tipped the block pad towards the window to check the words were indented enough to be legible. Looking through the window, her heart stopped to see the Renault pull in even sooner than expected. Stuffing the top sheet into her bra, she slammed the block pad back down, snatched up her pannier and fled the room. She ran to the far end of the corridor, down the service staircase and out into the street.

In the hotel lobby, a smiling Lothar told the receptionist that he would like to return a lost wallet to a colleague called Dieter Wetzel, if *monsieur* would be so good as to say in which room he is staying.

'I'm afraid he has gone out, *monsieur*.'

Lothar followed the receptionist's glance at the keys to the bulky fob lying in the Montgolfier Suite pigeonhole.

'Oh, well, in that case, I'll come back later,' said Lothar. 'Only, he must be beside himself, the poor man. May I slip a note under his door with my telephone number? I believe he told me he's in the ... Montgolfier Suite?'

'Do you know where to go? First floor, turn left.'

Lothar climbed the stairs. Before he got to the Montgolfier, he passed an open door swinging in the breeze. Stepping into the Blériot Suite, he found a girl's socks on the floor, an envelope with a London postmark and a letter inside. No sign of the girl, but she couldn't have got far. His eye landed on the block pad on the table and the indentations on its top page. He stepped across the room, picked up the pencil and rubbed the lead over the indentations. A message appeared in English. He tore off the page and went back out into the corridor. Outside the Montgolfier Suite, he slid a skeleton key into the lock. He looked up and down the corridor once more, and then clicked the door open, removed the skeleton key and entered the dead man's suite.

He locked the door behind him and set about erasing every last vestige of Dieter Wetzel. Pfennigs from the ashtray, Party card from the nightstand. With Wetzel's nail scissors, Lothar snipped the Wallheimer label from the neck seam of the herringbone jacket hanging in the wardrobe, and from its inside pocket he lifted the return tickets to Koblenz. From the sink, he removed the toothpaste, Doramad Radioaktive Zahncreme: *Thorium Makes Teeth Not Just Shine, But Glow!*

He thanked the receptionist again on his way out, climbed into the driver's seat of the Citroën and passed the block-pad message to Radio Man in the back of the van.

Radio Man awoke the radio transmitter. Amber light flooded its little dials. Silent needles swayed and settled. He tuned the antenna to the high-frequency channel and flicked the emission-control switch to *Voice*. Speaking into a circular microphone, its chunky brass mesh halfway to a suit of Saxon chain mail, he sent the coded call-sign for General von Manstein: 'Z X 1 E V M.' Then, he began his report: '*Eine feindliche Agentin hat DW getötet ...*'

Once the message had been sent, he clicked off all the switches.

Now, there was only one last item on the clean-up list. The little motorbike lady. Once she was disposed of, all the radioactive toothpaste would be back in the tube.

Little Green Woman

IDA CLIMBED A CINDER-BLOCK WALL in a back alley and dropped into a junkyard of car parts. She picked her way through piles of sprockets, engines, a punchbag and a dilapidated Sinti caravan, then entered the garage at its back door, through the colourful plastic ribbons of a fly curtain.

The bossman said, 'Get lost on your way back?'

'Two Germans are chasing me. I need your help.'

'Did they do that to you?' asked the little Chaplin one with the curly oil-black hair.

'No, that was another German.'

'Where's he?'

'Dead.'

'And the live ones?' asked Bossman.

'Hotel opposite. I can't get to the bike without them seeing.'

'Is one of them wearing a brown leather jacket?' said Chaplin, peering out of the main garage entrance.

'Yes.'

'He's on his way here, by the looks of it.'

In a flash, Bossman lifted a pair of green overalls from a peg and tossed them to Ida. Once she'd stepped into them, he kicked a board roller towards her. She lay on her back on the roller and scooted herself under a car. Bossman hung her battered brown leather pannier among a dozen others on a display rack.

Lothar made his way through the cobbled market square, weaving through stalls selling bread and cheese, fruit and vegetables, and sidestepping a peasant as she twirled a goose to wring its neck.

He stepped into the concrete box of a garage. Among the mechanics in green, he took the older one in the shirt and tie for *le patron*.

'*Bonjour, Monsieur Le Patron*, I'm looking for the woman who hired that Peugeot 350 cc parked outside the hotel. She owes me money. Lots of money.'

'She owes me money, too.'

'Still has the keys?' asked Lothar.

'Yes, she does.'

'Here's fifty francs. Let me know when she comes back. Another fifty when you do.'

The bossman trousered the fifty and asked, 'Where will I find you?'

'Across the street. Le Saint-Michel.'

'She has to return the keys by five or lose her deposit, so she should be here within the hour.'

Lothar knew this didicoi was lying to him. Why else did he stand so frozen, just waiting for him to go? Was the small woman on the motorbike not a client at all, but one of them?

Two little green legs projected from under a car. The didicois followed Lothar's gaze down to the legs. When he looked up, they were all staring at him in suspense, waiting to see what he would do next. Lothar squatted down, grabbed the green ankles and yanked. Castors trundled, followed by a bang and a cry.

From under the chassis emerged a short man with blood pouring from his nose, who shouted, '*Putain!* You whacked my face on the chassis!'

The *patron* shoved Lothar against the wall, with his forearm across his windpipe. 'What did you do that for, *salaud*?'

'I thought she was hiding under the car,' said Lothar. 'She's small like him. Forgive me. Another fifty when you find her.'

The mechanics watched him leave, then searched for the fugitive themselves, but she was nowhere to be found. Not under a car, not under a tarp, not in the grease pit, not in the caravan.

The bossman mimed a puff of sulphur. '*Pfft!* She just disappeared! *Pfft!*'

A poltergeist bowled a tractor tyre across the garage. The mechanics stood rooted to the spot while the tractor tyre rolled past them towards the grease pit, where it simply vanished. They heard a yelp. Like a human cannonball fired too far from the funfair, a woman in a helmet appeared from the grease pit.

'Easy to climb into a tractor tyre,' said Ida. 'Hard to climb out.'

Grabbing an arm apiece, Bossman and Nosebleed Kid hoisted her from the pit.

'He didn't sound German,' said Bossman.

'Well, he is,' she said. 'Can't believe he only offered you fifty.'

'Dead or alive!' cried Nosebleed Kid. 'Like in the Westerns!'

'Was the man you killed his friend?' asked Bossman. 'Is that why he's after you?'

'No, I discovered the Germans are about to invade France through the Ardennes, hitting Sedan first.'

The mechanics looked at each other in silence.

'Do you know when?' asked Bossman.

'Soon. This spring.'

'Will *les boches* go straight to Paris? Or will they stop to round up all the *tzigane* and Sinti?'

'No telling what a mad dog might do,' said Ida. 'Are you all Sinti?'

'Only the handsome ones,' said Nosebleed Kid.

'Here's what I owe you for that good Peugeot,' she said. 'Plus extra, if you will permit me to leave the motorcycle at Sedan railway station. This extra hundred is to cover the cost of collecting it from Sedan.'

'We're coining it today,' said Bossman, trousering the roll. 'But they'll be expecting you to go to Sedan, *mademoiselle*. So, if I was you, I'd go to Reims.'

'Sure you don't mind collecting the bike from Reims?'

'Well, I'd much rather you took a train from Charleville-Mézières, but that's asking for trouble.'

'Listen,' said Nosebleed Kid, 'who knows what twists and turns you'll have to do. Telephone us from whatever station you fetch up at, and we'll get the motorbike from there – Reims, Amiens, or wherever.'

'But not El Paso,' said Bossman. 'Not Santa Fe.'

'Dodge City for me, please,' said Nosebleed Kid.

Lothar sat in the Citroën with its slide door open. He watched the stunted didicoi, whose nose he had bloodied, collect the woman's motorbike from outside the hotel. But instead of taking it back to the garage, he pushed it through the market square. Lothar followed at a distance in the Citroën, driving at walking pace. He parked next to a call box in the cool of a stand of riverbank trees, near where a group of *vieillards* were playing boules, and watched the didicoi park the motorbike by the turn-off for the road to Sedan, then walk back into town.

Lothar lifted the *Feldfunk-Sprecher*, his portable walkie-talkie, from the passenger seat. 'He's left the motorbike for her on the Sedan road.'

'Wait there until she collects it, Lothar. I'll overtake her on the Sedan road and find a blind corner. You herd her from behind.'

A crocodile of schoolchildren blocked his view of the Peugeot 350. Lothar climbed from the van and walked across to the opposite pavement, so that he had a clear view of the motorcycle. Soon, the girl would fetch the motorbike that had been left for her, and he needed to be sure that she did indeed take the Sedan road. Once the children had all gone, he got back into the cab of the Citroën.

Moments later, the *patron* from the gypsy garage crossed in front of his windscreen and waved a cheery greeting.

Lothar leant out the open side door and said, 'Has she turned up yet?'

'I promise I'll tell you the moment I see her,' he said, resting his foot on the wheel he was rolling along the road. 'Hey, *mon copain*, someone's stolen one of your wheels.'

'What?' Lothar jumped out of the van and saw that a

car jack had replaced the van's nearside back wheel. He rounded on the *patron*. 'You did this.'

'Not me.'

'You've got my wheel there!'

'*Sans blague?*' No kidding. With the sole of his shoe, Bossman sent the wheel rolling down the riverbank.

Lothar swung at him, but Bossman ducked the blow and countered with a short punch to the liver. Lothar threw another punch. This time, Bossman caught his hand and twisted it behind his back. Lothar bent double in agony.

'Hey, remember I promised to tell you the moment I saw her? Well, there she is! Look!'

He steered Lothar by the arm until he was facing the right way. Lothar lifted his head in time to see a little woman in green overalls clip a pannier on to the motorbike, then mount up and ride off down the Sedan road.

The Nurses of Vendresse

AS IDA COLLECTED THE MOTORCYCLE from where Nosebleed Kid had left it, she saw the van wheel go bouncing down the riverbank and Bossman arguing with Lothar.

Riding along the Sedan road, she looked over her shoulder at the brown and cream wingtip racing to catch up. She peeled off the highway on to a service road that led back to the outskirts of Charleville-Mézières. When next she saw the Renault behind her, she ducked through a succession of narrow back alleys, then swung south-west for Reims.

She soon left the Reims highway for small roads and lanes, which wound through steep valleys and wooded hills, a topography better fitted to prey not predator. It was the very opposite of Dallam County, Texas, where the giant tarantulas of childhood nightmares hunted her across exposed moonscapes with nary a ditch nor gully in which to hide.

For all the Grand Est assured her of escape, it disturbed

her in another way. Riding through one village after another, she was troubled by the total lack of preparation for war. Yes, these villages were in the boondocks, but so were the sandbagged and barrage-ballooned towns and villages of Oxfordshire – your Abingdons and your Wallingfords. And, unlike Oxfordshire, the Grand Est region *shared an actual border* with Germany. Not until Ida rode into the town of Vendresse did she see the first sign of any preparedness.

Outside Vendresse's handsome town hall, between neat flower beds of pink, purple, red and yellow marguerites, begonias and marigolds, a dozen student nurses dressed all in white were gathered for an outdoor lesson. A senior nurse was demonstrating how to fashion a sling from a triangular bandage. At last, some war preparation – but how quaint! As if this were going to be a rough-and-tumble *Swallows and Amazons* sort of a war, in which news bulletins would tally the number of broken wrists and dislocated shoulders sustained on the frontlines.

She parked opposite the *mairie*, by a flint churchyard wall in the shadow of a yew. Blood, sweat and mileage had fairly glued the helmet to her head. She inched it off only with much profanity and stowed the blood-caked skid lid in the pannier, which she unclipped from the bike.

Conversation fell away as Ida walked through the celestial nurses.

'*Mon Dieu*, that's a very bad wound you have there, *mademoiselle*,' said the senior nurse. 'Were you hit by a truck?'

'No, I just took a corner too quick.'

'Truly? But you would not have a gash like this from the road, I'm sure.'

'Well, I think someone threw a rock at me from a bridge.'

'A rock.'

'Yes.'

'But there are two gashes here. So, did they throw two rocks?'

'One from the road, one from the rock. Anyway, from now on I'll always wear a crash helmet. I have learnt my lesson.'

'Is that your motorcycle over there by the church?'

'That's the one.'

'But it has not a scratch on it.'

'I wish it were the other way round,' joshed Ida. 'I wish the motorcycle was all scratched and dented, and there wasn't a mark on me. Ha ha!'

Nobody laughed.

'But, in fact,' said one eagle-eyed student nurse, 'your motorcycle did not entirely escape without a scratch, after all. Look at the pannier in your hand.'

Ida followed the young nurse's finger to three bullet holes. The bullets must have passed inches from her spine. She turned and dropped to her knees and then to all fours, vomiting in the marigolds.

The senior nurse sat Ida down on a chair.

'Gather round, ladies,' she said, 'and I will show you how to dress a head wound.'

The class muttered excitedly. At last, a proper injury to work on, and a gory one at that.

'First, one cleans the wound with iodine, like so ...'

Ida gasped at the sharp sting, then blew out a long breath.

The senior nurse recoiled, before speaking over the patient's head to her students: 'Now, here is another fact about field hospitals which your textbooks do not mention. Very often, a soldier's breath will absolutely reek.

The soldiers want to talk to you, of course they do. They are young men; you are pretty nurses. But their breath will stink of stale beer, fresh sick, rotting teeth and so on. Or, in this case, all three! So, the trick is to stand *behind* the patient when you apply the dressing. Then, if they turn to talk to you, you can firmly tilt and turn their head like so, just like a hairdresser at the salon!'

She placed one hand on Ida's chin to demonstrate the firm wrench of a patient's head to the forward-facing position.

'Another trick is to offer some mint leaves and tell them they have pain-reducing properties – which they do, but not for the patient. For you!'

Laughter from the celestial nurses.

Ida tried to explain this lapse in her usual standards of oral hygiene: 'I began the day with a thorough brushing of my teeth, let me tell you, but I've had quite a day of it, and the only reason why—'

Again, the senior nurse demonstrated the forward wrench of the patient's head. A student nurse handed Ida a few mint leaves, plucked from the town hall's herbarium.

Ida waved them away. 'No, thank you.'

'It's not for your benefit,' said the nurse. 'Take these leaves and put them in your mouth.'

And so the Dallas Zoo gorilla chewed her leafy meal while the school party gawped, and the vet tended the wound she got from fighting a rival ape in the cage.

The neat expertise with which Ida's wounds were cleaned and bandaged was almost worth the humiliating commentary.

For her part, the nurse was delighted with how the lesson had gone. Thanks to the sensation of this unexpected arrival, the students hung on her every word and were all taking turns to wrap bandages round each other's heads. At first, she waved away the money Ida offered. But when she saw just how much it was, she folded the francs into her apron as deftly as if she were tucking hospital corners. She dispatched a student to fetch a *sirop de grenadine* cordial, which Ida downed in one.

'Promise me you will drive your motorcycle slowly and carefully,' said the senior nurse, 'and please, I beg you, wear your helmet over your bandage.'

'My helmet?'

'Yes, the cream helmet you were wearing when you rode in.'

'Oh, *that* helmet. Yes, of course! I always do. Thank you, ladies. Thank you all.'

Glyn Gower and the Martian Invasion

―

A BELL RANG THREE TIMES on the seventh floor of the Peter Robinson department store, the Oxford Circus headquarters of MI14. This meant there was an outsider at the turnstile. At the third bell, there began what the office mordantly called the three-ring circus: from one end of the floor to the other, everybody quickly covered over classified charts and secret documents. Glyn wheeled a seven-foot-high screen on castors in front of a classified floor-to-ceiling wall map of Western Europe.

Colour-coded pins in the North Sea represented Royal Navy patrols, merchant ships and the last sightings of German U-boats. The pins were days old and obsolete. For some reason, he was no longer receiving naval intelligence. It was over a week since any arrived at his desk. Should he be worried? Were they on to him? Merry had warned him that he could be arrested for high treason. Had that day come? Was the fact that naval reports were no longer sent to him a presentiment of imminent arrest? No, he told himself. The pep pills were making him paranoid. That was all. He should try to cut down. No doubt he was out of the loop because of an administrative reshuffle, or because MI6 was trying to arrogate naval intelligence-gathering to itself ahead of the next funding review.

'Here we go again,' said Betsy Todd, walking past in her WAAF uniform and Senior Section Leader stripes.

'Who's it today?' Glyn asked.

'GPO engineers, putting in new telephone lines,' she replied. 'And this came for you. Landed on my desk by mistake.'

'Blimey, this has been round the houses, hasn't it?' he said. A palimpsest of rubber stamps recorded the manila packet's journey from Southwold Y Station to Arkley View Radio Security Service, before it had found its way to him.

Back at his desk, he opened the envelope and found a radio intercept on thin yellow paper. It began with the call sign ZX1EVM, which meant it was for the urgent attention of General Erich von Manstein, whose Army Group South was Glyn's bailiwick.

He smoothed out the yellow paper on his green vinyl desktop. After the call sign came the message proper, which he translated as he read:

Eine feindliche Agentin hat DW getötet.

A female enemy agent killed DW.

Wir haben ihre Nachricht nach London abgefangen.

We intercepted her message to London.

Nachright folgt. Zitat.

Message follows. Quote.

Then, to Glyn's surprise, the message switched to English. But, while the German was simple, the English was utter gobbledegook:

Martians land Jupiter's icy moon & Alien shelter. Only pretty ring time. O2 pumps no defence.

There came a reprise of straightforward German – *Nachricht beenden. Schlusszitat* – which Glyn translated as End quote. End message.

Then came an intriguing sign-off:

Agentin immer noch auf freiem Fuß.

Female agent still at large. Literally, 'free of foot'. *Auf freiem Fuß.* Footloose.

Glyn sparked up a Player's Navy Cut and set about deciphering the intergalactic English code.

Martians land Jupiter's icy moon & Alien shelter. Only pretty ring time. O2 pumps no defence.

As far as he recalled, Jupiter had more moons than his old jumpers had bobbles. The only Jovian moons he could name off the top of his head were the Big Four: Ganymede, Callisto, Europa and Io. In the *Iliad*, the gods kidnap Ganymede to serve as Zeus's cupbearer on Mount Olympus. So, was this perhaps a book code based on the *Iliad*? But, given Homer's silence on the subject of Martian attacks, Glyn dismissed the idea. He couldn't think where else there was a Ganymede and so he skipped to the next sentence.

Only pretty ring time.

This was from the Shakespearean ditty, 'It Was a Lover and His Lass', lately made famous by radio star and singing sensation Al Bowlly. In the Al Bowlly almanac, springtime was the only pretty ring time. Therefore, this message was about something due to happen in the spring, which meant it was imminent. Shakespeare's song comes from *As You Like It*, in which Rosalind disguises herself as a young man called Ganymede, and Celia dresses up as a shepherdess called Aliena. Well, that fitted with *Jupiter's icy moons* and *Alien*, but left him none the wiser. More perplexed than ever, in fact, since half the clues suggested an Elizabethan blank-verse comedy, while the other half suggested some kind of science-fiction epic, like *War of the Worlds*. He clacked his pencil against his teeth, then chomped on the middle like a horse's bit.

& *Alien shelter.*

Where did Ganymede and Aliena shelter? In the Forest of Arden, which was, if memory served, the Ardennes. And, if she was talking forests, then the O2 *pumps* were trees.

O2 pumps no defence.

So, Lady Agent Still At Large was warning that the trees in the Ardennes were no defence against the little green men from Mars. So far, so loony. And yet, when the Abwehr intercepted her warning, they sent its precious lunacy straight to Manstein, and to no man else. The Abwehr were sure this was something the general in charge of the invasion of France needed urgently to know about.

He took the pencil from his mouth and spoke the next words out loud.

'What do little green men have to do with General Erich von Manstein, chief of Army Group South?'

Martians ... Martians ... Martians ...

Aufmarschanweisung.

Our Martian Invasion.

His flesh turned cold. The whole room tilted and swayed. He heard her voice speaking the words of the message as clearly as if she were sitting beside his desk right now, in damp shoes, holding her cup of English tea with a ginger biscuit in the saucer and her sweet Texan voice teasing his German pronunciation: *Oh, I do believe I speak rather better*

German than you, Glyn. *The way you pronounce* auf-MAR-SCHAN-weisung *sounds like you're talking about Our Martian Invasion.*

Suddenly, the words *auf freiem Fuß* – still at large – were the most beautiful ever put to paper. Still at large meant still alive! Still at large meant Ida was out of their clutches. On the lam! *Auf freiem Fuß*. Running free. Yes, his girl was too clever for them! Just as, for better or worse, she was always too clever for him.

But where was the girl when she sent this? Behind enemy lines in Germany? Or in France? He remembered then that Ida had refused his request to be Dieter Wetzel's pen pal because she was going on a sabbatical to the Ardennes.

Dieter Wetzel! DW! *A female enemy agent killed DW*. Dear God! Somehow, in the Ardennes, Ida had crossed paths with Dieter Wetzel and, if the Abwehr were to be believed, killed him. Killed him and then sent a coded message. A message about Martians.

Our Martian Invasion. No one else in the world was in on that joke. Could it be that Ida had *tricked* the Abwehr into sending a message that Glyn himself would see? His eye fell on the telephone handset. *Hullo. May I speak to the Nazis, please?* She had entrusted him with this message. Trusted him to know her meaning.

What was she trying to tell him? Was she telling him that, having walked the forest floor in her own size fours, trees were no defence against several divisions of panzer tanks? Conventional wisdom held the Ardennes Forest to be a natural anti-tank defence, too thickly wooded to allow more than a foot patrol to hack its way through. Why would General von Manstein want to invade a forest?

Glyn heard the GPO engineers packing up to go. He

scooted the screen away from the floor-to-ceiling wall map of Western Europe.

The green Ardennes straddled the Franco-Belgian border. The Maginot Line stopped at the edge of the forest, level with Glyn's frown as he stood before the map.

What if Ida was right that trees were no defence? Perhaps because they were more spaced out than they appeared from aerial photography, or because panzers changed the rules of the game, since they could push most trees aside like bracken. In the moment of asking that question, the whole map seemed to shift and realign before his very eyes, in the same way a pair of 2D photographs became a 3D image under Merry's spectroscope. Suddenly he understood exactly what Ida was trying to tell him. Any day now, Manstein would invade the Belgian Ardennes, and then make a sickle-cut into France. By invading France from Belgium, Manstein would bypass the Maginot Line. It was a brilliant tactical manoeuvre. A masterstroke. That was his secret plan, the *Aufmarschanweisung*, the Martian Invasion.

Glyn's heart thumped in his chest.

The single greatest intelligence scoop of the war was in his hands.

He was about to deliver to the War Office the decrypt that would change the whole course of the war! An intelligence scoop that would scupper the German war machine! He and Ida were going to save France! But there was not a moment to lose. That message was intercepted at a Suffolk Y Station a whole day ago. If he lived to be a hundred, the next hour would be the most important of his whole life.

He phoned Austin, the head of MI14's Advanced Intelligence Section. The line was engaged. Glyn snatched his jacket off the back of his swivel chair. He would sprint all the way to Storey's Gate, Austin's Westminster office.

Just then, two hard-faced military policemen marched in. The iron Blakeys of their black boots rang out on the shop floor. It was unprecedented to see redcaps here. Why did nobody ring the three bells? Glyn wondered if he should shunt the screen back in front of the top-secret map of Western Europe. Those grunts weren't cleared to see its colour-coded pins.

'Which one of you is Gower?' barked one of the redcaps.

All heads turned towards Glyn.

'Glyn Gower, I'm arresting you under the Treason Act for destroying Royal Navy intelligence vital to the defence of the realm.'

'What? When? Not now, you're not,' said Glyn. 'An agent behind enemy lines has just discovered the German plan to invade France. I have to be at the War Office this instant.'

'Oh, *now* you want to share intelligence. Well, I'm afraid, Mr Gower, that you are under arrest, so it's a bit bloody late for that.'

Glyn shoved the redcap in the chest and ran for the turnstile, but the other one rugby-tackled him to the floor before he got there. Together, the two redcaps frogmarched him towards the exit.

Glyn pulled and writhed and shouted to his colleagues, 'An agent in the field has just discovered General Manstein's order of battle! Tell Austin that German panzers are about to invade through—'

The redcaps bent him into a strappado: arms steepled behind his back. Glyn screamed in agony and despair. He had failed Ida.

Ida Returns

MERRY HURRIED INTO ST PANCRAS station's oak-panelled ticket hall. She found Ida with a bandaged head, a yellow eye and so desolate an air that she ran to clasp her in her arms. They clung to each other while travellers moved around them. For a long time, neither spoke, until Ida, her head on Merry's shoulder, asked, 'Did Glyn pass on my intelligence?'

'Which intelligence was this?'

Ida jerked backwards and stared at Merry, holding her by the elbows. 'What do you mean, which intelligence was this? The Manstein Plan! Panzer tanks invading France through the Ardennes Forest *any day now*! *That* intelligence! The intelligence I risked my life for!'

'Oh, Ida, I fear, if he got it, he may have been arrested before he could pass it on.'

'Arrested! What for?'

'Withholding intelligence from the Royal Navy. Come, let me take you home.'

They took a taxi through the London dusk to Merry's small second-floor flat in Denman Alley. In its kitchenette, Merry tipped a paper twist of coffee granules into two cups and heated the steam kettle on the Belling.

'I'm on night shift tonight,' she said. 'Eight to eight. But, when I get to Wembley, the first thing I'll do is go over all our recent covers of the Ardennes.'

The light was failing outside. Merry pulled the blackout curtains of thick broadcloth across the flat's two windows. They'd stolen the curtains from the New Theatre in Oxford during the phoney war. The theft was in revenge for a production of *King Lear* performed in late Victorian costume. ('No one,' Merry had whispered to Ida backstage, as she folded the broadcloth into a firewood caddy, 'would ever set an Oscar Wilde production in Saxon times, with everyone carrying halberds, because it needs a world of handbags and left luggage offices – so why are we supposed to accept it the other way around? Why, Ida? *Why?*')

The blackout curtains drawn, Merry switched on the overhead light. From her canvas satchel, Ida pulled out the *Service Géographique de l'Armée* map and opened it on a table so rickety it swayed like a sea captain's. To Merry, the light in Ida's eyes was like that of a dog in a fight as she pointed out the cross-stitch of *La Ligne Maginot*, running the length of France's borders with Germany and Luxembourg, but stopping dead at the Belgian frontier.

'Let me take this to Wembley,' said Merry. 'When I get to work, I'll send a note to Austin, too, because he's very high up in Military Intelligence.'

'Which one? MI14, where Glyn was?'

'Well, I gather that Austin's sort of across all the MIs, from one to twenty – or however many there are. And, by the sound of it, he's rather dominating them, too, just as he dominated Oxford philosophy.'

'Well, isn't that the first bit of good news in a long while?'

'No,' said Merry. 'There is first and foremost the good news of your escape and your survival, and of how you cheated death.'

A long silence followed, then Ida said, 'I can't stop thinking that, if I'd taken another minute to uncuff my wrists, Merry, I'd be dead and buried and no one would have ever known where I was or what happened to me.'

'But you escaped.'

'I escaped.'

'And killed the slave that was a-hanging thee.'

'Ha! I knew I'd seen those curtains before.'

The Obdurate Keating of Wembley

AT WEMBLEY THAT NIGHT, in the Photographic Interpretation Unit's white offices, Merry selected from the shelves whatever aerial reconnaissance photographs they had of the land between Düsseldorf and the Belgian border near the Ardennes.

She arranged these 'stereo pairs' under the twin lenses of her stereoscope, working at ten-mile intervals east from the border. She restricted her search to sorties flown in early morning or late evening, when the shadows were longest. This way, although camouflage disguised a panzer from plan view, the tank might still cast a side shadow on to an empty road. Now and then, the low sun even gave away the camouflage netting itself, throwing its dapple-pattern silhouette halfway across the field, like an Asian cast net thrown from a sampan. This irony always delighted her – she would never have found many a field gun or fuel dump but for the long shadows cast by its camouflage net!

Her china-white pencil annotated a pepper-pot shadow

with the query, *Gun turret?* Here and there, she drew an arrow pointing to flattened grass. At one point, she circled the two ends of a long column of panzers on the westbound carriageway of the autobahn close to Aachen. Nowhere did she find a single piece of irrefutable evidence, but, by 7 a.m., when the trucks on the North Circular were casting their own long shadows over the roadside verges, she had amassed more than enough circumstantial evidence to confirm her belief in Ida's discovery.

She got up from her desk and stood beside her chair, arching her stiff back and rolling her shoulders. Draping her cashmere cardigan around her shoulders, she knotted the sleeves under her ancient pearls and took her findings to her boss, an archaeologist from Cambridge University called Keating, who'd been given a rank she could never remember, wing squadron captain or some such. To avoid getting it wrong, she presumed on academic collegiality and just called him Keating, which he didn't seem to mind.

As Keating studied her covers under his desk light, Merry saw her china-white annotations upside down in the lenses of his owlish glasses. She was keyed up and tried to calm herself by listening to the sounds of the nearby railway siding, where a shunter was being decoupled from a train. From the office corridor, a colleague shouted, 'Who blocked the bleedin' khazi?'

She studied Keating. Somehow, he looked as if he'd just begun his shift. His manicured hands were not inky from glossy covers, his ashtray was empty and his blue serge tunic was still belted. At length, he looked up, with a canny smile on his short face.

'Yes,' he said. 'There's just the requisite amount of matériel here for a decoy.'

'A decoy?' Merry exclaimed in a much louder voice than she had intended.

'Yes, it's a feint, isn't it? A feint designed to dislodge the British Expeditionary Force from the Dyle Plan.'

'I'm afraid I don't know what the Dyle Plan is, Keating.'

'No reason you should,' he replied. 'It's basically the strategy of concentrating our forces near the Dyle river, where we're now dug in. So long as the Allies hold the Dyle, the Germans cannot seize the Pas de Calais coal basin and Antwerp's petrochemical industries. Compared to coal mines and chemical refineries, the Ardennes seems to me to offer slim pickings indeed. And so, this is a feint, a decoy designed to lure the British, French and Belgian armies from the Dyle.'

'A one-hundred-mile decoy?'

'Not the whole way, no. Every now and then, I grant you, these covers do show an actual army base or an actual fuel dump or what have you, but that is a far cry indeed from the massed ranks of an invasion force.'

'What I'm rather struck by,' she said, tipping her head to one side as though they were not arguing but chatting companionably on a Rhine river cruise, and she were pointing out a charming detail on the riverbank, 'is that these isolated camps and fuel dumps appear to be in a straight line, don't they? Almost as though they form one continuous column from the Belgian border to the Rhine.'

'Haven't you rather imposed that line on the landscape?'

'No, I believe I have traced this column from a mosaic of covers. And if the covers have indeed discovered one continuous column, then one might estimate a force of at least a million men.'

'Well, let me stop you right there,' said Keating, leaning

back in his chair and awarding himself a private smile. 'You should have learnt ere now to halve estimates.'

Hark the bardic wisdom, she thought. Ere now. Were he not such a neophyte, he wouldn't be pretending to be steeped in ancient lore. Earlier this year, he was teaching the difference between Ionic and Corinthian columns. Now, he was the seasoned veteran whose deep knowledge came from the School of Hard Knocks.

She gave a quizzical smile and asked, 'Halve them? Why?'

'Simple, really,' he replied. 'If there's one thing the Central Interpretation Unit at the Air Ministry hates more than being told something they didn't know, it's being told something hugely significant that they didn't know.'

'But what if it's true?'

'Well, that's far from certain, and even if it were true, and you hoped to have a hearing for your pet theory, that is all the more reason not to talk about a million men.'

'Quite so,' replied Merry. 'May I therefore request that we duly halve our estimate, and you inform the CIU that we have discovered evidence of merely half a million men taking part in a decoy exercise on the Belgian border that continues in a camouflaged column of armour that stretches all the way to Düsseldorf?'

He narrowed his eyes and looked at her with an expression which was both spiteful and lacking in confidence.

Sliding his stereoscope over the covers again, he went through them one after the other, the frames and lenses of his owl glasses clacking on the stereoscope as he slid it here and there.

He lifted his head and scowled. 'All right. I'll pass it on to bloody CIU,' he said, in the resentful tone of someone having to do a disagreeable duty. 'But I already know what they'll say about this. They'll say exactly the same as me.'

Merry took a deep breath and smiled sweetly. 'Thank you for trying,' she said.

'You're knocking off now, aren't you?'

'My shift ends at eight, yes.'

'Well, I'm here until noon. Telephone me then and I'll let you know the verdict from on high, whether Central Interpretation have given the thumbs up or down to your Ardennes theory.'

Early light scythed through the large windows as Merry walked back to her desk. She sat, looking out the window, and asked herself if she had done right by Ida. Had she done enough? She was worried she had not. Keating's own scepticism would be sure to colour his report to the CIU. No doubt he'd frame it to imply that one of the office debs had a bee in her bonnet about the imminent invasion of France.

She recalled the ardent conviction with which Ida had spread that map on the deal table in Denman Alley, and how her wide frank eyes, so full of trust, had implored her to make sure that Berlin's greatest military secret was not ignored in London. That interview with Keating just now was not commensurate with those imploring eyes. What else could she do? Where else might Ida's secret get a hearing? Who else might give a thumbs up to her Ardennes theory?

Well, she thought, there was always British Military Intelligence Section 3's very own Oxonian. Any port in a storm. She listened to the sound of a plumber's metal tools clanking against porcelain. Sometimes, you just had to hold your nose to unblock the bleedin' khazi.

She phoned MI3 and asked to be put through to Vernon Alwynne.

*

Ida awoke to find her borrowed Viyella pyjamas soaked right through. She clicked on the bedside light to see if an upstairs pipe had sprung a leak, but the bedroom ceiling was dry. She was drenched in her own sweat and out of breath, as if she had been running for miles. Only then did she remember her nightmare.

She had dreamt she was Paul Revere's wife on that fateful night of April 18th, 1775, the turning point of the American Revolutionary War. Her husband's hour of destiny had come, but where was Paul? He was nowhere to be found. And so it fell to her, Mrs Ida Revere, to make the famous midnight ride. Sparks flashed from her horse's hooves as she galloped into Lexington, shouting, 'The redcoats are coming! The redcoats are coming!'

A furious housewife in a nightie and holding a lantern had stomped on to the porch of her frame house and hissed, 'Have you any idea how late it is, missy?'

Merry was still not back from work. Ida opened the stolen blackout curtains, made a coffee and shuffled around the house in Merry's long blue dressing gown. She avoided mirrors, since the dressing gown made her look like Dopey in *Snow White and the Seven Dwarfs* – after Grumpy had taken a pickaxe to Dopey's head down the gold mine, and Snow White had bandaged it up.

Just after nine, she heard Merry's key in the street door and her footsteps running up the stairs. She came in breathless and excited, blowing a windswept strand of hair from the side of her mouth. Her cheeks were red and flushed. She did not look like she had been up working all night. Her brown eyes were alive and sparkling with excitement.

'I've secured you a meeting with MI3. They're based in Gower Street, just up the road.'

'What time?'

'It's at eleven this morning.'

'That's less than two hours away! Who's it with again?'

'British Military Intelligence Section 3, MI3.'

'Which ones are they?'

'Geographical intelligence.'

'Meaning what exactly?'

'Finding out where who does what to whom, I imagine.' Merry opened her wardrobe door and clacked through its hangers. 'Now, after I got your Paris cable, I dashed up to Somerville and persuaded a porter to let me into your room. I must say, I was *keenly* disappointed to find that it had not been ransacked by Nazi secret agents. But I did some ransacking of my own and came away with this fast number.' She turned round holding a grey flannel suit.

'Oh, Merry, this is *the* single most favourite item of clothing I ever did own. It's from the high-tone Neiman Marcus in downtown Dallas. My dear grey suit!'

Merry hung it on the mantelpiece. 'I also filled a pillow slip with undies and sundries.'

'Thank you, Merry. Thank you. I am about to feel human again.'

'Do you know, after the war, let's set up an international relief organisation that takes only non-essential items to war zones and disaster areas: Max Factor lipstick, cami knickers and Turgenev, Billie Holiday and bone china – anything to make the displaced feel human again.'

'I'm in!' said Ida. 'Let's truck a load of Elizabeth Arden eight-hour cream across the border into Poland!'

She upended the pillowcase and shook her smalls on to

the sofa, then shucked off Merry's oversize dressing gown and stepped into her old reliables: a pair of workaday blue high-waist knickers.

'Plain bottoms, fancy top,' she said, clipping herself into a peach bra with ribbon bows on the straps and elaborate silver spirals on the cups. 'Only, how can I go to MI3 with my head all bandaged up? I look like I've had a course of ECT to stop me hallucinating tanks in the trees.'

'Bandage off? Show your wounds, like Coriolanus? It will bolster your case – show what this information has cost you and remind them that there's a real war out there.'

'No, thank you,' said Ida. '"I do beseech you let me o'erleap that custom; for I cannot … entreat them for my wounds' sake to give their suffrage."'

'Well, if you are not going to make a feature of your wounds, you must hide them.'

'A wig?'

'Oh, no – I have something much better.' Merry jumped up and left the room for a few minutes. When she returned, she handed Ida a pleated oyster-grey satin turban.

'It's beautiful,' said Ida, as the satin flowed over her hand.

'Try it on,' said Merry, 'but take the bandage off first or it will look crazy.'

'But what if my wounds ooze and I bleed all over your turban?'

'Then we're quits for your armchair on F Staircase.'

'That was you?'

'You didn't know?'

'No,' said Ida. 'I always assumed an old sow farrowed a litter of nine.'

Merry laughed her snorting laugh. It was endearing to

Ida that, for all Merry's poise, elegance and beauty, she laughed like an old sow pushing out the last piglet.

Ida fumbled with a safety pin on the crepe bandage with which the French nurse had dressed her wounds at Vendresse.

'Let me do that,' said Merry. She turned Ida away from the mirror so that her first sight of her scars would not be under the unforgiving ceiling light.

Slowly, Merry unspooled the bandage. When she saw the full extent of Wetzel's violence, her eyes filled with tears. She set her jaw and blinked them away. To start crying now would be unpardonable self-indulgence, for it would leave Ida feeling like a circus freak.

'What's good about this style of turban,' said Merry, in a perkier voice than usual, 'is that it's worn over the ears, so it covers pretty much the whole head.'

The bandage just above Ida's ear would not detach. Merry fetched her scissors and snipped away at Ida's hair where it was matted with blood and crepe.

'Been on yer 'olidays?' she quipped, but there was a catch in her voice. Silent tears rolled down Merry's cheeks. With a few more snips, the whole bandage came free. She kissed Ida's temple and, not disguising her grief any longer, said, in tears, 'My love, he nearly killed you.'

Ida held her hand, rested her head on her tall friend's shoulder and wept.

Merry passed her a cotton handkerchief from her cashmere sleeve. 'I'll give your blouse an iron, now.'

While Merry set up the ironing board, Ida stretched out the oyster satin and slowly lowered it over her head. Merry burst out laughing like a squealing hog.

'What's so funny?'

'You look like a cross-Channel swimmer!'

Ida stepped on to the sofa to see for herself. Framed in the mantelpiece mirror, she saw a woman in a swim cap and two-piece swimsuit. All she needed now were the goggles. She touched the pouchy, yellowed skin around her eye.

'Looks like I tussled with a shark off the Normandy shore.' She hopped down from the couch and stepped into her grey flannel skirt.

Merry spread Ida's cotton blouse on the ironing board, and said, 'Now, there is one thing about your meeting that you may take issue with.'

'Thing?'

'Man.'

'Who?' Ida looked up to find Merry giving her a subtle-is-the-Lord look. 'Oh, not Vernon Alwynne! Sweet Jesus, no!'

'He is the coming man in Military Intelligence.'

'Get out of town!'

'He's a rising star.'

'He's a knucklehead!'

'He may have been a duffer at Oxford, I grant you, but trust me when I say he's an altogether different creature in the intelligence world. Glyn told me Vernon Alwynne's a wizard at getting all the different agencies and ministries to talk to each other. He has the ear of senior mandarins and top brass at the War Office. Alwynne is the very man to ensure that all the key people get to hear the Manstein Plan before it's too late.'

Chin on knee, Ida laced her brown brogues over white ankle socks. 'Just how do you figure that?'

'Because,' said Merry, edging the flat iron around the collar of Ida's white blouse, 'the moment he hears the scoop you bring him, Alwynne will make it *his* scoop. He will want everyone who's anyone to know it came from him. He's climbed that greasy pole and wants to stay there – until they find him out. There, I've said my piece. You decide.'

'Can't we just go straight to Austin instead?'

'Austin's off sick. Pneumonia, or bronchitis, or pleurisy – one of those lung diseases, I forget which. I'll send a note to his home address in Cheyne Place today. But, if things go well at MI3 this morning, we may not need Austin and MI14 at all.'

Ida's heels rapped the bare floorboards as she paced the living room. Coils of light travelled over the ceiling. Merry looked up, puzzled as to where they might be coming from. Did she leave the electric Belling on? Were its glowing red rings reflecting on the ceiling? She checked, but the cooker was off. The sounds of Ida's pacing footsteps stopped, and the curlicues of light stayed as fixed as a ceiling boss. Merry suppressed an oink on tracing the coils on the ceiling down to the silver spirals on Ida's jazzy brassiere.

'Suppose I was Mrs Paul Revere,' said Ida, hands on hips.

'I beg your pardon?'

'Suppose it was I, lowly Mrs Revere, the humble wife, and not my husband, who galloped into Lexington at midnight, shouting, "The redcoats are coming! The redcoats are coming!" Would any man jack in the Massachusetts militia have listened to me, Merry? Do you think a single soldier in Washington's whole entire army would have paid me any mind at all?'

Merry looked her up and down and raised an eyebrow.

'Dressed as you are right now, my love?'

MI3

ITS WARTIME RECRUITMENT BONANZA had scattered Military Intelligence across London. Vernon Alwynne's MI3 was quartered in a Georgian townhouse off Gower Street.

Ida had mixed feelings about this townhouse. It wasn't the top floor of a department store, she'd give it that, but it wasn't the War Office either. And that's where her information deserved to be. Ida wished she were being hustled along the busy warren under Whitehall, where Prime Minister Neville Chamberlain might beckon her through a reinforced steel door, saying, *Now, tell Winston exactly what you told me.* Only then would she be sure that she was doing right by the great secret vouchsafed her. Instead, she found herself standing on the tasteful Persian rug of what could be a private residence, while Vernon Alwynne perched a broad buttock on a broad desk and told her what the problem was.

'The problem is you have no proof. If you came bearing

photos or enemy documents or some such, then we'd have something beyond mere surmise. But I can't very well go up to my boss and say, "Scuse I, General, an American gal I know met a Jerry tomb raider who spilled the German order of battle to her. Long and short of it is, sir, our Yankee Mata Hari says the British Expeditionary Force should reinforce Belgium." You see my point? If you had documentary proof, that would be different. But, for want of proof, how are you any different from all those Girl Guides who report German parachutists landing on the village green?'

This remark about Girl Guides left her dumbfounded. A crass argument is often harder to answer than an intelligent one, for it collapses those common assumptions of sense on which communication depends. Alwynne smiled to see her lost for words, as if he were a brilliant logician, a Bertrand Russell or a J. L. Austin, who had caught her in a cleft stick of her own contradictions.

Once more, Ida tried to explain that Dieter Wetzel was General Manstein's attaché, but Vernon Alwynne was no longer listening. Over her shoulder, his eyes were following all the comings and goings of the office, which was where the real action was. When he did finally turn back to Ida, she sensed it was because his inner clock had just dinged, telling him he'd given her enough time.

His way of getting shot of her was to pretend to be bringing her in, to act as if he were admitting her to a secret star chamber. He led her out into the corridor, where he dropped his voice to a conspiratorial whisper.

'Look, I shouldn't be telling you this, but such an attack through the Ardennes has already been anticipated. Just on the off chance. The French and Belgian armies have reinforced defences west of the Maginot Line. It's called the Dyle Plan. Very hush-hush. Shouldn't have told you even half so much. Probably be hanged, drawn and quartered at Traitor's Gate, God help me! They'll fry my tongue before my eyes for having blabbed! Keep it under your hat, there's a good girl. If Jerry twigs that we know what he's planning, he'll be on to all those brave French soldiers lying doggo. Wheels within wheels and so forth. I do thank you for coming in. It was the right thing to do. It was the proper thing to do. I'm only sorry your intelligence was not quite the bombshell you hoped it would be.'

National Gallery

WAITING OUTSIDE THE NATIONAL GALLERY, one look at Ida told Merry all she needed to know. She had seen her friend look confused before, but this was a sort of deep-tissue disorientation, an existential bewilderment one might never shake off.

'Oh, that colossal duffer! That oaf! I'm sorry I put you through that, Ida. You were right and I was wrong. Damn and blast the man!'

Merry checked her watch. Almost noon. She stepped into a phone booth by St Martin-in-the-Fields and dialled Keating at Wembley. The heavy door sealed her inside with the smell of damp ashtray. When Keating came on the line, she pushed in her coins at the pips.

'I'm afraid I have to tell you,' said Keating, 'that the Air Ministry shares my opinion, but with knobs on. Knobs, bells and whistles too. They scolded me. Said Wembley was a nest of useful idiots. Said the Wehrmacht was counting on fifth columnists to spread false rumours of an attack through Belgium so as to divert our forces away from the Germans' real point of attack. Said Jerry would be cock-a-hoop to know we were spreading their misdirection to the higher echelons of British intelligence. I really stuck my neck in the blender for you. Could have saved myself a lot of unnecessary bloody ache and humiliation had I but followed my own instincts. Are you still there? Hello?'

'We will know just whose idiocy has been useful to whom ere long, Keating. This time next week, one of us will still be working in intelligence, while the other will be back in the Fitzwilliam, lecturing on the caryatids of the Erechtheion.'

She hung up and left the phone booth.

Placing a hand on Ida's shoulder, she said, 'I'm so sorry, my love. It's like the international situation in reverse – the American jumping up and down and the English unable to grasp the urgency of the situation. Shall we try the American Embassy?'

'Why would they believe me any more than the British? I just don't understand: how can I know something so huge and yet no one else wants to know?'

As they walked across Trafalgar Square, Merry wondered how it could be that Ida, so modern, so funny, and the owner of possibly the only pair of blue jeans in England, should end up like a character from ancient myth. A Cassandra, fated to utter true prophecies never believed. She who descends to the underworld to trick a monster and cheat certain death to obtain a secret that she cannot share. She who lives to tell the tale that no one wants to hear.

They queued on the steps of the National Gallery for Myra Hess's lunchtime concert. By the time they had paid their shilling, all the seats were taken, so Merry and Ida joined all those sitting on the wooden floor, leaning their backs against the denuded gallery walls. Ugly, discoloured oblongs marked where priceless pictures once hung.

'Where did they take the paintings, Merry?'

'To a Welsh cave.'

Ida jerked at the chinking sound of a chisel hewing cave art from wall – but it was just the aluminium legs of stackable chairs being put out for the overflow audience. There were still not enough seats to go round, so the women stayed where they were. On the floor between them, Merry placed a gas-mask box from which she produced spam-and-pickle sandwiches, a thermos and two tin cups.

'Let me try Austin again,' she said.

'You said he was off sick,' said Ida.

'I shall go directly to his flat in Chelsea. If he's not there, I'll give his wife Jean a note for him. If they're both out, then I'll see her next week at St Hilda's.'

At that moment, applause greeted Myra Hess, who sat down at a giant Steinway and began to play. Ida couldn't listen to the Bach partita; Merry's breezy suggestion depressed her too much. To think it had come to this: after trying the higher echelons of MI14, MI3, Wembley's Photographic Interpretation Unit and the Air Ministry, now they were reduced to passing a hopeful note in a St Hilda's tutorial!

Ida lay her head on Merry's lap and looked up at the vaulted skylight. What a ridiculously fragile structure to put on a roof in these days of sandbags and concrete bunkers! And where was its criss-cross sticky tape? What was to stop the Luftwaffe opening their bomb bays above this preposterous skylight to sprinkle *eine kleine Kristallnacht* over the gutted gallery? Those bombers would likely take off from France, the Reich's new runway, since no one ever listened to her. She'd tried everything. Nothing worked. No one listened.

Ida sat up and stretched her legs in front of her. If the world was turning a deaf ear, she could at least pay Myra Hess the courtesy of listening to her. The second piece in her programme began – Brahms's tender and thoughtful Opus 118, Intermezzo in A major – and Ida leant her cheek on Merry's shoulder.

As the intermezzo filled the bare gallery, she realised that everybody shared the same dread of an approaching evil they couldn't control. The upturned faces of the wartime audience seemed to hang on every note, every bar, every phrase. It was uncanny how Myra Hess, in her playing, seemed to divine exactly what Londoners were feeling, what they needed to hear. Ida recognised a distinguished Viennese Kant scholar and his wife. No doubt they were not the only refugees in the audience. And, unlike her own continental suffering, theirs was no mere sabbatical.

Standing against the opposite wall, a man in a black wool coat was staring at her. Was his stare prurient, she wondered? Was he staring because her head was on another woman's shoulder, and had been, just now, in her lap? Ida sat up straight and fixed her gaze on the pianist for a few moments. When next she checked, he was still staring. She met his stare; he looked away. But a moment later, she felt his eyes on her again.

After the concert, while the audience was filing out, she took her time brushing breadcrumbs from her skirt so as to let the gawker get ahead. She wanted to follow him into Trafalgar Square, not have him follow her. The gawker placed a dark grey homburg on his head and joined the exit crush. Once out in the fresh air, however, he was nowhere to be seen.

The UV Man

MERRY AND IDA WALKED arm in arm back to Denman Alley, with Ida looking over her shoulder at every junction, still uneasy. She'd been stared at by men before, but this wasn't like that. She sensed she was a different kind of quarry now, and that the man in the homburg was from the same firm as Radio Man and Lothar.

'And now I shall sleep the sleep of the just,' said Merry, balancing her tall frame on the rickety deal table while she pulled off each shoe. 'Ken's put us both on the guest list at the Café de Paris, so, if you're not here when I wake up, I will see you there at nine tonight.'

Ida dozed on the couch. Waking at dusk, she leant against the window frame and looked down at the Soho afternoon. Seen from above, all hats and headscarves were the same. She wondered how Wembley's aerial reconnaissance photos could ever tell a shipyard from a sheep dip at 10,000 feet. But then her stomach lurched as she saw an arrangement of shoulders and homburg that was unquestionably the man from the concert. She jerked back against the wall. He had followed them all the way here from Trafalgar Square, despite her thinking she had thrown him off. When she next peeked out, he was gone. She went to the kitchen window and saw him trying the gate that led to the back fire escape. He looked up at the window. She ducked beneath the counter. The sudden movement hurt her head. Cowering by the sink cupboard, she asked herself, what did he want from her? Why had he followed her here? She was appalled to think she might have drawn Merry into danger.

Returning to the living-room window, she saw that he had taken up position halfway down the alley, where he could survey their front door. This gave her an idea. If she went out into the blackout, could she draw him away from Merry's flat and then lose him in Soho's streets? Ida scooted round the apartment, collecting her things. She belted her raincoat and stuffed one of Merry's cloche hats into the pocket.

The darkness was thickening, now, and she tiptoed down the stairs to the street door and silently turned the latch. She whirled out of the door, pretending not to have spotted him, and turned sharp right, away from where he stood and towards a dog-leg at the foot of the alley. Once round this dog-leg, she broke into a run. At the end of the alley, she crossed a courtyard, then a busy street, and found herself in another alley. She heard footsteps all around and could only hope Homburg was somewhere nearby and not still lurking under Merry's window. 'Piccadilly Commandoes' – hookers – haunted doorways and alleys. In a side street, four men lugged wooden crates of spirits up from a basement cellar. Was this a burglary? Or honest toil under cover of darkness? But, if they weren't stealing those crates of bottles, then why all the whispering? She stumbled over a kerb and cursed herself for her lack of a blackout torch or one of those luminous wands. Turning a corner, the night seemed suddenly much darker and quieter. She couldn't see much further than the end of her arm, forcing her to inch forwards, looking out for luminous kerb paint. She was about to turn left into Coventry Street when some instinct made her press her back into a doorway and perch on the step with her heels against the locked wooden door, standing stock still. Waiting.

She heard raised voices. Two men and a woman. It was a quarrel on the corner. She poked her head round the brickwork of the doorway. The altercation was happening in the middle of the street, blocking the traffic. The reedy blackout headlights of the jammed cars illuminated the scene. She saw an English Tommy pushing and shoving Homburg for shining his torch right in his girlfriend's face. Homburg squared up to him. Passers-by pulled them apart.

Ida took Merry's dark cloche hat from her pocket and slipped it on over the light-coloured turban. Now, she followed Homburg up a side street, but quickly lost him to the blackout. Her heart started thumping. He might be lying in wait to lunge out of the night any second. A truck crept by. In the weak beam of its hooded headlights, Homburg rematerialised, walking towards Berwick Street. Relief flooded her body. She was the seer, not the seen. The hunter, not the hunted.

'Luminous flowers!' barked a Berwick Street stallholder, hiding her light under an awning. 'Get your blackout-busting flowers over here!'

'A dozen carnations,' said Ida, 'and two dozen sprigs of

luminous heather and broom, please.' The florist tried to slot a bonus UV rose into her buttonhole, but Ida waved her off. 'Oh, it's not for me.'

Keeping to the pavement, Ida tracked Homburg past displays of fruit and bread. He flicked on his blackout torch, which joined a constellation of small, dancing, hooded lights up and down the street. As she walked, she rubbed the ultraviolet flowers to powder between her gloved palms.

He turned into a wider street with double-deckers coming and going each way. He had his back to the street, searching the pedestrians among the jouncing lights of their torches. Ida hopped on to the running board of a bus and passed within inches of his back. She leant out and, from the flat of her palm, blew phosphorescent confetti all over him. Sensing movement, he spun round, so that the last specks of ultraviolet pollen dusted his face. Ida hopped off the bus further down the street. A rowdy crowd of drinkers stood on the pavement outside a pub, drinks in hand, and she squirmed her way in amongst them to wait for the show. The pub-goers laughed and heckled as Homburg stomped by, all lit up like a honky-tonk riverboat.

'Make way for the Pearly King!'

'Put that light out!'

'Get run over much, do yer, cock?'

She followed him at a distance for another couple of blocks, until he stopped in a side street. Glowing and raging like a laboratory experiment gone wrong, he banged his homburg on a sandwich board. She watched him from across the street as he took off his sparkling coat. He flailed it against some railings, but the luminous spangles stuck fast. He turned the coat inside out, but when he tried to put it back on, his arms got stuck in the sleeves. The more he struggled, the more he wedged himself in. Elbows pinned to his sides, only his fingertips peeked from the sleeves. He looked like a T-Rex: big body and tiny, useless arms. He twisted and writhed, grunted and roared. Ida knew it was now or never.

She charged across the street and shoved him with both hands. He fell backwards down some steel basement steps, clattering and thumping and wholly unable to break his fall. She hung on to the metal handrail to stop herself tumbling after him. He was still conscious, but woozy.

She crouched down beside him, put her hands around his throat and growled, 'I don't know exactly who the hell you are, but let me tell you this: the one thing that could make the British believe I know something worth knowing is if you kill me, but I ain't willing to pay that price.' She stamped back up the steps, then turned. 'So leave me alone. Or next time I'll kill you, like I killed him.'

She'd reached the top of the steps when his gloved hand clamped her ankle. She kicked back like a bronco, but now he was on his feet and right behind her. He put her in a headlock and dragged her along the pavement. A leather glove covered her mouth. He pulled her into an alley. With both hands around her neck, he hoisted her off the ground. His grip tightened. She struggled for breath. She tried to kick him. His bodyweight trapped her legs against the wall.

A thud. He staggered and let go, stumbling out of the alley and into the street, where he fled into the passing traffic.

Holding a torch the size of a truncheon, a Piccadilly Commando removed the cigarette from her cherry-red mouth.

'He roll you for much, ducks?'

'Pardon?' Ida croaked.

'How much he take, love?'

'He wasn't after money.'

'A strangler? I shoulda brained him!'

'Something like that. You saved my life, just now.'

'All in a night's work, Yankee Doodle. You all right from here?'

'Yes, thank you. Only, where's the Café de Paris, please?'

'You're a game bird, ain't yer? Heh heh! Jest five doors up, Yankee Doodle. I may pop in myself, later, if I have a good night, and I shall expect you to stand me a fancy cocktail and all!'

'I'll line up the daiquiris.'

'You're my girl, Yankee Doodle! So long, pardner! Yee-hah!'

In the Ladies' restroom of the Café de Paris, Ida entered an oasis of bright light, shining white sinks and silver-framed mirrors: the perfect opposite of the blackout. Everything visible, clear and safe. She sat in a velvet armchair, almost a throne, and let the tears come, pulling paper tissue after paper tissue from a diamanté box. As the fight fuel left her body, she felt tremendously weary. Her head throbbed, and her guts sank at the prospect of having to watch over her shoulder every minute for this assassin, this German sleeper agent or fifth columnist. The Abwehr must have found her name on the hotel register at Le Saint-Michel. Did he first identify her at the National Gallery? Or had he been following her for longer – biding his time, waiting for his chance? She hauled herself out of the velvet armchair and washed her face and neck with almond-scented soap. Stepping out of the bright white light of the Ladies' into the dim, purple corridor, she walked towards a pair of double doors, which she hauled open just as Ken Johnson belted out the refrain from 'Give Me My Ranch – El Rancho Grande': 'I love the ro-de-o dearly!'

And there at a table sat Merry, tapping her wristwatch and mouthing, 'You're late!'

All of Their Panzers Are Missing

―

'HOW ON EARTH HAVE YOU managed to lose track of seven entire panzer divisions?' Lieutenant-General Sir John Dill, vice chief of the Imperial General Staff, glowered at the Military Intelligence section heads in the briefing room. 'How could hundreds of tanks simply vanish? Do you mean to say they could be absolutely anywhere? Anywhere at all? Well, perhaps I should ask the question a different way. Are any of you able to name one place where these tanks definitely are not? Is there anywhere we can say for certain is *not* threatened by these panzers?'

'Chelsea Bridge Road was pretty clear half an hour ago,' said Austin.

'That's a start, Austin. Thank you. But, now you're back, I want your Advanced Intelligence Section to locate these seven missing panzer divisions, and I want you to report your findings to us at nine o'clock tomorrow morning.'

Well, that was a costly quip, thought Austin, as he walked up Regent Street. The Monday morning meeting between CIGS, the chiefs of the Imperial General Staff, and the

Military Intelligence section heads had been a chance for him to catch up on all he'd missed since he'd come down with pneumonia. Hospitalised for two nights, he was then laid up in bed at home for another fortnight. If the Advanced Intelligence Section was still located in Storey's Gate, Westminster, he'd be at his desk by now and making a start on finding those lost tanks. But, during his illness, they'd suddenly lumped AIS in with the rest of MI14 on the top floor of the Peter Robinson department store, so now he had to walk all the way to Oxford Circus. His ravaged lungs prevented him from striding anywhere near so quickly as he wished. Impatient spasms jolted his legs, as if he were stepping, here and there, on an unearthed electrical cable.

In the second week of his illness, Merry had sent him the most extraordinary note. If true, it was the single most cataclysmic piece of intelligence he had ever seen. But did the note only seem momentous because powerful doses of sulfapyridine had left him chuckle-headed? After all, how could a note brought up by one's wife on the tea tray be more momentous than all those Ultra decrypts? According to Merry's note, the Manstein Plan had been vouchsafed to Ida Marshall, the American tutorial fellow from F Staircase, who'd heard it from Manstein's attaché (now dead), before she tricked the Abwehr into communicating this intelligence to Glyn Gower (now in Wormwood Scrubs). Ida Marshall herself was currently recovering from a blow to the head. *The Brain-Damaged Thoughts of Oxford Philosophers, A Critical Survey.* Was the damage to her head as severe as the chemical cosh to his own?

On the top floor of Peter Robinson, Betsy Todd met him outside the lift in her serge blue WAAF uniform with its officer stripes on the sleeves.

'Welcome back, sir, and welcome to the new place. Let me show you to your desk.' They clicked through the turnstile. 'How was this morning's CIGS meeting, sir?'

'Bloody,' said Austin.

'Was it about the missing panzers, sir?'

'Exclusively.'

'We've been working on that, sir, and I'm pleased to be able to report that we have a couple of leads.' They came to a steel desk with a green vinyl top, on which sat a small beribboned bottle of Courvoisier. 'Here you are, sir. We clubbed together to buy you some brandy to aid your convalescence.'

'Thank you, Todd.'

'How long have they given you, sir?'

'The doctors?'

'CIGS. To tell them where the missing tanks are, sir.'

'Until first thing tomorrow.'

Betsy Todd handed him two manila files. 'We believe the missing panzer divisions are either in Pilsen or Offenburg,' she said. 'It's all in these files. Once you've plumped for one or t'other, we'll compile a full dossier for tomorrow, sir.'

'Thank you, Todd.'

Austin sat down at his new desk to read his team's detailed findings, but soon found himself skipping whole paragraphs. This was most unlike the Forensic Austin. The Details Man. The Great Assimilator of Inhuman Quantities of Information. This was not something he ever did. And yet, here he was, sliding half-read pages to the side, one after another.

On May Day, in a Pilsen marshalling yard, Czech railwaymen observed German troops loading one hundred tanks on to a low-loader freight train going west to Stuttgart.

Be that as it may, thought Austin, it's still a thousand tanks short of an answer.

The second report described a build-up of armour south of Offenburg, a small town in south-west Germany, close to the French border. He studied an aerial reconnaissance photograph showing imperfectly camouflaged 55-calibre gun barrels hidden under trees and hedgerows south of Offenburg. There was no telling if these were tank guns or, as seemed more likely, field artillery. And there weren't enough of them. Besides which, if this was an invasion force lying in wait, where were the tents, latrines and fuel depots? Where was the churned-up ground?

He was aware of his team casting looks his way, and so he pretended to read another couple of pages. When at last he closed the files and sat back in his chair, they all came towards him.

'We've been running a sweepstake, sir,' said Todd. 'Which do you choose? Pilsen or Offenburg?'

'I'm afraid, neither.'

'If not Pilsen or Offenburg,' said Todd, 'then where would you like us to focus our search instead, sir?'

'I need you to find me the contents of Glyn Gower's desk.'

Todd exchanged worried looks with her team. Had Austin suffered a kind of brain flu?

'You said CIGS wanted to hear from us first thing tomorrow, sir, so shouldn't we present them with all the Pilsen and Offenburg evidence, and let them decide?'

'The tanks are not there.'

'Have you discovered something, sir?'

'No, but Gower did. And it'll be in his desk.'

'Well, you're sitting at it,' said Todd. 'That's his old desk.'

Austin opened one steel drawer after another. Empty. Empty. Empty.

'Where did you put the contents?'

'It'll be in one of those boxes stacked over by the window, sir.'

'Quick as you can, please,' said Austin.

Unpacking one cardboard box after another, Betsy Todd felt humiliated. She came to work this morning in eager anticipation of one of the most exciting days of her career. She had expected to spend the day compiling a dossier for the chiefs of the Imperial General Staff. But instead, she now found herself, along with the rest of the AIS team, going through cardboard boxes, searching for the personal detritus of a disgraced former colleague.

'Building a play fort?' joked the commissionaire, as Todd re-stacked a pile of boxes.

When, after an hour's search, she finally found the box containing the contents of Glyn Gower's desk, she quietly excised a flirty postcard she had sent him from Brighton, with lipstick crosses hardly smaller than the sticky tape on the windows. Then she carried the box over to Austin.

Austin immediately upended it all over the green vinyl desktop. Out spilled pens, pencils, pep pills, a Café de Paris cocktail menu, half a pack of Player's Navy Cut cigarettes, a creased snapshot of a bluestocking in a barn with strands of straw in her crown plait, a cloakroom ticket, a crumpled envelope covered in dockets and rubber-stamps, a Graham Greene paperback with the back cover missing and a tin of lavender brilliantine.

Humouring the mad monarch, Todd asked, 'Is it everything you hoped it would be, sir?'

Austin cut her a look. But, the next moment, he did indeed see what he was hoping to find. From the crumpled envelope he pulled the yellow radio intercept that Merry had told him about.

'Yes, it is! It's here! Thank you, Todd. Excellent work! That will be all.'

'Thank you, sir,' said Todd, and went away, seething.

Austin swept the other junk aside to study the yellow intercept annotated in blue ink.

Gower had underlined ZX1EVM three times. Quite right, too. The fact that Abwehr agents in France sent this message directly to General Erich von Manstein was of the first importance. Clearly, the message was of urgent concern to the chief of Army Group South.

Eine feindliche Agentin hat DW getötet.

An enemy agent (female) killed DW.

A lasso of blue ink looped DW and tethered it to the top corner of the page, where Gower had written *Dieter Wetzel*. According to Merry's note on his tea tray, this Dieter Wetzel was once a visiting fellow at Keble.

Wir haben ihre Nachricht nach London abgefangen.

We intercepted her message to London.

Nachright folgt. Zitat:

Message follows. Quote:

Martians land Jupiter's icy moon & Alien shelter. Only pretty ring time. O2 pumps no defence.

Austin twisted the paper this way and that as he tried to read Gower's scribbled decrypt. Gower took the word 'Martian' to be a pun on *marschan* in *Aufmarschanweisung*. This seemed a bit of a stretch — unless it was a prearranged code word between the two of them. Overall, however, the workings seemed sound. From *As You Like It* to the Forest of

Arden to trees being no defence, contrary to received military wisdom.

'Very clever, Mr Gower,' muttered Austin. 'But not half so clever as our *Agentin immer noch auf freiem Fuß* – your old flame Ida Marshall, the girl in the barn with the straw in her hair.'

He lifted the receiver to make his first ever call from his new phone, asking to be put through to Air Chief Marshal Hugh Dowding, commander-in-chief of RAF fighter command.

After ten minutes of crackle and clicks, Dowding's deputy assistant came on the line. Austin requested a spy plane over the German–Belgian border south of Aachen. Though it was an extraordinary request, it was likely to be granted, given that CIGS were chasing round like blue-arsed flies in search of the missing panzers.

Austin got up and went to stand at the brown-paper-latticed windows, looking down at the West End buses and shoppers.

If the spy plane found those missing panzers on the Belgian border, Austin would be spared having to explain to the War Office why he'd junked the best data of the combined intelligence services on the say-so of his wife's tutor, a convict and a Texan on sabbatical.

Dill and Dowding in the War Office

IT WAS VERNON ALWYNNE'S FIRST VISIT to the War Office. He wasn't entirely sure to what he owed this honour. He'd been told that Austin had specifically requested his presence, which he found a tad perplexing. At Oxford, Austin had made no secret of his low opinion of Alwynne's academic ability. But this wasn't academia, this was the real world, where Austin must have got wind of how Alwynne was pulling up trees, how he was building a reputation for getting the different agencies to talk to one another and join the dots. Cometh the hour, and all that. And now here he was with his feet under the table, not just with Lieutenant-General Sir John Dill, not just with the gnomic Austin, but with Air Chief Marshal and commander-in-chief of RAF Fighter Command Sir Hugh Dowding, who was expected any minute.

'Dowding's just on the blower, Austin,' said Dill.

'Righto,' said Austin, packing his briar pipe.

Alwynne was astounded by the clubbable informality

here. Austin seemed to have gone from Sherlock to Mycroft Holmes. No longer the lone exponent of deductive reasoning, but the very brains of the state. Someone who could respond with a 'righto' to the vice chief of the Imperial General Staff.

'Oh, Alwynne,' said Austin, lighting his pipe. 'Heard anything from Ida Marshall?'

'The American girl from Somerville?'

'That's the one.'

'As a matter of fact, I have, Austin.'

'Oh, yes?'

'She came to see me, claiming to be in possession of the German order of battle no less. Problem was, it was the one from the last war. You know, where Jerry invades plucky Belgium, then swings south through the Ardennes to invade France.'

Austin shook out his match. 'Nothing worth passing on, then?'

'Alas, no. Did I mention she'd had a blow on the head? Not the full shilling. Monomaniacal.'

At that moment, the rangy figure of the air chief marshal strode in.

'Any panzers for me, Austin?'

'Yes, Sir Hugh. The third, fourth and ninth panzer divisions are in North Rhine-Westphalia, parked in woodland south of Aachen, forty-one miles east of Liège.'

'How many tanks in total?'

'Eight hundred and eight. And, thanks to the reconnaissance plane you kindly scrambled for us at short notice yesterday, Sir Hugh, we also have aerial photo reconnaissance showing German troop movements on the Belgian border.'

From a slim leather folder, Austin took out a photographic contact sheet with Merry's china-white annotations stating the locations of the armour parked from the Belgian border all the way back to Düsseldorf. Dill and Dowding bent over the contact sheets.

'The German army in the wild,' said Dowding. 'Is this an invasion force, Dill?'

'It all points to a blitzkrieg attack on Belgium,' said Dill. 'But to what end? Why?'

'To avoid the Maginot Line and invade France,' said Austin. Dill and Dowding stared at him.

'Are you saying,' asked Dowding, 'that the invasion of Belgium is the first step of the invasion of France?'

'Intelligence received from an agent in the field,' said Austin, 'suggests that, once Manstein has subdued Belgium, he will do a sickle cut down through the Ardennes into France.'

'You make it sound like the work of an afternoon, Austin,' said Dill, voice of the land army. 'But what's to stop Army Group South getting bogged down in Belgium for years, just like in the Great War?'

'This time, they're coming with panzers and Messerschmitts,' said Austin. 'Makes all the difference.'

'To which end,' said Dowding, 'the Luftwaffe have concentrated a thousand fighter planes in Düsseldorf.'

'That ought to do it,' said Dill.

'I should cocoa,' said Dowding.

'Now, if I'm Manstein,' said Dill, 'and I find myself in Belgium at the head of an intact army, what do I want to do? I fancy I shall want to split my forces. I'll order half to drive west to kettle the BEF at Dunkirk, and half to race to Paris à toute vitesse.'

'We could be looking at the fall of Paris within weeks,' said Dowding.

'What I'm more worried about,' said Dill, 'is the total annihilation of the British Expeditionary Force within days.'

'Hang on just a tick, sirs,' interjected Alwynne.

They'd all forgotten he was there. Dill, Dowding and Austin turned to see him hopping from foot to foot, knowing it wasn't for him to speak, but possessed (such was his fate) of the one essential fact that they were all missing.

'Aren't we all getting a little ahead of ourselves, here? After all, Germany has not even declared war on Belgium – and is probably keen not to stir up another hornet's nest, I should have thought.'

The long ensuing silence was broken finally by Dill.

'Did I hear you tell Austin you were given advance warning of Manstein coming through the Ardennes?'

'Yes, Sir John.'

'Then why the bloody hell didn't you share this information? You might have saved the entire British Expeditionary Force had you passed it on. Not to mention France and Belgium.'

'Women's gossip, sir. Hearsay. Entirely uncorroborated by any other source.'

'Corroborated in writing by my deputy at MI14,' said Austin.

'On prison notepaper,' snapped Alwynne.

'What?' Dill exclaimed. 'Why prison notepaper?'

'Because, Sir John,' said Alwynne, 'Austin's deputy, Mr Glyn Gower, was sent to jail for his criminal failure to pass on information vital to the war effort.'

Knock. Knock. Knock. Austin tapped out his pipe, and asked, 'For his what?'

'Failure to pass on information vital to the war effort,' said Alwynne.

'Did he quash advanced intelligence of the Manstein Plan? Or was that you?'

Alwynne's mouth opened and closed like a landed fish.

'If we were in the field,' said Dill, quietly, 'I could have you shot. Now, get out and stay out!'

1941

The Troglodyte Theory

TWILIGHT IN SOHO on a Saturday night. Ida swatted away a cloud of tortoiseshell butterflies and hawk moths, anxious to keep them out of her new victory-roll hairdo.

'What's with all the butterflies, Merry?'

'The Blitz has put the bird population to flight, and so London is lousy with them.'

On the crossroads at Bateman and Frith streets, they ran into Ken 'Snakehips' Johnson on his way to the Café de Paris, dressed in a Humphrey Bogart mac and bowtie, a folder of sheet music under his arm. Merry invited him to join them for supper.

'I'd love to, Merry,' said Ken. 'You've no idea how much. But if I'm not there by seven it all falls apart, and I might not even have a band any more. I've put a new song in the set and they're all grumbling about having to learn their parts.'

'Then you'll need a stiff drink first,' said Merry, taking his hand and all but pulling him towards the Dog and Duck.

He kissed her hand and let it go. 'The new song is the least of it,' he said. 'Those broken-down musicians bring me all their problems, which all have to be fixed before they take to the stage.'

'You sound like their chaplain,' said Ida.

'Chaplain, psychiatrist, lender of last resort. I'm telling you, one tenth of my job is music and the other nine tenths is pastoral care. Hey, let me put you both on the guest list for the second set and we'll have a proper chinwag after the show.'

'I'd like that,' said Merry.

'Thanks for putting us on the door, Ken,' said Ida. 'That's most kind of you.'

In the middle of the empty crossroads, he pirouetted and began a serenade:

> 'Ida! Ida! Sweet as apple cider,
> Sweeter than all I know.
> Come out! In the silvery moonlight,
> Of love we'll whisper sweet and low!
> Seems like I can't live without ya!
> Listen, please honey, do,
> Ida, I idolise ya,
> I love ya, Ida, deed I do.'

An approaching coal truck honked its horn to get him out of the way, and, when it passed, Ken Johnson was nowhere to be seen.

At half past nine, an air-raid siren's wail sent Ida and Merry hurrying into Leicester Square Tube station. They were halfway down the first flight of steps when they heard a boom and felt the earth shake.

'That sounded rather near,' said Merry. The crush of people seeking shelter meant they couldn't go any further down. They were stuck where they were. 'I hope nobody above us panics and starts a stampede.'

But, instead, by some invisible signal or ripple effect or synchronous decision like the ones that direct murmurations of starlings, everybody sat down where they were. Merry and Ida sat on the steps. Lower down, people sat on the escalators and, below them, people lay on the platform and on the tracks and halfway up the tunnel.

'Do you know about the troglodyte theory, Ida? It's why the home secretary Herbert Morrison was against Londoners using the Underground to shelter from bombs. His big fear was that we'd revert to troglodytes, to cavemen and women.'

'Was he worried we'd all start painting fabulous murals and taking care of the elderly?'

'Once in, we'd never come out again. He really believes that we're only a few nights of sleeping in the Tube away from picking up where we left off ten thousand years ago, and all the intervening years would vanish like the mastodon.'

When the all-clear sounded, they emerged from the Tube to the sound of clanging fire bells. The Charing Cross Road could not be seen for smoke and dust. Unable to see each other, they stood holding hands outside Wyndham's Theatre.

Ida coughed and fumbled for Merry's hip flask of brandy. The memory came to her of standing next to Wetzel in La Grotte Ardennes as they waited for the dust to reveal their first view of an Upper Palaeolithic mural. When this gauzy scrim cleared, would she find London churned under its Pliocene clay, with no buildings left standing between Wyndham's and the sea? Maybe Herbert Morrison was right.

'Sometimes,' said Ida, 'do you feel that the forces of

darkness have already won? I mean, all the bright, hopeful things have been scattered, the children banished, the paintings carted away to a Welsh mountainside, the flowerbeds in the public parks dug up and replaced with anti-aircraft guns, Somerville turned into a convalescent ward and all the handsome men sent packing. I can see where he's coming from with his troglodyte theory. I went into that cave in the Ardennes to find proof of prehistoric goodness, and what I found was a man gone ape. And not just him. My whole world shrunk to "kill or be killed". So much for my fancy notions, as my mother would say.'

They could hear passers-by coughing and stumbling close, almost on top of them.

'Had it not been for prehistoric human kindness,' said Merry, speaking out of the cloud, 'you'd have had no thigh bone with which to hoick that grenade at your captor. And then you'd have died underground and no one would have known.'

Slowly, the scrim of dust lifted to reveal not Pliocene churn, nor wandering troglodytes, but a pretty much unchanged West End. As Ida and Merry reached Soho, however, rubble and rescue teams sent them up unfamiliar side streets and back alleys. A large man stumbled towards them, covered in masonry powder.

Merry stopped him, placing her hands on his shoulders. 'Are you all right, Mr Bowlly?'

'You'd think they'd be safe in a basement,' he said. Tears rolled through the powder on his cheeks.

'Who?'

'The band. The dancers.'

Merry swayed. Only her grip on Bowlly's shoulders kept her from fainting. She had a terrible presentiment. It was a point of principle at the Café de Paris never to stop for air-raid sirens because the management believed that the venue was so deep underground as to be as impregnable as Churchill's war room.

'Is Ken safe?' she cried out.

'He was in the middle of a song, and now he's dead,' said Bowlly.

Merry broke down sobbing in Ida's arms.

'Did you actually see him hit?' Ida asked over Merry's shoulder. She was sure it was all a mistake. Bowlly was shell-shocked and confused. He stood there blinking, unable to answer her simple question. He didn't know who was alive or dead. After all, how could Ken serenade her on a crossroads at twilight, and be dead just a couple of hours later?

Al Bowlly made to walk away, but Ida was anxious not to let him wander off on his own in so distracted and bewildered a state.

'You must let us walk you home, Mr Bowlly. Is it far? Where do you live?'

'Duke's Court, Jermyn Street.'

'I know the way,' said Merry, wiping her eyes and squaring her shoulders.

They walked down Haymarket. At Duke's Court, Merry took Bowlly's front-door keys and led him up the stairs. She sat him in an armchair, opened his drinks cabinet and placed a tumbler of bourbon between his trembling hands.

Then Ida and Merry hurried from Duke's Court back to the Café de Paris. They had both been expecting Coventry Street to look like Coventry, but the Café de Paris appeared largely untouched. A few windows had been blown out. A burnt and ragged curtain blew in the breeze. Bodies were being stretchered into a mortuary van, but this was nothing like the apocalyptic scene they'd feared.

'I knew it,' said Ida. 'Bowlly's just shell-shocked. Ken's alive. You'll see.'

They stood at the crowded barrier, watching as the electricians unplugged their arc lights. Nobody else was coming out, dead or alive. The crowds began to disperse. An air-raid warden in a black helmet, a woman their own age, banged brick dust from a black binder on the wooden barrier.

'Excuse me,' said Ida. 'How come the building looks untouched?'

'Oh, it was the most rotten luck you could possibly imagine,' the warden replied. 'A parachute mine slipped down a ventilation shaft. It only exploded once it hit the basement. The poor old dancers took the full brunt of the blast.'

'How many dead?'

'Thirty-four and counting.'

'Thirty-four,' gasped Merry.

'Many more injured, of course. Were you in there? Only I'm working my way through the guest list and there's a few still missing.'

'We weren't inside,' croaked Merry, in an ashen voice, 'but our names may be in your book.' She took the binder from the warden and began turning its dusty, gritty pages, the ledger of the living and the dead. 'Yes, this must be us,' she said, and handed back the ledger. 'You may put us among the living.'

'Which ones are you?'

'We're there in blue ink,' said Merry. 'The last two names.'

'Righto,' said the warden. 'I shall cross you off my list. A reprieve for the Misses Merry Havoc and Apple Cider.'

And then it was Ida's turn to break down in tears.

The Lascaux Debate

FREDDIE AYER WAS BACK IN OXFORD. Flamboyant, philandering, celebrity philosopher A. J. 'Freddie' Ayer, bestselling author of *Language, Truth and Logic*. Taking a break from his hush-hush espionage work, Fast Freddie was here on a flying visit. He was supposed to have been debating Collingwood, the Waynflete Professor of Metaphysical Philosophy, until Collingwood suffered a mild stroke at the prospect. A young man in a hurry, Fast Freddie hated being at a loose end. He wanted to make his night in Oxford count. If he couldn't debate Collingwood, he would debate Ida Marshall at the Oxyrynchus Society. Apparently, this American girl was peddling mystical claptrap about an innate moral sense inherited from prehistoric times. Such was the unkempt garden of wartime Oxford philosophy. Freddie would debate her at eight, banish metaphysics from the academy, and catch the last train home.

Ida spent the afternoon before the debate in the Bodleian Library, studying journal photographs of the newly discovered Lascaux cave paintings in the south of France. She pored over the journal's full-colour plates. The Lascaux fauna might have been the work of the same artists who painted the animals in La Grotte Ardennes. Did this mean itinerant painters transmitted a style of painting? Or was the whole tribe on the move through France, painting where they overwintered? She read how the Upper Palaeolithic painters would sometimes balance powdered pigment on their palms and blow the powder on to the cave walls. She remembered leaning from the running board of a double-decker to blow a palm load of fluorescent confetti all over her Abwehr stalker.

For all Lascaux's jaw-dropping wonders, however, its murals lacked many of the glories of La Grotte Ardennes. For one thing, the Lascaux fauna was more ranch than safari. Long on bison and horses, short on hyenas and rhinos. A Texas livestock holding. For another, the Lascaux murals lacked dancers. There was, it seemed, only ever one Upper Palaeolithic depiction of dancing, and those dancers had perished in the explosion. Blown to smithereens, like Ken Johnson and the subterranean dancers in the Café de Paris.

'We have heard Miss Marshall,' said Freddie, 'eloquently describe how cavemen had all the domestic virtues. If true, the picture she paints would force us radically to overhaul our understanding of early humans in the state of nature.'

The Oxyrinchus Society debate was held under the oak beams of the All Souls senior common room. About thirty of so fellows and tutors of the university philosophy faculty were seated, and as many again stood around the panelled walls. A fug of cigarette and pipe smoke hung in the air.

Freddie and Ida sat in two armchairs. Behind them, Ida

had hung a white tablecloth from one of the picture rails. The oblong outlines of framed paintings bulged under the tablecloth. On a small table sat a projector borrowed from the Pitt Rivers.

'Miss Marshall has given us a vivid picture of how cavemen would care for one another in sickness and in health. Here was no mere tribe, but a society. But here is my question for you, Miss Marshall: are you able to produce one single piece of evidence to support this idea of prehistoric solidarity, of concern for weaker members of the group, of medical care and solicitude among cave dwellers?'

There was a long silence. Ida felt all eyes upon her. But she had come prepared. She switched on the projector and asked them to dim the lights. The projector shone an empty bright circle on the white tablecloth. Between her thumb and forefinger she held the slide of the mended femur, the same one she had discovered in the Pitt Rivers all those years ago, on the day she met Dieter Wetzel.

'This is my evidence,' she said. It came out sounding grander than she meant, and that was unfortunate because, when she slotted in the slide and the image landed on the white tablecloth, the audience burst into laughter at the bathos of so large a claim being followed by so poor and inconclusive a photograph of a muddy bone in a puddle.

When the laughter died down, Freddie expressed the audience's sentiment perfectly, saying: '*This* is your clincher? *This?*'

'Circumstances prevented me excavating the bone so that it could be more forensically studied in Oxford, but I can report that a very definite and clear fracture callus suggests that the bone healed during the lifetime of its owner.'

Now, her own words rebelled against her. To say 'owner' was an own goal, she knew. Who talks about owning their own bones?

After a pause, Freddie Ayer showed her what a proper clincher looked like: 'Quite apart from the lack of verifiable prehistoric evidence,' he said, 'I wonder how you can have managed to miss every Pathé newsreel since 1939, for how else can you maintain your cosy belief in innate human goodness and an inherited moral sense?'

Ida looked at him and then out at the audience. She could think of no riposte. The one thought in her mind could not be spoken: how she envied Collingwood his stroke.

F7 Tutorial

WITH SO MANY PPE TUTORS away on war service and requiring cover, Ida's workload far exceeded her pre-war levels of tutoring, marking and lecturing.

Female students did not seem to mind having Ida as substitute, but the dwindling band of male undergraduates rebelled. The emasculation of not yet seeing active service in a world war was one thing, but being taught by a woman rubbed salt in the wound. Or lack of wounds. Bad enough to go up to an Oxford devoid of marquee names – Austin and Ayer seconded to the secret service and Isaiah Berlin dispatched to Washington – but to have this slip of a thing foisted upon them was an insult. The student newspaper, *Cherwell*, ran a mocked-up still from *The Perils of Pauline*, with Ida's face superimposed over Pauline's body, which was strapped to a table with a giant rotary saw about to cleave her skull in two. Caption: *Radical Improvement to Oxford Philosophy Announced for Michaelmas Term*. But mostly the young men voted with their feet. When

Ida walked into the several-hundred-capacity Sheldonian to give her lecture on 'Jean-Paul Sartre versus the Delphinium', there were only five students there, all women.

She invited them back to F Staircase, where she abandoned the lecture for something with the flavour, she hoped, of one of FDR's 'fireside chats' – except about philosophy, rather than the Emergency Banking Act.

The students found various roosts and perches in her odd-shaped room. Ida served them tea and biscuits, provided ashtrays, and learnt their names. Then she sat on a wooden chair at the corner table, where Austin had once knocked the dottle from his pipe, and began the 'fireside chat' version of her lecture. Or rather, what with coal being so dear for the duration, the 'two-bar electric-fireside chat'.

'I'd like to start, if I may,' said Ida, 'with an astonishing claim that Jean-Paul Sartre makes in his latest book. He says, "A nauseating sloppiness characterises the natural world." The first thing to say about this wild claim, it seems to me, is that stringent selection pressures categorically rule out sloppiness from most of the animal kingdom. A sloppily constructed beaver dam will kill the kits in winter, for instance.'

What the wartime intake craved, she had discovered, was a Big World Picture or a Giant Explanation Machine. They were hot for existentialism, Marxism and positivism. They didn't want Analytic pulling apart, they wanted Continental synthesis. No matter how many points she scored against Continental philosophy, Ida never could dislodge its hold on her students' minds. Just as she had lost the intelligence war, so now she was losing the philosophy war. They wanted top-down not bottom-up philosophy, so to speak. But then Ida remembered how, through having actually set foot in the Ardennes, she had understood that the forest was not the panzer barrier that aerial photography and top-down military orthodoxy believed it to be. And she began to form the notion that the living world, natural history, plants and animals, might be the way to hit a home run against the wartime vogue for grand explananda – hence the title of her talk: 'Jean-Paul Sartre versus the Delphinium'.

'Why,' she asked, 'does Sartre act as though he never saw a spider's web in his life? Why bother? Why pretend the dainty precision of the delphinium doesn't exist? Or that swifts aren't pinpoint navigators? I mean, a child of five could tell him that ant colonies are models of ruthless hygiene and rigid hierarchy, but all Sartre sees is slop. Now, my question to you is: why?'

'Because nature worship too easily lends itself to blood-and-soil nationalism,' said Helen, from up on the mini-landing, her legs, in grey woollen tights, sticking through its banister rail. 'And so existentialism is here making a clean break with bourgeois philosophy.'

'Is it a clean break?' asked Ida. 'Or is it a continuity? Think of John Locke saying that "Nature and Earth furnish only the almost worthless materials." That's a pretty similar sentiment, isn't it?'

'That's not continuity, that's coincidence,' said Lotte, the post-doc sitting in the tatty grey armchair. Her wavy black hair was neatly side-parted and she wore an indigo dress with a crisp, white collar. 'It would only be continuity if they were both speaking from the same set of beliefs, which they are not.'

'An excellent point,' said Ida. 'However, I want to argue that Locke and Sartre do in fact share a belief in the old Graeco-Christian idea that we are too good for the earth. And not just them, of course. When Fichte is upset by what he calls "the sluggish atmosphere of forests", he has inherited the same world picture, which blinds him to the existence of such forest critters as woodpeckers, pine martens and squirrels, each the very opposite of sluggish.'

'But existentialism is an avowedly atheist philosophy,' retorted Lotte.

'I hear you,' said Ida, 'but, when you throw religion out the door, it comes in through the window.'

'So, what you're saying,' said Helen, on the landing, 'is that, since there's no hope of escaping religion, we should just bow down and worship the Lord anyway?'

'No,' said Ida, 'I'm saying the way to escape religion is not to embrace it, which is what Simone de Beauvoir does when she says, "There is nothing natural about man."'

'No, no, no, that's the opposite of religious,' said Jane, who was smoking a Woodbine on the third step up from the sunken floor, the same step where Glyn used always to roost. 'De Beauvoir is saying that people have the power to make or remake themselves or their institutions any which way they choose. This is liberating and it couldn't be more secular.'

Recalling how Merry would sometimes emphasise a point by standing up and leaning on the F7 mantelpiece, Ida now attempted the same. But five foot is not six foot, and Ida's elbow was by her ear, so it was with considerably less than Merry-level panache that she delivered what she hoped to be the coup de grace.

'To say there's nothing natural about humans,' she said, 'is to say there's nothing animal about humans, and that's a pre-Darwinian idea, right? A religious idea. The idea that we are made in the image of God or of angels, but not of chimps or baboons. That's what I mean when I say, "Throw religion out the door and it comes in through the window."'

'But you can hardly call the existentialists Christian,' said Woodbine Jane.

'This philosophical stowaway is older than Christianity,' said Ida. 'It has its roots in an ancient Greek idea – but, even then, it was a hotly contested notion.'

The great thing about being in F7 was having her own books to hand. She pulled out Plato's *Critias* and asked Jane to read a passage:

'"Once, we had plains full of rich soil and forested mountains, with lofty trees of many species. Moreover, the soil was enriched by the yearly rains from Zeus, which were not lost to it, as now, by flowing from bare land into the sea. Instead, the loamy soil absorbed the water to provide each district with abundant springs and streams, whereof only the shrines remain to mark where these springs have all dried up. Now, the soil is so thin, the rocks rise to the surface like the ribs of a sick man."'

'Thank you,' said Ida. 'So, here's Plato, who made his name saying the natural world doesn't really exist, now deploring how much of it has disappeared. He sounds like nothing so much as a soil scientist *avant la lettre*. That's quite the volte-face, isn't it? But his repentance comes too late. The genie is out of the bottle. Ancient Greece has let loose the virulent idea that the earth is not our real home. A vector for this disease is the Gospels, written in Greek, and so Platonic repudiation of the living world is all over the New Testament like a rash. Colossians and Corinthians instruct us to set not our affection on things of the earth. Jesus curses a fig tree, and the Church Fathers preach *contemptus mundi*, contempt for the earth. And it is all in strict accordance with early Plato and recent Sartre.'

'No,' said Jane, *Critias* still spread in her lap. 'Sartre is honestly describing a forbidden emotion, one which he knows he is not supposed to have. A forbidden thought. In saying what we really think and what we really feel, he's boldly going against the usual pieties.'

This comment elicited unanimous agreement from the others. Ida looked from one face to another and saw opposition in each one.

'Seems all my cherished ideas are having what they call a bad war,' she said. 'Clearly, I need to think about this some more. Well, now, ladies – what say we do this again? Same time, same place, next week?'

After they left, Ida tidied away their cups, plates and ashtrays, and noticed that she was smiling. She was surprised by how much she had loved teaching this impromptu seminar and the company of these bright women. She didn't expect her students to seize on her insights. After all, if nobody listened to her when she had advance knowledge of the Wehrmacht's order of battle, why would anyone embrace her insistence on the elementary philosophical blunders of Jean-Paul Sartre? Or the importance of John Dewey to the present moment? But it was not nothing, she remembered, to contribute to the ecology of ideas.

And she still had hopes of bringing the nitty-gritty of the natural world, the facts of life on earth, to bear on philosophical problems. She wondered what Merry would make of this idea. Perhaps there was even a connection between this approach and Merry's photographic interpretation work, with its close attention to what was actually to be seen down on the ground – as a way of telling a hawk from a handsaw and a goat from an oil silo.

1942

Boot Camp

ON 11 DECEMBER 1941, Germany declared war on the United States of America. At the start of 1942, Lieutenant Colonel J. L. Austin recruited Ida Marshall into the Advanced Intelligence Section of MI14. Merry accompanied her to the top floor of Peter Robinson and, during the interview, sat on a desk with her long legs on a chair.

'There are two necessary preconditions to fulfil before you can join us at AIS,' said Austin, standing before Ida. 'You must enlist in the Signal Corps of the US Army Air Force, and you must complete the RAF officer cadet training course at Wilmslow with the Women's Auxiliary Air Force.'

'So, I'll train with the WAAFs, but I'll actually be part of the US Air Force?'

'That's not so unusual. Poles, Czechs, Kiwis, Free French and Canadians also undergo officer cadet training at Wilmslow, before joining their respective air forces. The US Signal Corps has made exceptional provision for you to do your basic training over here and not over there.'

'Why are you sending me for a soldier, Austin?'

'They call me "sir" here, you know.'

'Fancy.'

'The rules and regs say I may recruit Allied service personnel, but not foreign civilians. Plus, we all have to do a bit of basic training.'

'I never did,' said Merry.

'Why not?' Ida asked.

'Brains. I was just given the address of an outfitters in Regent Street. Walked into the fitting room a civilian, came out a flight lieutenant in full get-up. The standard-issue uniform chafed mercilessly, however, so I walked straight from Regent Street to South Molton Street, where the family tailor swapped out the lining for a silk one *and* sold me my indispensable loupe – so, I suppose, in the end, there was some practical benefit to the uniform rigmarole.'

'If it's any consolation,' said Austin, 'Glyn has had to put in a few months of training at RAF Alconbury.'

'Did it take long to secure his release?' Ida asked.

'No, a single telephone call to the prison governor. Could have phoned earlier, but I thought Glyn might benefit from a second week in pokey. Character building.'

Ida spent the months of January and February on the officer cadet training course at RAF Wilmslow, in Cheshire. Each day, as part of the world war against totalitarianism, thirty women in identical blue boiler suits ate identical chow in a barracks canteen before filing into the lecture hut to listen to a man in uniform.

One afternoon, an adenoidal captain from the Corps of Royal Engineers gave them a slideshow presentation about German weaponry and munitions. With clicker and pointing stick, he talked them through the enemy arsenal, slide by slide. His inventory of German armaments was so extensive that Ida suspected him of being a fifth columnist, come to destroy Allied morale by showing how completely outgunned they were.

The captain clicked to the next slide. 'This is the M39,' he said, 'or, to give it its full name, the Model 39 *Eihandgranate*, which means "egg grenade", for obvious reasons, as you can see from its shape ...'

She looked up. The metal swan's egg loomed as large on the projector screen as when it had sat primed at the end of her nose in the cave. Her head swam.

'The M39 is a nasty piece of work,' said the captain. 'This is not your honest-to-goodness Mills bomb or stick grenade. Oh, no – the M39 is designed for booby traps. Here, at the base of the grenade, is a little ring, you see.' He tapped his pointer on the screen. *Rat-a-tat-tat.*

Ida flinched.

'Through this little ring, Jerry will thread tripwires. Now, it only takes a minuscule amount of force to pull the pin and detonate the M39. The slightest pressure will do it. You can pull that ring out with fly-fishing line, or even with what tailors call gossamer thread.'

Knocking over chairs, a hand over her mouth, Ida stumbled for the door. Outside the hut, she fell to her hands and knees and threw up all over the concrete.

Through the wall, she heard him say, 'Was that the Yank? God in heaven help us, if they're all like that!'

She mopped up her sick, sluiced mop and bucket, and went to the empty, silent dorm. She sat on her metal tube bed with its grey wool blanket. Her hands were trembling. If she pressed them flat on her thighs, it stopped, but, as soon as she lifted them, it began again. Not just her hands. Every few seconds, she found herself nodding a few quick, small nods. The hands you might not notice, but the head was an all-out catastrophe. Trembling hands could be physiological, but a nodding head looked like straight-up lunacy. If she screwed her neck into an uncomfortable position, the nodding stopped, but only until she untwisted her neck.

She went to sick bay to see if the medics would dish out some pills or sign her off, but there was no medic on duty. The medicine cupboard was locked, but not so the admin drawer, where she found a sheaf of leave-of-absence passes. Hands shaking, she scrawled illegibly, wasting several sheets before she managed to fill out date and time, and forge a medic's signature.

She wheeled a bicycle to the red striped barrier and showed her forged pass at the guardhouse. The guard waved her through.

The country lane she cycled along was smooth tarmac, but her head nodded as though she were riding over cobbles. After a couple of miles, she came to a crossroads and a pub called the Goat. They still had Scotch in the countryside, so she ordered a double. The nodding slowed, but did not disappear. She could keep her head straight for minutes at a time, punctuated by a series of slow, emphatic nods. She ordered another Scotch, and whatever that handsome young farmer was having.

She played bar billiards against the young farmer, beat him best of three then necked with him in the beer garden. That slow, emphatic nod had its uses, letting her come on all Barbara Stanwyck and vampy.

It was dark when she cycled back to base. Her bike

light's grinding dynamo sounded like a drummer's brushes, the rhythm section to the medley she belted out along the country lanes: 'Wayfarin' Stranger', 'Don't Fence Me In' and 'How About You?'.

She wondered if she could still cycle no-handed. Whisky and all, she found that she could indeed. Not only that, but her hands were no longer shaking. This joyful discovery set her spirits soaring. She cycled along, making slow wing-beats, a condor flying home to her mountain-cliff cave. All in all, she was returning to RAF Wilmslow in far better fettle than when she had left a few hours earlier.

Upon her return, however, the RAF camp lit up with arc lights as if she were a low-flying Messerschmitt. There were shouts, jeeps and radio traffic. She found herself bundled into the stockade. Five days' solitary in a five-by-five windowless cell. *Don't fence me in.*

Ida never could bring herself to explain to her dorm buddies why she fled the slideshow. The last eighteen months had taught her that the bigger the fact, the less she'd be believed. But, for want of an explanation, the other cadets kept their distance, seeing her as not quite officer material, not likely to last the course, soon to be kicked out for indiscipline or lack of nerve, or both.

A letter came from Merry. In February, the Photographic Interpretation Unit had moved from Wembley to Medmenham.

Dearest Ida,

The contents of the Aircraft Operating Company on the North Circular have been boxed up and trucked to

RAF Medmenham, a stately home made of chalk on the banks of the Thames, close to Kenrick Johnson's Marlow. (One sees why he fled.)

Medmenham is a grandiose wedding-cake of a building, with mock-Tudor chimneys and turret towers, set in sixty-five acres. Home from home, in other words – ha! – except Kirklockham is Millstone Grit sandstone, not chalk. (Will you come home with me one day? Meet my people? See why I fled?) Top brass lodge in the big chalk house itself; lowlier staff are billeted in the nearby villages, or stabled in rows of Nissen huts, which lengthen daily. Would you believe there are now 1,700 of us toiling in Medmenham's PIU? I myself, I'm happy to say, am a day boarder, commuting from Paddington to my desk in the East Tower. The print library here holds half a million bird's-eye views of the Reich.

I enclose some reading material so that you are not too dull a companion when next we meet. Boot camp deadens the brain, I imagine. Here, in this parcel, you shall find Wittgenstein samizdat smuggled out of Cambridge, Nietzsche's 'Twilight of the Idols', and the latest issue of Analysis, which includes my piece 'On Facts and Values'. The origin of this essay, I believe, is the row I had with Glyn in the Café de Paris that time. Have you heard from that notorious jailbird? How is he? Send him my love when you do.

I miss you more than you miss me.

Love Merry

The upside of nobody talking to her at RAF Wilmslow was that Ida got a lot of reading done. Several times over, she read Merry's piece, 'On Facts and Values', which – even more than her letter, somehow – seemed to bring her presence right into the room. She could see her incline her long neck. She could hear her dulcet voice, deceptively gentle as she mercilessly dismantled an argument, in this case the stick-to-the-facts empiricism that Ayer and the positivists thought they'd invented, and which had browbeaten enthusiastic freshers out of any confidence in the possibility that moral philosophy was a respectable, worthwhile or even possible endeavour.

> Facts and values are not discrete. What we decide to call a fact depends on what we value. We value facts that can be falsified over those that cannot. We value facts derived from the patient sifting of intelligence data over the inspired hunch of a brigadier general in his desert tent, or the divine afflatus of a Mussolini in the map room. We place our trust in the consensus decision of committees, be they never so tedious, rather than in truths revealed to the pure of heart. We compile and collate data from multiple sources, rather than seek out a pre-eminent fount of wisdom. When contradictory facts collide, one fact very often yields to the other by reference not to more facts but to that wider set of truths we call values. We organise competing facts by appeal to these fields of ramifying values and larger truths. For example, the statistical fact that the female skull is smaller than the male is of no value when awarding a degree – except at the University of Cambridge, which still denies women degrees on the basis of this disinterested calculus. These fields of ramifying values we call facts of life.

Rereading *Twilight of the Idols*, Ida wondered if Nietzsche's maxim 'what doesn't kill me makes me stronger' was to blame for the training-camp doctrine of 'break 'em down to build 'em up'. Ida never held with this particular maxim, anyway. Seemed to her, what didn't kill you just weakened you for the next blow. Dieter Wetzel didn't kill her, but he left her nerves so ragged that a mere slide projection of a hand grenade set her head nodding like a Clay County pumpjack. She'd call that weaker, by any measure.

As it happened, one of the set-piece break-'em-down events on the RAF Wilmslow officer cadet training course was the forty-eight-hour endurance test. Two nights in the woods, with no map, no compass, no water, no supplies. When their turn came, Ida and three other women – two from Czechoslovakia and one from Poland – were driven at dusk in a lorry with the tarp down. Against orders, Ida peeped under the tarp a few times. There were no signposts, of course, but plenty of other useful landmarks. A glimpse of a water tower. The vibrations of a cattle grid. They were driven for an hour, but most of the journey time, Ida suspected, was just going round and back over the same roads. Why else that recurring smell of slurry at the foot of a hill that always needed the same double declutch into first gear? And didn't an hour's drive in England invariably take you to the sea, anyway? Or maybe Berlin? At the end of this hour-long rigmarole, however, when the truck's handbrake squeaked and the sergeant major dropped the tailgate and ordered them out, they were neither by the seaside nor on Kurfürstendamm, but on the edge of some woods, where they were ordered to put on blindfolds.

They marched blindfolded in single file, each with her hand on the shoulder of the cadet in front, like the soldiers in John Singer Sargent's *Gassed*. When the sergeant major removed their blindfolds, the women found themselves in a small clearing deep in the woods. He left them with a stern warning that theft from any farm or allotment would see them kicked off the course. He then walked off in the direction of the truck and, a few minutes later, they heard it start up and drive away.

Together, the women built a bivouac from branches and walled it with underbrush and dry bracken. Once their tipi was complete, they spread a jacket on the ground, on to which each cadet pooled the contraband she'd smuggled in her socks or bra. The Eastern Europeans' haul amounted to a torch, two matchbooks, a penknife and a pocket compass. From under the insole of her left boot, however, the American produced only a solitary, damp pound note.

'But there is nowhere here to buy anything,' said one of the Czech women.

'We are miles from anywhere,' said the other.

'In this itty-bitty country?' Ida protested. 'Oh, come on, now, ladies. Why, we're close to everywhere.'

Lena, the Polish woman, shook her head in pity at the sorry pound note. Patiently, she tried to explain the American girl's mistake to her.

'In the forest, you do not buy,' she said. 'No, you forage. I forage,' she said, tapping her chest.

Carrying two empty haversacks and an empty water canteen, Lena set off to forage. Now it was Ida's turn to shake her head with pity at this forlorn hope. Did Lena really imagine these Cheshire woods would be the al fresco deli of Białowieża? Was she expecting to return with a wild boar slung over her shoulder and her pockets stuffed with truffles? How could she so wildly overestimate the nutritional properties of an English wood? It was in Oxfordshire's Wytham Woods, after all, that Ida first heard the phrase 'sod this for a game of soldiers', when Glyn finally gave up his three-hour search for in-season mushrooms.

Sure enough, a long hour later, Lena came crashing through the undergrowth.

'Not so much as a hazelnut,' she fumed. 'Not even a stream to drink from! We shall have to suck raindrops from leaves! This land is cursed, I tell you – cursed!'

'Ladies,' said Ida, 'might I have the loan of a torch?'

'Oh, yes, I am sure you will find the banquet I missed just around the corner,' snapped Lena. 'It will all be so easy in this little bitty country, just as you say. Oh, yes!'

Ida followed the torch beam through the trees, wishing Lena weren't so cross with her. She should have clarified what she meant by 'itty-bitty'. Not geographical sprawl so much as ever-changing topography. European landscapes rang the changes. Every few hundred yards, a whole new biome appeared. From limestone hill to chalk down, all within a hop, skip and jump. The spirit of Micawber was in the very hedgerows. How could something not turn up?

It was the very opposite of the north Texas panhandle, on the edge of the Great Plains. When she was nine, she'd got lost in scrubland that changed so little mile after mile that she began to fear she was not walking at all, but treading air a few inches off the ground and going nowhere, only hallucinating movement.

In her last year at Dallam County High, she had to translate a passage from Blaise Pascal's *Pensées*. When Ida came to the phrase 'the eternal silence of these infinite spaces terrifies me', she assumed Pascal must have been one of those French adventurers, like Lafayette or de Tocqueville, who centuries ago travelled through the Great Plains, and maybe got lost like she did along the way. If so, he'd captured the spirit of the place perfectly. When, a few lines later, she saw that Pascal was only writing about the Milky Way, she felt hoodwinked. She didn't believe Blaise Pascal, either. Did the eternal silence of infinite spaces really terrify him? Was every night out ruined – simply ruined – for him by the lowering stars? Or was he just striking a pose for those dark-eyed salon ladies?

Half an hour in the all-too-finite space of a Cheshire woodland, by contrast, brought her to a metalled road with a cattle grid. Half a mile along this road, she arrived at the concrete water tower she first glimpsed from under the tarp as the truck bumped its way to the woods.

The water tower afforded many more handholds and footholds than the walls of All Souls, and her blue overalls were better suited to climbing than a taffeta ballgown. On top of the water tower, she blew on her cold hands, then stuck them in her armpits. Slowly, she revolved on the spot, until she saw dimmed lights converge less than a quarter of a mile away. Where there were fireflies, there would be grubs. She climbed back down the water tower. Twenty minutes later, the landlord of the Goat declared, 'You're becoming quite the regular!'

The dishy farmhand was not in, alas, but she was here on business, anyway. To which end, she bought a bottle of wine from the landlord and a brace of pheasants from a poacher. From the cold fireplace in the empty public bar, she trousered several lumps of coal. From the restroom, she stole two packets of toilet paper – the cheap British kind that rustled and came in *decimo sexto*.

A sweet elderly couple gave her a lift in a startlingly fetid station wagon. Sitting in the back seat, Ida tried to work out all the ingredients of the stench. Her list got as far as camphor moth balls, leaking battery acid, mouldy dog blanket, urine and rotten milk, before they rattled over the cattle grid, where she thanked them for the lift and walked back through the woods to the bivouac.

'A midnight feast for the girls from occupied Europe!' she announced, and threw the brace of pheasants down at their feet.

'How did you kill them?' Lena asked.

'I foraged,' she said. She tossed a lump of coal from her pocket on to the dying campfire, sending up a flurry of sparks.

'And I suppose you mined this, too,' said Lena.

Ida took the wine bottle from inside her boiler suit. 'Like I trod these grapes with my own two feet.'

When she returned from camping in the woods, she found a card from Merry.

Dear Ida,

I have been sacked from the chalk house. I have never been sacked before and find myself swamped in shame to a quite incredible degree. I'm rusticating in Oxford in my old Walton Street digs most of the time, save the occasional day shift at Austin's West End Emporium. Please darken my door just as soon as you possibly can.

Head to toe, x love M

It did not seem possible that Merry, of all people, could be, of all things, sacked. How maddening of her to say she had been fired, but not say why! Not even a hint. Ida could scream. Merry, sacked? Merry. Sacked. How could that even be?

In her last week at RAF Wilmslow, there came a letter from a less dedicated correspondent: Glyn. She lay on her metal dormitory bed to read his looped and flowing handwriting.

Dearest Ida,

I heard from Austin you were at RAF Wilmslow. How does camp life compare to F Staircase?

For my part, RAF Alconbury compares most favourably to A Wing. While the other conscripts moan about being cabined, cribbed, confined, I find camp life to be the very sunlit uplands promised by Churchill. It helps to come, hot foot, from Wormwood Scrubs, don't you know?

That said, there was an ugly incident yesterday. There were three of us standing at the top of the parachute tower, which was rocking and creaking in the wind, one hundred and fifty feet up. The instructor repeated very clearly what we had to do, emphasising the importance of counting to three before pulling the ripcord. To demonstrate, he jumped first, shouting out the count in an unhurried way: 'And one ... and two ... and three.' But then his parachute failed to open and he 'Roman candled'. We watched the beetling medics stretcher his body into the green rectangle of an ambulance. While I was asking a flight sergeant if we should all climb back down the tower steps now, in case the other parachutes had also been packed incorrectly, he pushed me off the platform mid-sentence. I believe I could murder that flight sergeant and never feel a moment's remorse.

Even though my prison stretch was all of two weeks long, I did the best thing I ever did in my life when I was there, which was to teach a daily English class to a couple of dozen men. I was shocked by how many prisoners were illiterate. The heartbreaker is that several inmates were definitely Oxbridge material, but for the small trifle of not being able to write 'bum' on a wall. Not that that held Alwynne back, what? But I believe that, after the war, all this will change.

I know you dismiss Hegel's Zeitgeist as astrology, but I do believe there is a Spirit of the Time. It seems to me that we are living through a Great Shake Out of discredited ideas. Things are simply too serious to allow for all the old jiggery-pokery, and so the body politic is shaking off everything and everyone that is hollow and false and rickety ... But maybe this is nonsense, because my wits have atrophied for want of your conversation.

Hey, Ida, do you realise that our last written communication was the note you sent me via the Abwehr Express! Do you know how the Abwehr signed off? Their last words were these: 'Agentin immer noch auf freiem Fuß.' And that's how I think of you: 'free of foot'. Free from English conformity and restraint. Free to do things in your own way. Free to make your own weather − which inspired me to have a go, for a little while at least, until I lost my nerve. Five-foot, free-foot Ida!

The one time we ever went dancing together was the night I stopped trying so hard to fit in at Oxford. The foxtrot bored you at Hertford May Ball and so you tried to teach me a dance called the Texas Tommy. You hitched up the sea-foam skirts of your ball gown and banged your heels together in midair. At first, I was mortified – you were wearing brown boots under your gown – but, as I copied your hillbilly hoedown, the game of trying to look like I belonged at Oxford no longer seemed worth the candle. Suddenly, it ceased to matter that my mother drives a mobile library for a living, and that my All Souls fellowship was almost certainly due to a clerical error. Anyway, that was why I was vexed that you went to a May Ball without me – the night you came in through the window.

What are you reading, Ida? Me, I'm reading my fellow jailbird Boethius's 'Consolations of Philosophy', written in solitary confinement when he was under sentence of execution from King Theodoric. Boethius counsels prison inmates to focus on consoling thoughts. For me, one consolation above all others sustained me through the darkest nights of my incarceration. Looking through the bars of my cell, I thought: 'Well, she won't be climbing in through this window!'

I experience a similar consolation looking out the window of a Wellington bomber at 4,000 feet: 'She ain't climbing through this one either!' As the Hun's ack-ack fire rocks the crate, I tell myself, 'Glyn Gower, you are safe at last!'

Anyway, I had best be careful not to antagonise you, now that you carry live ammunition. Esp. as the rifles and sidearms issued to the USAAF are no doubt superior to the muskets and fowling-pieces with which we have been supplied.

How happy I would be to see you again, dear Ida, armed or unarmed, in uniform or out of it. Until then, I wish you all the love and goodness in the world.

Your old and battered, but, I hope, improving beau,

xxxx Glyn

Her eyes filled with tears of joy. All that was good about him had come through his ordeal intact and whole, and all that was dreck had fallen off. It could be done. Perhaps she could do it too.

Blue Packard

―

ALIGHTING AT KETTERING STATION, Ida folded her Ordnance Survey one-inch to the mile map of Northampton and District and set out to hike the four miles to USAAF Grafton Underwood. This was her last day in a WAAF boiler suit. Today, she would swap RAF Wilmslow's dowdy dark blue for smart olive drab. Today, she would be kitted out in her USAAF uniform.

She crossed a flood meadow and vaulted a five-bar gate – a cinch, after two months scaling the twenty-foot-high cargo net on the Wilmslow assault course.

Halfway across the stepping stones of a shallow river, she crouched down to study a white-clawed crayfish scuttling over pebbles, its bronze armour flashing in the gin-clear water. She felt she was restocking her mind after the sensory stultification of barracks life. A plain old roach scoping for mayflies seemed as superb to her as a coelacanth or manta ray.

She entered a copse studded with signs saying *Private*

Property, Keep Out and *Trespassers Will Be Prosecuted*. The English had taken down every sign except those they held most sacred. Yard by yard, the land grew flatter as she drew closer to the aerodrome. The public bridleway emerged from the copse on to a long runway. She looked out at a scatter of squat buildings, a row of jeeps, each with a white star stencilled on the hood, and Old Glory hanging limp on a flagpole. There were no airplanes in the hangar, just a spectacular, preposterous, shiny blue Packard drop-top with gold trim and white-wall tyres. The polished Packard blazed in the sunlight like the bronze scales of the crayfish in the river.

In a green two-storey corrugated-iron shack, under a hand-painted wooden sign saying *119th Quartermaster Company*, Staff Sergeant Renfro from Lubbock, Texas told her he'd been expecting her. The grizzled, slow-moving Renfro handed her a pile of neatly folded olive drab, on top of which sat a pair of bronze ingots, and a cap like a French kepi, before directing her to an adjacent tin shack to get changed.

Her actual name was stitched on to the shirt above the pocket, and the badge of the US Army Signal Corps on the sleeves. The fact that her US uniform fit perfectly, when almost nothing else ever did, seemed significant. It was as though this time and place and purpose had always been waiting for her.

She walked back towards the Quartermaster building, passing the motor pool, the GIs wolf-whistling.

'Where's the rest of your platoon, darlin'?'

'One riot, one ranger,' she replied, and stepped back into the 119th Quartermaster Company hut.

'Where's your bars, lieutenant?' said Renfro.

'My what?'

'Your second lieutenant shoulder bars.'

'Oh, those little bronze ingots?'

'Yes, ma'am.'

'I couldn't figure out how to get them on.'

'Will you permit me?' He attached the bronze bars to the stiff cotton epaulettes of her starchy new jacket. 'Now you're a second lieutenant in earnest, ma'am.'

'I was hoping for a little more ceremony, dontcha know?'

'Ceremony or no, ma'am, you are now an officer of the United States Air Force, which means you cannot let the men talk to you like that no more.'

'Understood, sergeant.' Her eye fell on an A5 envelope on his desk addressed to RAF Alconbury. 'Is there an internal postal service between air-force bases, sergeant?'

'You're looking at him.'

'Where's Alconbury?'

'Thirty miles east. The 8th Air Force will move there this summer.'

'Who's that Packard drop-top for?'

'Bob Hope.'

'Get out of town!'

'USO concert tour. And I gotta trust one of the lunkheads you just passed to deliver her to London without a scratch.'

'Stage door of the Palladium?'

'No, the embassy, ma'am.'

'Good luck with that, sergeant, driving on the left and all.'

'Keeps me awake at night, I don't mind tellin' ya.'

'You know, I drove all through England till the gas ration came in.'

'How about that, ma'am,' he said, going back to his clipboard.

'Come to think of it, I even drove to a reception at the embassy one time.'

'Is that a fact, ma'am?'

'Gotta tell you, sarge, the one-way system by the embassy is a doozy.'

'Is it, now?'

'I only hope one of your lunkheads is up to it.'

'You are a smooth one, lieutenant,' said Renfro, slotting his pencil behind his ear.

'Oh, no, I am but a plain-speaking, simple soldier, much like you. And, as one blunt soldier to another, I ask you, Sergeant Renfro, did the brave boys of the one-one-nine come all the way over here to do valet parking? Hell, no! Do you know what I say, sergeant?'

'I have a feeling I soon will, ma'am.'

'I say this. I say, put the little lady behind the wheel of Bob Hope's vanity wagon, and let those good old boys go fight the Germans, which – God dammit – is why they're over here in the first place, am I right?'

He unhooked a set of car keys from a peg board on the wall behind him. 'I'm too old to survive being busted down to private, ma'am, so, I beg you, please drive extra careful and deliver this top-dollar automobile in pristine condition to the US embassy.'

'Sergeant Renfro, I promise you that Mr Bob Hope will see this fine sedan exactly as she leaves this hangar.'

'Thank you, ma'am.'

'And, you know what, Staff Sergeant Renfro, why not let me drop this big old envelope off for you at RAF Alconbury en route?'

'It ain't en route at all, ma'am.'

'But it's only thirty miles, you said. Why, that's closer than Tahoka!'

'Closer than Tahoka.' He chuckled. 'Why do you want to go to RAF Alconbury?'

'I believe it will be prudent and beneficial to do a short test drive to check the engine's running smoothly before the long drive to London.'

'What's his name, ma'am?'

'Glyn Gower.'

'Known him long?'

'We were at Oxford together.'

'What are his prospects?'

'He was in intelligence at MI14, but now he's a navigator in a Wellington.'

'That's a dangerous job he's got there. Will you take some advice from an old man, lieutenant?'

'Yes, Pop.'

'Tell him what you feel. Do not waste one precious second. Not a one.'

Renfro walked the second lieutenant out to the hangar. On seeing the bars glint on her shoulders, the startled men stood to attention, all jokiness gone, and stared straight ahead.

'That's right, you rowdies,' growled Renfro. '*Ten-hut!* And you stay like that till I'm back!'

Ida sat in the Packard and peered over its enormous white steering wheel. Renfro handed her the keys and a cyclostyled map of the route to RAF Alconbury.

'This here, ma'am, is one of the last ever automobiles to be made in the United States.'

'How come?'

'FDR done told Ford, General Motors, Chrysler and Packard to stop making cars. Period.'

'Just like that?'

'Executive order. Cease and desist. From now on, ma'am, every car plant in the whole entire country has to make tanks and planes.'

'We're always told change comes slow, but, look at that, they can switch it up lickety-split when they have a mind to.'

'This war has changed the rules of the game, ma'am.'

'Some of them.'

'I'll phone ahead to Alconbury and warn them of your approach, ma'am. Tell them to get out while the getting's good and evacuate the base before your arrival. Heh-heh. You may find them all gone when you get there.'

'Hopefully not Mr Gower, sergeant.'

'Hopefully not Mr Gower. Safe journey, Second Lieutenant Marshall.'

Long Barrow

IDA DROVE THE LAST MILE at five miles per hour, due to the children from Alconbury village who were perched all over the car. Some stood or knelt on the back seats, others crawled over the trunk or stood on the running board. There were two children in the passenger seat, giving her conflicting directions and shouting over each other to be the one she listened to. For the sake of fairness, she tried to favour the one who wasn't wearing her cap.

'There it is, miss! RAF Alconbury!'

Ida saw the low-slung humps of a row of Nissen huts. The corrugated iron benders were roofed in turf, which gave them the look of Neolithic long barrows. Next, she saw wings and tail fins and a watchtower with radio masts.

Before she had even stopped the car at the red and white checkpoint barrier, the children hopped out and hared off into a field. Ida put her discarded cap back on her head and watched them rip up spring cabbages, tossing them into the air and seeing how far they could clobber them with a stick.

The RAF Alconbury checkpoint barrier raised and a soldier saluted, no questions asked, as if he'd been expecting her. He directed her to the station commander's office, where she parked up and climbed out of the Packard. A wing commander stepped out briskly in peaked cap and ribbon bar, spare and bow-legged like a jockey. He returned her salute and then shook her hand warmly.

She handed him the envelope. 'Here's your eviction notice, sir.'

'And a prettier bailiff there could not be. Thank you, lieutenant.' He pronounced it 'leff-tenant'. 'Now, Grafton Underwood tell me your orders are to courier some operational intelligence to London. And I am given to understand that this intelligence must not be written down, cabled or sent by radio, but communicated to you verbally by our Flight Sergeant Gower from PI. Have I got that right?'

Silently, Ida blessed sweet Sergeant Renfro for this cover story. His Southern tact had spared her the salacious winks and smutty jokes that would have attended a pretty bailiff asking to have a private word with her lover. Former lover.

'Yes, sir. It's connected to Flight Sergeant Gower's former work at the Advanced Intelligence Service of MI14, sir.'

'You will find Mr Gower in the furthest bomber on the runway, lieutenant. He's just working out how to beat the traffic to Hamburg.'

Her palms sweaty on the large white steering wheel, Ida drove the gaudy Packard down the runway and parked beside the last Wellington. She scaled a wooden ladder, walked along the bomber's wing and slid over engine hump to fuselage. There was Glyn, behind yet another diamond-pane window. Not All Souls' ancient leads, nor Peter

Robinson's criss-cross sticky tape. No, this time she found him behind a chunky geodetic aluminium alloy. Glyn had his own little desk in there, across which he was sliding a hinged protractor, possibly working out the trigonometry to get that cap at an even jauntier angle. He wore his garrison cap, or 'Molly cap', at two o'clock on the side of his head. Perhaps all the brilliantine held it in place. He still hadn't looked up from his maps and slide rules, so she stood to one side of the window, where he could not see her face, then banged her fist on the thick Perspex.

'Probation visit! Open up! Parole officer!'

When she peeked in at the window, he had gone. Seconds later, over her right shoulder, the cockpit's Perspex ceiling slid back and Glyn's head popped out the top, his eyes shining with joy.

'Ida!' He vaulted out of the window and kissed her on both cheeks like a Frenchman – but not a lover, or even a former lover. 'What are you doing here?'

'Your station commander thinks I'm gathering top-secret intelligence for MI14.'

'But why are you *really* here?'

She told him how she'd been to three bases in one day, having left RAF Wilmslow for USAAF Grafton Underwood and brought the envelope to RAF Alconbury.

'What are your hopes of third base, ma'am?'

'I must say, it's a comfort to find you safely behind a desk for the duration.'

'I almost never fly, now. Once a year, like Santa. I'm just covering for the navigator, who's getting married. I used to do the odd recce in a Blenheim, but since the switch to Mosquitoes and Spitfires, the pilot just takes the photos himself, pressing what used to be the trigger. So now you find me, for the most part, that least romantic of things: the ground crew.'

Ida placed her hands on the top of the ladder, hooked her shoes on the outside of the side rail and performed a controlled slide without once touching the rungs of the ladder. The whole way down, she kept her gaze locked on his ever-widening eyes.

'Where did you learn to do that?'

'RAF Wilmslow,' she replied. 'Your turn.'

'Not on your nelly,' he said, climbing down the wooden rungs. 'Now, let me show you my actual, earthbound desk.'

They crossed the runway towards the Nissen huts. The asphalt was ridged and buckled here and there, either by extremes of heat and cold, or because it had been made with the wrong sort of bitumen.

'Good grief! Why are you driving that perfectly hideous car?'

'Standard issue. Aren't you scared about flying off in that Wellington today?'

'After the Blenheim, it feels safe as houses.'

On the edge of the runway, parked on a verge of brown grass, they passed a decommissioned twin-engine plane covered in green mildew and encrusted with guano. Its tail end was covered in a mossy tarpaulin, but the rest was exposed to the elements and the birds.

'How one misses bird shit now the Blitz has put them all to flight,' said Ida. 'This shit-encrusted airplane gives me a Proustian nostalgia for *la vie entre deux guerres*.'

'This is the Blenheim,' he said, in a bitter voice.

Ida stopped in her tracks. 'Hold on – you mean, you flew in this?'

'Yes,' he said, 'and this is where I sat ...' He whacked the flat of his hand against the transparent nose cone, sending a Perspex panel rattling in its frame.

'Nothing but Perspex around you? You must have been terrified. The whole flight, you were there?'

'Except for take-off and landing,' he said.

'What happened then?'

'There's a gimcrack fold-down navigator's seat, side-on to the pilot, in the cockpit. Then, after take-off, you crawl down into the "snot bubble", as we used to call the Perspex nose-cone.'

'Seems F Staircase's architect was called up to serve in aeronautical engineering.'

'Of eighty-nine reconnaissance sorties flown by Blenheims, forty-eight men were lost.'

'Why's it such a death trap? Is it very slow?'

'Fully one hundred miles per hour slower than an Me9. Not only was this bastard a death trap, it was a useless death trap, because its cameras froze at altitude and didn't unfreeze when you came down low for the photographs.'

'Is it all Spitfires and de Havilland Mosquitoes, now?'

'Yes, but these are Spitfires gutted for speed. They rip out its guns, its armour plating and radio to give it a top speed of near-on four hundred miles per hour – and that's even after they've fitted it with a larger fuel tank, so it can fly further over enemy territory.'

They came to the last Nissen hut in the row. He held a black tarpaper-covered door open for her and said, 'Welcome to First Phase Photographic Interpretation.'

Ida had been expecting something like the dorms at Wilmslow. Instead, they entered an office where twenty or so men and women, in roughly equal number, were working quickly and quietly at trestle tables. A young private pegged dripping photographs to a line suspended above a sink. Red light seeped under a door marked *Dark Room*. Here and there were bulky Teletype 19 teleprinters, the size of Wurlitzers, with QWERTY keyboards instead of piano keys. As they passed, one teleprinter began humming and whirring and spooling out a chameleon tongue of pink paper that a WAAF flight sergeant impatiently slid between her thumbs.

At a far desk, a woman called out, 'Is it there?'

'No ... and no ... and no,' the flight sergeant replied, as she searched and searched through the ticker tape's fine print, letting vast coils spool by her feet. 'Yes! Yes, here it is!' She tore off the tape, kicked away the tendrils of pink paper entangling her shins and hurried to the other woman's desk.

'The whole place has the air of the newsroom of a daily paper,' said Ida.

'Right down to the smell of print,' he said.

'There's none of the leisurely, donnish air that Merry describes at Medmenham.'

'And for good reason,' he said. 'Unlike Third Phase Brahmins, your First Phasers work against the clock, all day, every day. From the moment a Mosquito touches down, we have two hours tops to rip out and print the film, analyse the photos and send a teletype to whomever has been screaming loudest and longest for the information.'

'Who are your customers?'

He took her to a wall-mounted blackboard at the end of the hut. Names and numbers were neatly painted along ruled white lines. The client list was imposing: War Office, Air Ministry, Admiralty, SHAEF, Ministry of Economic Warfare, MI14 and Joint Photographic Reconnaissance Committee – RAF Medmenham.

'Now, where it says MI14,' said Ida, 'that's just Merry, right? Nobody else does photographic intelligence at Peter Robinson.'

'This whole set-up,' he said, 'is all just an elaborate ruse so that she and I can exchange love letters. I didn't think you'd see through it so fast. Now I have to send these out-of-work actors home.' From a drawer in a scuffed teak desk, he took out a pack of Navy Players and a lighter. 'What gave the game away, might I ask?'

'That airplane covered in bird shit. I thought, if this is a real RAF base, they'd have proper airplanes.'

He laughed and led her out into the sunlight and round to the far side of the Nissen hut. They leant their backs against the sloping turf walls of the bender and felt the March sun on their faces. Since Photographic Interpretation was the last hut in the row, they enjoyed an uninterrupted view of bare brown rolling fields. Between the hut and the fence lay a lawn speared by early crocuses. They shared a cigarette.

'I'm about to start a new job in London,' she said. 'In a department store.'

'I know the one.'

'I believe you were arrested there once.'

She turned and rested her head on his chest. When she kissed him, his lips and neck were already warmed by the sun.

He took off her Signal Corps kepi and ran his fingers through her hair. His fingertips traced the bumpy scar tissue above her ear.

'Lobotomy scar,' she said.

'You'll fit right in at British Military Intelligence.'

'I start tomorrow.'

An Exchange of Gifts

―

WITH NO SIGNPOSTS TO GUIDE HER, Ida drove approximately south-east until she recognised the village of Girton on the outskirts of Cambridge. She knew the road from Cambridge to Oxford. Two hours later, the sunlight blazed against the gold trim of her hubcaps and the bronze bars on her shoulders, as she parked right outside Merry's Walton Street terrace.

'I'm trying to work out why that uniform suits you so well,' said Merry, at the front door. 'Perhaps it's because you've always had an erect, upright stance. Shoulders back, chin up ...'

'And spoiling for a fight.'

'Heavens, what an extraordinary car! Can you give me a lift to London? My two-seater has no petrol.'

'Tell me why you got the sack,' said Ida, on the London Road, just after Shillingford.

'Must I? I warn you, this is a very ugly tale, from which no one emerges with any credit.'

'Oh, goody,' said Ida, in her best Joyce Grenfell.

Merry kicked off her shoes and pushed her stockinged feet against the dashboard.

'Well, I was still getting my legs under the table at Medmenham, but I had an excellent team under me, all quick studies. I loved the ethos of the place, which was like a sort of campus university, rather bohemian, ballet dancers and film producers. The base even has its own entertainments officer. Each week, there's some sort of concert: a gang show, a piano recital – sometimes whole plays and operettas. And all to a very high standard, thanks to all the West End types. Professional set designers employed by day making models of Hamburg's industrial area would spend the evening making replica Japanese houses for *The Mikado*. They even have big-name ENSA acts from outside, too. None of us had ever been taught how to salute and so there was none of that. Nobody, so far as I know, had ever done a lick of military training.'

'Get to it, girl! Why were you sacked?'

'So, the Medmenham idyll was shattered with the arrival of a new station commander called Carton. Like the receptacle. Group Captain Carton was most keen to impose military discipline – shiny shoes, parades, you know, square bashing, kit inspections. Anyway, one day, they were having some sort of parade, while I was leading my shift from the huts to the main house, when Carton shouts at us. Now, my mother always told me that, if a man shouts from a distance, one should pretend not to have heard.'

'Why?'

'An acquaintance should know better than to be so rude, and if he's a stranger then it lets you put some extra yards between you. And so, I kept on walking, and told my team to do likewise. We'd made it to the print library when Carton burst in with a face of thunder, shouting that the parade was mandatory, and that all seventeen hundred personnel were required to participate. It was meant to start in twenty minutes and yet, here he found us, nowhere near ready for the big event.

'I said, "Can't you get by with sixteen hundred and ninety-two? You see, we are working flat out to find the exact location of the battleship *Tirpitz*, and I'm afraid neither I, nor my team, can spare the time." Then he told me to stand up.'

'Like he was about to punch you?'

'Yes, that's just what I thought, Ida. I really thought he was about to punch me, right there and then, in front of my whole team. Instead, he decided to give me a carpeting, shouting in my face, spittle flying, accusing me of this, that and the other. It's strange how keenly his words stung, even though they were, I think, baseless.'

'Perhaps what stung,' ventured Ida, 'was what Austin would call the "speech act" of being denounced, rather than the denunciation itself ... ?'

'Yes, I think that's it exactly. I was being humiliated in front of my team. Oh, it was vile, Ida.'

While Ida focused on overtaking a tractor, Merry let her mind go back to the actual words that Station Commander Carton had shouted at her in the print library. She remembered them all with ghastly fidelity. Why, she wondered, does unpleasantness etch itself indelibly, but sweet moments vanish from the mind without a trace?

'The uniform means nothing to you,' Carton shouted. 'Nothing but fancy dress. Brave men are fighting and dying in that uniform. And they would be fighting and dying in far greater numbers but for drill. Drill is what turns a ragbag into a fighting unit. This has proved true for hundreds of years, but you come sauntering along one summer, fresh from your sheltered little world, a world that was won for you, I might add, by the blood of young men in these same uniforms that you so disrespect, young men who fought as one mind and one body precisely because of the discipline and drill and training which you, with your airs and graces, Lady Muck, find so unbecoming and beneath you.'

She was cowed. No one had shouted at her like that since she was a day boarder, aged twelve. She was shrivelling like a salted slug. Then, suddenly, she asked herself how she would respond had he been arguing like this in the Jowett Society. The next instant, she found herself smiling, awaiting her turn to speak.

The smile made his bluster seize up, even as he concluded his diatribe: 'You are part of the armed forces, yet you seem to think the armed forces are part of you. If this was only your own lofty opinion, it would not poison the barrel too much, but I look around at your shabby, slutty, slaggy shower of misfits, all these ragged-arsed librarians, and I see you have infected them with your contempt.'

'If I may just say one thing—' ventured Merry.

'What can you possibly have to say for yourself?'

'May I speak without interruption? Thank you. Nothing that happens here – nothing – originated in the regular RAF. You had to be dragged kicking and screaming towards modern techniques of reconnaissance and interpretation – by which time, the Luftwaffe were way ahead of us, thanks to your scandalous dereliction of duty. In 1940, my old boss, a canny Australian civilian, offered you the facilities and expertise of his Wembley aerial reconnaissance firm, but you lot slammed the door in his face. This won you another whole year in which to enjoy your bizarre cleaning rituals. And now, when you see seventeen thousand former civilians working round the clock to make up for lost time, do you hang your head in shame? Do you vow to make amends for your grievous blunder? Do you try to help? No, you do not. Unbelievably, you seek to drag us away from urgent war work to waste yet more time on your mind-numbing square-bashing, which the squaddies, with good reason, call "bull".'

'Oh, what do you think the regular RAF are doing here? Are we just old retainers? Glorified groundsmen?'

'Bingo,' said Merry. 'Hallelujah. You got there in the end. Sweep the paths, change the light bulbs, paint the rocks white if you must, but stay out of the way.'

'You think that's my duty?' Carton was trembling the way a rocket seems to wobble on its launch pad in the moment before lift-off. 'You think an RAF station commander has no higher duty than that? Well, let me tell you—'

The print library phone began to ring. An insistent single ring.

'Answer that,' snapped Carton to the young WAAF who stood beside it, eyes front.

The WAAF's hand trembled as she lifted the receiver. She answered the phone in a whisper, then looked back at the group captain, swallowed hard and said, 'Sir, it's Mr Duncan Sandys, financial secretary to the War Office, sir.'

With an imperious click of his fingers, Group Captain Carton held out his hand for the phone.

'Beg pardon, sir,' said the WAAF. 'It's for Merry, sir.'

Merry took the handset from the WAAF and placed

her hand over the mouthpiece. 'I'm afraid I must take this call in private, Group Captain Carton, because you are not security cleared at this level. If, however, it turns out that Mr Sandys is calling with news of an exciting breakthrough in button-polishing, I'll be sure to let you know.'

She could see that Carton was pulled in two directions. He did not dare keep a senior minister of the war cabinet hanging on the other end of the line, and yet he could not let her gross insubordination go unpunished. His mix of rage and irresolution reminded Merry of a bull deciding whether to charge or turn tail.

In the end, he bellowed, 'The moment this call ends, you will come to my office and bring everything in your desk with you.'

Merry gave him a three-fingered Brownie salute, which she recalled from her last time in uniform. Carton slammed out of the room.

'Hello, Mr Sandys,' said Merry. 'Oh, no, we're not being bombed. The wind just slammed a door. How may I help you … ?'

At this conclusion of Merry's tale, Ida slapped the steering wheel, laughing with delight. She honked the car horn a few times too, disturbing Friesians in a field.

'I made an enemy of Carton,' said Merry, 'just as I made an enemy of Keating at Wembley. I don't like to be at odds with people. I think of you as being much more the sort of person who accrues enemies, and yet, somehow, I find it to be true of myself. I wonder if this is due to your influence.'

'That's our exchange of gifts,' said Ida, with a satisfied smile.

'Our what?'

'Friendship is an exchange of gifts. You taught me the tact and diplomacy for which I am now a byword among nations, while I gave you the gift of being less emollient and more combative.'

'That doesn't sound like a fair swap to me at all.'

They overtook a column of military trucks on their way to RAF Benson, then slowed down again when they came to a village which they deduced to be Nettlebed.

'Being a passenger in a left-hand drive, one feels oddly remiss,' said Merry. 'When other motorists see me lolling about on the right-hand seat, how they must despair of women drivers.'

'Quartermaster told me this might be one of the last ever cars to be made in America.'

'Really? Why's that?'

'FDR's abolished the car industry for the duration! How about that?'

'How about that indeed,' said Merry, crossing her long legs in the footwell as if they were having this discussion in Somerville's senior common room armchairs – an association which the car's luxurious crush pile carpeting rather encouraged. 'Once you're at war, nobody even pretends to believe in laissez-faire economics, do they? I think that's why Londoners have been so stolid throughout the Blitz. They already know everything has changed. They've seen the government commandeer banks, hospitals and private land for war, and they shall expect them to do the same for the peace.'

'All very well in practice,' said Ida, 'but does it work in theory?'

'Life is going to be very much more equal after the war, but first we have to win the war – and that is far from certain. The whole thing's balanced on a knife-edge.'

'Balanced on my sweet ass! Ever since America entered the war, there's only one winner.'

'You're insane.'

'Listen to Lady Haw-haw! The great state of Texas alone has twenty Ruhr Valleys. The Mesabi Iron Range another fifty.'

'Coal production doesn't win wars, for God's sake,' said Merry. 'Has your head wound reopened?'

Ida laughed. 'Since we're going to the US embassy,' she said, 'let me tell you about the row I got into on my last visit there – keeping to the theme of ugly spats with powerful men. I should caution you that one person *does* come off well in this story, but it sure ain't me.'

'Oh, goody,' said Merry, not having to travel quite so far to sound like Joyce Grenfell.

'It was their New Year's Eve party,' said Ida, 'and I was introduced to an American expat called Tom, who had showroom-dummy hair and was a Merton College alumnus, and once read philosophy at Harvard, where he specialised in Aristotle.'

'I think I know who he may be.'

'It took me a little longer than you, because I may have had a couple of cold drinks.'

'Sparkling ones?'

'Yes, they were cold. Yes, they sparkled. I said, "Hi, Tom – where ya from?" Tom said he was born in St Louis, but his accent was pure Boston Brahmin. He was halfway through telling me how much he detested Oxford because it was a sort of mausoleum when the penny dropped, and I realised that this Tom was no ordinary Tom, but—'

'Thomas Stearns Eliot.'

'"Oh, it's you," I said ...'

'Oh, it's you. Do you know, my students forever quote *Burnt Norton* in tutorials. They just love your line about "human kind cannot bear very much reality".'

'Very nice to hear,' said Eliot.

'And then I tell them how wrong you are.'

'Ah, I see. So, you tell your students that people love reality and can't get enough of it? That they shun escapism in all its forms, which explains why the cinemas stand empty night after night?'

'No,' said Ida. 'I caution them against the fallacy that, if one's conclusions are not bleak, one must have dodged the truth in some way. Very often, obfuscation and sentimentality lie in the other direction, in a melodramatic attachment to the hard-knocks fallacy.'

'But what if reality truly is cold and hard?'

'Sometimes it is, but I tell students not to overlook the easy reality, the sweet, soft truth and the warm and cosy fact of the matter. I tell them it's the *denial* of reality that folks cannot stand.'

'And how do you teach your students about the great tradition of eminent philosophers, from Plato right up to Freddie Ayer, who all argue that we have no contact with the so-called reality of the outside world?'

'I teach them that that is a very wicked thing to say.'

He leant closer, as though his bat-ears' sonar detected the tasty thrips and lacewings of error. 'Wicked? Why wicked?'

'To tell people that their whole experience of the outside world is a hallucination constitutes an act of colossal psychological violence.'

'Not if it's true,' said Eliot.

'But is it?'

'The science confirms that we have no direct access to the outside world, but only to sense-data.'

'Science my ass! It was all said by Bishop Berkley back in the seventeen hundreds! So, of course a High Church Anglican like you just laps it up.'

'The idea of reality being too much for us is also found in Freud, who is not, I think, a member of the Anglican communion.'

'Denial of reality is what folks really cannot stand.'

'Yes, you've said that. But I'm sure I don't know what you mean.'

There it was: the proud incomprehension of Oxford philosophy. *I'm so clever, I don't understand you.* Only made ten times worse by his Boston Brahmin accent. Here were Northern vowels to make Abraham Lincoln secede from the Union – though, of course, it was T. S. Eliot who actually seceded from the Union, having renounced his US citizenship to become a subject of the British crown – all the better, she supposed, to play the echt Anglican conservative and strike the dégagé pose about the frightfulness of reality; all the better to say, in true Oxonian, *I'm sure I don't know what you mean.* She told herself to calm down. Be more like Merry. The scalpel, not the broadsword. But her dander was up.

'Then let me explain,' she said, her voice quivering with passion. 'Being kept in the dark is intolerable. If I'm held in jail and do not know if my case will ever be heard; if no one will tell me if my village still stands; if I do not know in which prison my children are held, or even how many of them are still alive; if I do not know if my husband has been killed by firing squad or granted a stay of execution

– all this is denial of reality and it is absolutely *unbearable*.'

Eliot laid a gentle hand on her forearm and smiled sympathetically. 'I only hope the new year is less torrid for you than this one has been,' he said, and left to rejoin his friends.

Ida emptied her glass and swiped another flute of fizz from the drinks table. Catching her reflection in an ornate mirror, she was now reminded that she was wearing the conical party hat with a crepe tassel that flick-flacked like a burlesque dancer's, and she knew her defeat to be total. What great oration could survive the wearing of a conical party hat? 'Four score and seven years ago, our fathers brought forth on this continent a new nation, conceived in liberty, and dedicated to the proposition that all men are created equal ... Oh, sorry, I forgot I was still wearing it. Came straight from a shindig at the White House. How's everybody doing today?'

Ida changed down the gears as the Great Western Road took them through the outskirts of London and the traffic thickened.

'Oh, Merry, he knocked me into a cocked hat. That's the cold, hard, awful bitter truth of it! I remember wishing, if only I were you, if only I could be Merry, then I'd have kept my poise and won.'

'But I think you were right in your riposte to him,' said Merry. 'You lost the battle but not the war. People always talk about deluded optimists, but what about deluded pessimists? Despair can be as mistaken as hope.'

Old Tat

IDA AND MERRY'S STEEL DESKS formed an L-shape in the corner of the top floor of Peter Robinson's. Their view over central London would have been grand but for the brown sticky tape criss-crossing the windows.

The two of them were just hanging up their coats when Betsy Todd heaved on to Ida's desk a cardboard box full to the brim with crumpled postcards, faded holiday snaps, back issues of German magazines and yellowed newspapers.

'Oh, I don't think that can be for either of us,' said Merry, in her smooth, emollient voice. 'We've only been here five minutes.'

'Colonel Austin said to bring this box here,' she replied. 'So, here it is. Oh, and here *he* is.'

Austin walked towards them, dressed exactly as at All Souls, in pinstripe and glasses, with a look of amused intrigue on his face.

'Welcome to the Advanced Intelligence Section, ladies.

Ah, you have the boxes. Excellent! Here, you will find crucial intelligence about the German littoral.'

'In this box of old tat?'

'And many more like it! I want you to compile detailed information about Germany's coastline.'

'But isn't that rather a job for PI?' asked Merry.

'Ah, but what I want is *precisely* what the photographic interpreters and aerial reconnaissance cannot see,' said Austin.

'But what,' asked Ida, peering doubtfully into the box, 'can anybody learn from postcards, holiday snaps and the like?'

'Roughly speaking, everything.'

'For instance?'

'For instance, before the tenth of May 1940, it was a perfect axiom of high command that the Ardennes formed a natural anti-tank defence. Every spy-in-the-sky modified Spitfire, every photographic interpreter at Medmenham, every War Office briefing knew, everyone positively knew for a definite fact that the Ardennes was impenetrable to tanks. Only you knew different. Now, why was that? What made you so special?'

'Nothing special,' said Ida. 'I just walked through the forest.'

'And only by walking through the forest did you see how easily tanks could slip between trees. Aerial photography showed an impenetrable canopy, but the view from the forest floor was different. Let's try a lucky dip,' he said.

Austin kept his eyes on Ida as he reached into the box and pulled out a crumpled black-and-white holiday snap. 'What do you see here?'

'A man diving off the rocks,' said Ida.

'Nothing else?'

'Well ... Perhaps, if the ocean here is deep enough for a grown man of average size to dive from an elevation of about fifteen feet, then you can deduce the anchorage boundary for ships.'

'Brilliant,' said Austin.

'Swot,' said Merry.

'Am I in?' asked Ida.

'In? My dear girl, it was you who created this position.'

'I did?'

'You were the one who showed us the value of the sort of nitty-gritty we can get from these boxes.'

'You singlehandedly took all the glamour out of espionage,' said Merry. 'Whenever I spend an entire week slogging through boxes of dog-eared German trade journals, I bless the day you were born.'

An air-raid siren began to wail. And then another and another, until it seemed whole postal districts were howling.

'Let's have a dekko from up on the roof,' said Austin.

'Shouldn't we go to a shelter?' Merry said.

'Almost certainly. Only, I do like to watch the raids. See what we're up against.'

Stepping out on to the roof, they found a sky so cloudless they could see clear to the East End. They walked to a rusty iron railing at the edge of the roof, where they stood three abreast, like spectators at the greyhound track. No sight of enemy bombers anywhere.

'False alarm,' said Merry, and turned to go.

'No, here they come,' said Ida, shielding her eyes with one hand and pointing to a scattering of tin tacks in the air with the other. Together, they watched the tin tacks swell into German bombers banking over Holborn.

'Heinkels and Dorniers,' shouted Austin over the noise of the bombers' engines. The planes kept formation as they flew east. Against the bombers' massive bass drone, the ack-ack from the anti-aircraft guns sounded as tinny as BB guns. 'They're heading for Surrey Docks.'

They watched the bombers drop stick after stick on the docklands. Whole buildings collapsed silently as in a Buster Keaton film. Seconds later, dust, smoke and fire arose over untold dead Londoners, while the Heinkels and Dorniers vanished over the Thames estuary, not one plane lost.

They stepped through the hatch and climbed down to the seventh floor, back to the box of old tat with which they hoped to stop the mighty German war machine.

Sommerzeit

IDA OPENED ANOTHER BOX FILE and lifted its spring clip. The first thing she took out was a parish newsletter called *Das Senfkorn*, the mustard seed.

Das Senfkorn served the parish of Peenemünde. The village priest thanked his flock for attending in such numbers the funeral of a nine-year-old boy, who was run over on his paper round by a truck in the month of March, when the mornings were still dark. A poorly reproduced photo showed local school children presenting Peenemünde's *Bürgermeister* with a petition arguing that *Sommerzeit*, or daylight-saving hours, should be brought forwards from April to March in order to protect children from the overnight traffic of heavy goods vehicles. Upon receipt of the petition, the *Bürgermeister* told *Das Senfkorn* that 'The Reich has set *Sommerzeit* to start in April, which safely protects all German schoolchildren, to say nothing of farmers and factory workers. This tragedy did not befall the boy on his way to school, but when he was working hard to support his family in the early hours before light.'

Ida was stunned that the *Bürgermeister* was blaming a family's Protestant work ethic for the death of their son. Then, rereading the lines, she started to wonder whether his cold words were due not to a heart of stone, but rather to a need to sidestep the big question of why there were so many nocturnal trucks passing through this little village.

She passed *Das Senfkorn* across her desk to Merry, and said, '*Warum die vroom vroom?*'

Merry lifted her face from her stereoscope. 'Hmm?'

'What's with all the big rigs trucking through the boondocks every night?'

Merry hauled herself to her feet and rubbed the small of her back. She took the church newsletter to the window. Leaning sideways against the radiator, one foot resting on the other, she read about the little village of nocturnal juggernauts. The name Peenemünde rang a bell. She laid the parish newsletter on the brick windowsill and went to the card index box on her desk. Flicking through the letter P cards, she found what she'd jotted down one night in Wembley: *Peenemünde: odd ski-jump structure. Poss. rocket launcher (?) Request sortie.*

It came back to her now. She'd spotted a peculiar swooping ramp near the north-eastern Baltic shore. It was the same night she'd reprieved a nanny goat from being targeted as an oil silo. Her sortie request had been ignored or denied, she couldn't remember which – it amounted to the same thing. Now she knew she needed to study that site again.

She picked up the phone and called Medmenham to ask if they had any more recent covers of the Peenemünde municipality. An hour later, they called back to say they had none. Chewing the side of her lip, Merry beckoned Ida and together they crossed to Austin's desk.

'Two years ago, at Wembley, Austin, I saw a very odd, very long structure in a village called Peenemünde. Now, there's a heavy traffic of lorries in the same place. Medmenham say they have no recent covers of the place.'

Austin was unscrewing the sections of his pipe. 'When you saw this structure, what did you think it was?'

'I'd never seen anything like it,' said Merry.

'But if you had to guess its function ... ?' Austin blew through the hollow pipe stem to clear it of dottle.

'Well, I wondered,' began Merry, somewhat apologetically, 'if it might have possibly been a ramp for launching rockets, perhaps.'

Austin knocked the empty bowl of his pipe on the desk and smiled. She could not tell if he was smiling to himself or at her. In fact, he was trying to work out how much he was permitted to tell her about the Luftwaffe's new rockets. Austin was one of the very few people outside Bletchley Park who were cleared to read Ultra decrypts that came from cracked Enigma codes. Recent Ultra decrypts had found the Luftwaffe buzzing with talk of V-rockets. He decided he could tell her all the intelligence he knew, just not its provenance.

'The Luftwaffe have been developing a rocket called the V1. *Vergeltungswaffen*. We have no idea where these V-rockets or V-weapons are being developed. And so, the more excited the Luftwaffe sound, the more they talk of successful tests and long-range accuracy, the more nervous the Air Ministry and the War Office become. Now, back then, did you request a sortie to the putative launch pad?'

'Yes, but no dice.'

He reached for the phone receiver. 'Let me see if I have better luck.'

One week later, Austin was still picking up the phone and requesting a sortie over Peenemünde. Still no dice. It became such a routine start to their day that, each morning, as she came in through the turnstile, Merry raised her eyebrows at Austin, and he shook his head, like two professional bidders at an auction house.

After a week of this, Ida joined the two of them at Austin's desk and asked, 'Why's Benson so backward in coming forward?'

'They're dead against MI14 being able to request sorties at all,' said Merry. 'They want it all to come just from Medmenham. So much neater on a flow chart.'

'And they see Peenemünde as a low-priority request,' said Austin. 'Oh, they tell us it's because they're in the thick of critical reconnaissance elsewhere, but that's just their way of saying they have better things to do than dance to the tune of the department-store people.'

'But they do know it's rockets we're talking about here, right?'

'They certainly do.'

'So why the foot-dragging? I just don't get it.'

'Well, I suppose,' said Austin airily, 'there is also the small matter of Merry having been sacked from Medmenham by the man who is now station commander at RAF Benson.'

'Carton?'

'The very article.'

That night, Ida went home at six and waited up for Merry. She came in at about eleven and slumped down in the armchair, staring straight ahead. What with the coal ration, it was not so unusual for a person to sit down still wearing hat, coat and scarf, but it was unusual for Merry, she who always did things just so. Because Merry had poise, her exhaustion was not at first apparent, but, the previous evening, on their way home from the Sun, Merry had almost stepped under a bus. Ida had snatched her backwards just as a double-decker chugged past, lifting their fringes.

'How much sleep did you get last night?' Ida had demanded in the exhaust fumes' backdraft.

'About three or four hours.'

'You nearly killed yourself.'

Yesterday morning, she'd started early. Tonight, she'd finished so late she must have been last out of the building save the nightwatchman. Ida pulled her forwards to help her off with her things.

'You could cooperate a little,' she said.

'I feel like a prawn being shelled,' said Merry.

When Ida tugged off her black coat, Merry's slender frame in her houndstooth tweed fell back into the armchair like a much heavier woman, sending up dust.

'What happened to the UV armband I gave you?'

'Oh, it must have fallen off,' said Merry, pretending to notice its absence for the first time.

'And the luminous gloves?'

'Aren't they still in the pockets?'

Ida folded Merry's flared black coat. She felt in the pockets and found the UV armband next to the luminous gloves, which were still in their paper wrapping.

'Why are you burning the candle at both ends?'

'*Vergeltungswaffen.* Austin's very worried about V-weapons. And, while we're waiting for fresh snaps of Peenemünde, I've been scouring old covers for other possible launch sites.'

'Would you translate *Vergeltungswaffen* as "retribution weapons", or "retaliation weapons"?'

'Either way, what strikes me is the pretence of self-defence – as if *we* started the war. Attackers have a psychological need to pose as outnumbered defenders. Gordon of Khartoum and Rourke's Drift are the tales you tell when you bring the Gatling gun to Africa.'

'And Custer's Last Stand, circled wagons and the Alamo, when you bring it to America.'

Ida fixed Merry sardines on toast and a whisky. She watched as Merry munched her sardines with the simple-minded contentment of the geriatric ward, then set aside her empty plate and closed her eyes.

'Do you want the paper?'

'No, thank you, my eyes cannot look at another thing.'

'Let me put you to bed.'

'If I go to bed now, I shall only lie awake all night with my head churning and jabbering in a fever of black-and-white plan views of German sports fields that may or may not be grassy runways. Will you be so good as to read to me, Ida?'

'What shall I read?'

'Anything,' she said, her eyes still closed. 'Are you staring at me?'

'Yep.'

'Why?'

'You look like you're about to cross the road.'

Merry oinked softly.

Ida ran her finger along the bookcase and found Wilfred

Owen. She sat down on a wooden chair and opened the book.

'*Move him into the sun,*' she began.

'Good choice,' murmured Merry.

'*Gently its touch awoke him once,*
At home, whispering of fields unsown.'

Ida silently closed the book and recited from memory, the better to study Merry.

'*Always it woke him, even in France,*
Until this morning and this snow.'

She noted how Merry's jaw hung slack and her arms fell either side of the armchair. How drained must she be not to even prop her elbows on the armrest?

'*If anything might rouse him now*
The kind old sun will know.'

Merry's face looked like a death mask. This discombobulated Ida so much that she forgot where she was in the sonnet. She opened the book and tried to find the right page. She heard Merry's dulcet voice:

'*Think how it wakes the seeds –*
Woke once the clays of a cold star.
Are limbs so dear-achieved, are sides
Full-nerved, still warm, too hard to stir?
Was it for this the clay grew tall?'

Merry opened her brown eyes and met Ida's gaze. They spoke the final couplet together:

'*O what made fatuous sunbeams toil*
To break earth's sleep at all?'

'This time next week,' said Merry, 'we'll be done with Peenemünde. Will you come with me to Kirklockham?'

'With all my heart,' said Ida.

'Do you ride?'

'Medora Danes – where am I from?'
'Ha! Well, we'll ride at Kirklockham.'
'That sounds like heaven.'

Ida took Merry's hands and pulled her out of the armchair. They hugged.

Merry stroked Ida's back and whispered in her ear, 'Thank you, dear heart. That was beautiful.'

'What was?'

'All of it.'

She kissed her cheek and went into the bedroom.

The Death Trap

EARLY THE NEXT MORNING, Ida tiptoed into Merry's bedroom, switched off her alarm and set the hands of the clock back a couple of hours. When Merry came into work, she narrowed her eyes at Ida but looked rested. She hung her hat and coat on the hook against the white-painted brick wall by the L-shaped corner desk. She turned to look at Austin, who was standing by the window, lighting his pipe. True to their morning ritual, Merry raised her eyebrows, and this time – at last – he replied with a chipper nod.

'Hallelujah!' said Merry.

'That's the good news,' said Austin. 'The bad news is that RAF Benson can only spare a Blenheim. They made it clear it was that or nothing, so I said yes to a Blenheim, but now I feel like a murderer.'

'But I thought their cameras froze at altitude,' said Merry.

'That, at least, has been fixed,' said Austin, his cheeks hollowing as he sucked his pipe into flame. 'They've now been fitted with a special gubbins that diverts hot air from the engines over the camera. So, if they do come back, they will at least have some photographic covers to show for it.'

'Well, we need those pictures by hook or by crook.'

'And – who knows?' said Austin. 'The crew may get lucky.'

'When do they fly?'

'They are just waiting for the planes to be fitted with the new lenses, which should only take a day or two.'

'Well, I feel like a murderer, too,' said Merry. 'Poor sods.'

'Hey, I saw a Blenheim once,' said Ida. 'All covered in bird shit. But why even get the Blenheim out of mothballs when you have Spitfires and Mosquitoes? Why go back to the age of steam?'

'That's probably my fault for being so insistent,' said Austin. 'RAF Benson don't think the far-flung peninsula of Peenemünde is worth the risk of losing a Spitfire, but they want to stop me phoning them every day.'

The turnstile click-clacked. Ida looked up and saw Glyn walking towards them in uniform and Molly cap. It was his first time in the building since his arrest, and so he shadow-boxed his way towards them, head darting this way and that, pretending to be on the lookout for military policemen lying in ambush behind every desk and filing cabinet. Ida met him halfway – not least to stop this pantomime.

'Ida,' he said. 'I've come because I have twenty-four hours' leave and tickets for tonight's revue at RAF Mad Mayhem.' He put his mouth to her ear and whispered, 'And I've booked us a room at the Dog and Badger in Medmenham village.'

'How did you get *Out of the Blue* tickets?' asked Merry,

coming towards him and kissing him on both cheeks. 'It sold out ages ago.'

'I'm well in with the ents officer.'

'Greetings, Gower,' said Austin. 'How's life in Cambridgeshire?'

'Oxfordshire now, actually, Austin,' he said, shaking his hand. 'I've been shuttled along the varsity line from Alconbury to RAF Benson. But I've been allowed out for twenty-four hours while they await a special delivery from Leuchars.'

'What's the special delivery?' asked Ida.

'A new thirty-six-inch lens for one of the Blenheims.'

'Yes, we were just pitying the poor sods who will fly in those death traps,' said Austin.

'One of those poor sods is me.'

'But you're ground crew,' said Ida. 'You're First Phase PI.'

'The antique Blenheim needs a two-man crew. I have to hold the pilot's hand and snap the snaps.'

'This is the Peenemünde sortie,' said Merry, gravely.

Glyn looked spooked. 'How did you know?' Then the penny dropped. 'Because it was your idea.'

'We didn't think for a minute that this would entail a Blenheim,' said Merry. 'And we didn't know it would be you.'

'It shouldn't matter who it is,' said Glyn, stoutly.

'But it does,' said Ida. 'Is it that airplane I saw covered in bird shit?'

'I spent yesterday chipping off the guano and greasing it for speed.'

'When do you fly?' Austin asked.

'Tomorrow, sir. Sixteen hundred.'

Austin turned to Merry. 'Do we have any covers of German defences on the Baltic littoral?'

'No,' she replied. 'They're all in Medmenham's print library.'

'Go there tonight,' said Austin. 'Fetch me covers of all the coastal gun batteries and radars on Glyn's flight path. I'll ask Bomber Command to knock them out.'

'Is there time, Austin?' asked Ida.

'It's tight,' said Austin, 'but, if Dowding say yes to a bombing raid tomorrow morning, there's just enough time.'

Merry began packing her stereoscope and loupe into her gas-mask box. 'I'll need your imprimatur to get in, Austin,' she said. 'What with my being persona non grata there.'

'Righto,' said Austin, and he sat down to write a formal requisition slip. 'Will you phone with map coordinates about midnight, Merry?'

'It will actually be far quicker to get the physical covers to you in person,' said Merry.

'Quicker than reading out a list of map coordinates over the phone?'

'The information on the print-library cards is primarily visual,' said Merry. 'For years, First Phase plotters such as Glyn have glued map sections to the back of photos on which they circle the radar masts and gun batteries we need, and send them to Medmenham. My job tonight will be to collate these and then draw circles around any they may have missed – or, at least, as many as I can. What we'll bring to you is visual information which Bomber Command can reproduce and distribute to their navigators.'

'Point taken. But the question still remains: how will you get them to me in time?'

'I don't know,' said Merry.

'I do,' said Ida. The three of them turned round to find Ida already in her olive US coat, her battered satchel slung across her shoulders. 'There's a US base at Daws Hill, seven miles from Medmenham. I'll requisition a swift conveyance with a full tank, and then, when Merry and Glyn have combined their Third and First Phase skills to ferret out the covers, we'll hightail them to you at Cheyne Place.'

'I'm afraid there's another problem,' said Merry. 'And a rather serious one, too.'

Ida, Glyn and Austin stared at her.

Merry looked at each of them in turn. 'Even with a special requisition slip, the maximum number of files anyone may take from the print library at a time is three.'

'How many do you need?' Austin asked.

'More like twenty-five or thirty.'

'So, we shall have to steal them,' said Ida.

'All the pandemonium may help us,' said Merry.

'All what pandemonium?' asked Glyn.

'The print library is used for a dressing room when there's a show on,' she replied. 'Only performers are allowed entry. A chit from Austin will get us on to the base, but not into the print library, not when there's a show on.'

'Can you get your ents officer friend to add us to the bill?' asked Ida.

'It's rather last minute,' said Glyn, 'but he does owe me one. What shall I say you're doing? Knife-throwing? Bullet-catching?'

'Why don't you tell your ents officer friend,' said Merry, 'that we're performing a piece called "Our Decoy Strategy". We'll figure it out when we get there; the important thing is to get inside the print library.'

Austin handed Merry an envelope. 'Here's my imprimatur to get you through the gate. Once I have those covers, I'll phone Dowding and request a raid.'

'Is it likely,' asked Glyn, cursing himself for the catch in his voice, 'that Dowding will agree to a raid at such short notice?'

'The War Office are very concerned about long-range rockets,' said Austin.

'But that's an ongoing concern,' said Glyn. 'What makes you think he'll respond to a topical request?'

'If he does, you'll have Ida to thank. And Merry, too.'

'How so?' asked Glyn.

Austin resettled his brown-framed glasses on his thin, sharp nose. 'Back in May 1940, Dowding was incandescent that nobody alerted him to Ida and Merry's intelligence about panzers coming through the Ardennes. So, now, when the two of them come warning of long-range rockets, he's bound to make sure everybody scrambles.'

'See you at the chalk house, Ida,' called Merry. 'Come on, Glyn.'

'Now, you had better scramble, too,' Austin told him.

The Gang Show

―

ARRIVING IN THE PRINT LIBRARY at RAF Medmenham, Glyn was aghast at the bustle and confusion all around him. Whether he lived or died would depend on whatever intelligence could be extracted from this place in the next few minutes, but how in God's name would it be possible to collect anything at all from this chaos of costumes, props and music cases? When a huddle of woodwind and string musicians ran through the chord changes of 'Till the Lights of London Shine Again', Glyn felt like a man drowning in Margate while still in earshot of the carousel's pipe organ. RAF and WAAF uniforms lay scattered here and there, slung over the backs of chairs or folded on tabletops, as if the German army had reached Marlow and sparked a mass desertion, with everyone pretending to have been civilians all along. A voice somewhere called out: 'Act One Beginners.' Twelve people siphoned out through the side door that led down to the stage. It was in keeping with the topsy-turvydom that almost no one came and went through the main-entrance double-doors, but a busy traffic went in and out through that side door. From downstairs, he heard applause followed by the *thump-thump* of a double bass and the high notes of a clarinet.

His head spinning, there seemed to be only one locus of quiet efficiency – and that was Merry. With a single graceful motion of her forearm, she swept a litter of make-up boxes, sheet music and feather boas into an empty mailbag. On the desk space she had cleared for herself, Merry spread out the flight plan that Glyn had dictated to her on the ten-past-six Great Western from Paddington. In a low voice, she asked Glyn to fetch files for the first half-dozen place names on its itinerary. As Glyn caddied files to her, his First Phase expertise enabled him quickly to discard irrelevant files. On the section of shelf labelled *Aerial Masts and Decoys*, for instance, he knew to ignore any pages not specifically to do with radar. Transmitters and jammers could stand, and so could Rommel's asparagus, those tall metal poles planted in fields to keep Allied gliders from landing, like pterodactyl spikes. Only radar masts needed to be knocked out. And so, from a fat ring-book bulging with some sixty pages of covers, he filleted just seven pastel-green radar files. Each radar file contained a stereo pair, a reproduced map section and a small swatch of typewritten legend. He carried the seven files at shoulder height, like a waiter, back to Merry.

Merry stooped her blond head to the stereoscope, searching for any radar masts that First Phase might have missed in their first pass at Aerial Masts and Decoys. Giving the appearance of having done with the file, she slipped it first on to her lap and then, after checking nobody was watching, from her lap into the open mailbag by her feet.

Then she asked Glyn to fetch the next set of place names on the flight-path itinerary.

Absorption in the task kept Glyn's dread away for minutes at a time. He envied the off-duty PIs getting into costume, envied them their certainty of living through the next twenty-four hours. He felt like a ghost. Perhaps he already was one. He was already invisible to the two women quick-changing at the end of the alphabetised map drawers. One of the women, changing into a gold lamé ancient-Egyptian costume, was momentarily topless. The other woman, dressed only in a camisole, stood on one leg to hook the strap of her heels. She rested her hand on the V–Z section for balance and bent over for the other shoe. Glyn froze with a photo of Zeebrugge harbour in his hand. He heard a creaking sound and turned to find Ida clenching her fists in brown leather gauntlets.

'Will you,' he said, 'begrudge me a last look at all things lovely in my last few hours?'

'Last few minutes, if I catch you again, boy.'

Merry had just identified a new cluster of radar aerials in a defensive arc in Mecklenburg when someone put their head round the door and cried, 'Robb Wilton's on!' The print library emptied as everyone rushed downstairs to see the music-hall star perform his 'The Day War Broke Out' sketch. Suddenly, the trio found themselves alone in the print library. Now, they could forego all clandestine pussy-footing. Glyn snatched up the mailbag from the floor and opened it out. Ida and Merry chucked the remaining files into the bag. Nobody noticed the woman come in. The first they heard was her loud denunciation.

'What on earth are you doing?'

Her voice rang as clear and pure as her skin. An idealistic

fresher in round gold-rimmed glasses, she would have made a good Major Barbara.

Before they could think of how to placate her, she stepped out on to the main landing above the grand staircase and shouted, 'There's people stealing covers from the print library!'

Ida shut the double doors behind the zealot and jammed a window pole through the pull handles.

'Glyn, tip that bag out on the floor!'

He upended the bag. Out fell the files, along with the make-up and other actor detritus that Merry had earlier swept in.

Outside, Major Barbara was rattling the doors. 'Stop thief! Stop thief!'

Ida emptied the USAAF panniers of crash helmets, gauntlets, slickers and thermos flask. They transferred the stolen files from mailbag to panniers. Major Barbara's hue and cry had summoned men who now began shoulder-slamming the door.

'You're the decoy, Glyn,' said Ida. 'Keep them on you until we get clear away.'

'See you in the Dog and Badger,' he said.

Ida and Merry, each holding a US Air Force pannier stuffed with stolen files, ran to the side door that led downstairs to the ballroom's backstage area. At the door, Ida turned and threw Glyn the motorbike key.

'It's the big green hog in the bike racks. White star on the gas tank.'

The thudding against the double doors ceased. Glyn heard Major Barbara hotly explain to newcomers what she'd seen. Slowly and silently, he slid the pole from the pull handles and laid it on the floor. He flung open the double doors, grabbed the mailbag and ran into the corridor, blowing past Major Barbara.

'There he goes!' she yelled. 'Quick! He's got stolen files in his sack!'

Glyn bounded up two flights of stairs and along another corridor, at the end of which he found a bright red Davy Descender fire-escape hoist mounted to the wall. He wound the fire-escape cord around his shoulders, climbed on to the windowsill and abseiled from the third-storey window, bouncing his toes off the chalk walls. Spotlights cast by hand-held torches speckled his descent.

He was hauled down the last yards and thrown to the ground. Taking kicks to his ribs and punches to the head, he hung on to the mailbag until he was flipped on to his back and had it wrenched from his grasp and handed to Station Commanders Carton and Keating, who now stood above him on the lawn.

'Stealing classified documents is a capital crime,' said Carton, his breath steaming like a bull's in the night air. 'You could hang for this. Name and rank.'

'Flight Sergeant Gower, sir.'

'Stand up, Gower. Gather round – I want witnesses. Many witnesses.'

Everybody held their breath as Carton reached into the bag. He drew out helmets (two), pairs of gauntlets (two), rain capes (two), thermos flask (one), sheet music (one) and feather boas (two).

'All right, Gower. You were seen stuffing documents into this mailbag. Where are they?'

'No, I was not stuffing documents *into* this bag; I was getting documents *out* of this bag. I was returning First Phase documents from Benson. Returning, not purloining. I suppose what made me look suspicious or conspicuous was that I'm the only one doing any work in all this carnival.'

'Sir, he has two female accomplices,' said Major Barbara.

'Does he, now? Where are these women who aided and abetted you?'

'I'll tell you exactly where they are,' said Glyn, wiping the mud from his hands. 'They're onstage right this minute, performing a sketch in *Out of the Blue*, and I shall miss my friends' performance because of your insane blunder.'

'Perfect timing,' said the master of ceremonies as Merry and Ida arrived in the wings, stage left. To thunderous applause, Robb Wilton exited stage right. The master of ceremonies strode onstage. 'Let's hear it once more for the legendary Robb Wilton! Follow that, as they say! Well, here with that unenviable task are the Misses Apple Cider and Merry Havoc, who will perform a sketch entitled "Our Decoy Strategy". Please welcome them on to the stage!'

'Now what?' Ida whispered, stowing the panniers under a blue-lit props table.

'I shoot the gun, and you catch the bullets!'

The downstage footlights shone up at a tall English officer in blue, next to a short American officer in olive.

'Ah sure am mighty curious to know more about your decoy strategy,' hammed Ida.

'Well, it's like this,' said Merry, with ingenuous enthusiasm. 'We've made thousands of cardboard tanks and placed them in fields in Kent.'

'Cardboard tanks.'

'And all these dummy tanks are painted in green and brown camouflage markings, and their guns are made from the cardboard tubes from inside old wallpaper rolls.'

'I see. What else have you Limeys made?'

'Papier-mâché Spitfires. And we've also constructed a huge dummy barracks made of crêpe paper stretched between two willow hurdles.'

'May I enquire as to why y'all have done all this?'

'Well, you see, we know that Luftwaffe spy planes are taking aerial reconnaissance photographs and our hope is that, when these photos are developed in Berlin, the German high command will take one look at them and say, "There's no point trying to invade Britain – the whole country's made out of craft materials."'

The audience erupted into long and sustained laughter.

'I have a few questions, ma'am,' said Ida.

'I rather thought you might,' said Merry.

'Now, about these papier-mâché Spitfires ... what happens when it rains?'

'They turn into Blenheims.'

'May I tell you about the decoy strategy we've been working on up at little old Daws Hill?'

A cheer went up from the Americans in the audience at this mention of their base. 'Our decoy strategy,' said Ida, 'is designed to make every Luftwaffe photographic reconnaissance pilot believe he has punctured the space-time continuum and travelled back through time to the sixteenth century.'

'How does this work?'

Ida snatched up two black cloaks from upstage and passed one to Merry. Together, they swung their cloaks over their shoulders.

'First, we get 'em to dress old-timey, like so, and to use old-timey weapons, such as the halberd.'

'And the pikestaff?'

'And the Enfield No. 2 revolver.' Improvising, Ida seized a large book lying on a pirate's chest. 'Now, as part of this time-travel decoy,' she continued, 'Whitehall panjandrums and war leaders will be pictured carrying around this ancient book from a simpler age, long before modern warfare.'

'Is it the First Folio?'

'No, ma'am.'

'A book of spells?'

'No, ma'am.' With a malicious glint in her eye, Ida handed Merry the book – and, with it, the whole burden of finding a punchline and a way out of this sketch. 'Here, read the title yourself.'

There was nothing written on the stage prop, but Merry first pretended to inspect the book's spine, before reading out its title: '*The Battle Tactics of Field Marshal Bernard Montgomery.*'

Her extempore punchline elicited a huge back-of-the-room laugh, followed by spontaneous applause.

The women bowed low, which brought the hoods of their cloaks over their heads. They pantomimed not being able to see their way as they exited stage right.

Merry threw back her hood, took Ida's hand and led her behind the painted backdrop, crossing to stage left. It felt strange to be invisible to the audience, despite being only inches behind the master of ceremonies as he introduced the Medmenham Jazz Quartet, who began a smoky, downbeat version of 'Till the Lights of London Shine Again'. Merry and Ida retrieved the panniers from under the props table, cracked a fire escape and found themselves out on the wide, misty lawn, from where they could just make out Glyn being interrogated by Carton and a small knot of inquisitors. The two Oxford philosophers put up their hoods and ran down the lawn towards the river. Ida tripped over the hem of her cloak and rolled over. She tore off the cloak and, once more, they ran for the riverbank.

Holding both bags, Ida stepped into a punt and sat down. Merry launched the punt off the grass bank into the river, then hopped on to the till, pole in hand. She punted with practised ease, letting the pole slide through her fingers, pushing at the riverbed, and then hoisting it up again, lobbing it from hand to hand. Once they had gained the middle of the river, the tide ran with them, and Merry held the pole horizontally in both hands, like a tightrope walker, letting the river do all the work. Ida looked at her standing on the till in her cloak, timeless and modern, magnificent and daft.

'Sirrah, the love I bear thee,' said Ida, 'bids me pray ye be found no traitor, even though thou hast stolen these Star Chamber papers, for which thou wilt be hung at Tyburn on the morrow.'

'M'lady, I would as lief be hung for a traitor,' said Merry, 'as lose sight of thee in this boat, with thy bosom heaving and thy sweat stewed and reeking like a polecat or fitchew.'

Using the pole as rudder, Merry steered them towards a tributary. She punted along a narrow, overgrown creek until they came to a rusted metal footbridge. They moored the punt and walked along a grass alley behind some allotments, coming at last on to the Henley Road.

As they walked the road, a lorry came towards them, its blackout lights throwing two chalk stripes on the black tarmac ahead of it. They leant their backs against a tall hedge. After the lorry passed, Ida could not see Merry, but heard her giggling in the undergrowth.

'I fell through the hedge! Haul me up, will you?'

Ida mimicked her voice: 'It's always so vair, vair hard to get oneself out of a hedge backwards, don't you know!' A dog started barking somewhere nearby. 'He thinks there's a wild boar on the loose.' She hauled a snorting Merry to her feet and brushed the leaf litter from the back of her skirt.

The Dog and Badger

ON THE TOP FLOOR of the Dog and Badger pub, Merry opened the door to a long, triangular attic room. She found she could only stand straight in the dead centre of the room, under the long oak beam at the apex of the ceiling.

'Well, that's one way of getting a girl into bed.'

'Could have made a dandy love nest,' said Ida, ruefully.

'I don't know,' said Merry. 'Isn't it rather too much like being inside a Toblerone?'

Merry threw her cloak on to the bed's old gold eiderdown quilt. Ida hung up her tunic in the wardrobe, took off her uniform tie and rolled up the sleeves of her olive shirt. Then she took out the stolen files and laid them in a long row on the carpet, next to the slanting grey wall. Merry set out her stereoscope on the table beside the kettle and tea tray. In the low-ceilinged room, the two got to work to identify the radars and coastal gun batteries that would have to be destroyed if Glyn was going to fly there and back safely in a lumbering old Blenheim. They went on in silence, side by side, for an hour, until a scatter of pebbles sprinkled the dormer window.

Ida went downstairs and found Glyn under the porch. They kissed in the misty air, a passionate, desperate kiss. She found she was crying. He kissed away her tears, feeling suddenly strong and brave and capable.

'I've got your crash helmets in the bag.'

'I never heard you arrive.'

'That's because I didn't dare start the engine. I pushed it the whole way here.'

Upstairs, Ida went to the closet, picked the pockets of her uniform jacket and turned around with her hands heaped with sachets of powdered chocolate, a chocolate bar, a soft pack of Lucky Strike and a sealed brick of ground coffee.

'Swag from the PX,' she said. 'I didn't break it out earlier because I was saving it for the late-night sugar dip.'

Glyn set the electric kettle to boil and spooned hot chocolate into a floral-patterned, bone-china pot. Merry got up from the desk and lay on the bed, her head propped on a bolster at the headboard. Sitting at the foot of the bed, Ida lifted Merry's legs into her lap and massaged her feet between her thumbs.

'Two years ago, Glyn,' said Merry, 'how I castigated you for not passing on naval intelligence, and now look at us, stealing classified documents. War has changed our standards of behaviour.'

'Do you mean that, when put to the test, all our fancy Oxford beliefs turn out to have been hollow?'

'No, I don't think I do,' said Merry. 'I mean that the same values are expressed differently at different times.'

'That sounds like rationalisation of wrongdoing,' he said, as he poured the boiling water into the china pot.

Merry sat up on the bed. 'The more you cling to your values in wartime, the more you may find yourself performing an action you could never have anticipated beforehand.'

'How so?' said Glyn, handing Ida and Merry each a cup and saucer of hot chocolate.

'If our values had just vanished like spit on a griddle,' said Ida, 'would we even be in this room together right now, with both of you in danger of arrest for treason?'

'Not you, too?'

'*Civis Americanus Sum.*'

Glyn lit an American cigarette. He found it very much smoother on the throat than Navy Cut, its taste less bitter.

'Isn't it odd,' said Merry, blowing on her hot chocolate, 'how Austin never questioned our need to do all this extra work for Glyn's mission?'

'That's because he doesn't want you to spend the rest of your life thinking you sent Glyn to his death by spotting the rocket sites.'

'Or didn't want *you* to feel guilty for finding that newsletter about the trucks in Peenemünde.'

'Could be he is thinking about both of us,' said Ida. 'And authorised the bombing raid to save us both from guilt.'

'Maybe so,' said Merry. 'Yes, quite possibly.'

'Aren't you rather overlooking the central figure, here?' said Glyn, exasperatedly exhaling smoke through his nostrils. 'Is it not the case that all this extra effort is so that I don't die?'

'Oh, yes, right – that,' said Merry. 'Sorry, yes, of course.'

'No doubt,' said Ida, sipping her hot chocolate.

'Let's get back to it,' said Merry, setting down her cup and swinging her feet off the bed.

One hour later, Merry announced that she had plotted the last Peenemünde cover. 'Now, we just need to get all our work to Austin at Cheyne Place.'

Glyn stood outside the Dog and Badger in unlaced boots, watching the women prepare for their journey on the green Harley-Davidson with its white star on the fuel tank. He felt unworthy of all they were doing to win him safe passage. Ida hooked the panniers rammed with Medmenham files to the side rack. Merry – comical in khaki rubber rain cape, helmet and goggles – hugged him and then climbed on to the pillion.

Ida came to him. 'Good luck, old beau.'

'And to you.'

She held his face between her gauntlets and kissed him on the mouth. She mounted the Harley and kicked it into life with a single boot-swing.

Glyn watched the night snuff out the last dot of their tail light before he climbed up to the attic room, cobwebbed with cigarette smoke. He kicked off his boots and lay on the bed, hands behind his head, looking up at the single beam.

The love he felt was new. Love used to be the word for obscuring the girl from view, for mislaying Ida and Merry among a welter of half-remembered love songs, poems and Hollywood films, a way of smearing the lens, so to speak, like those preposterous 'Vaseline close-ups' that, quite rightly, drew derisive catcalls at the flicks. What was different, it seemed to him, was the way that this love sharpened his understanding of them, like the 3D lunge in the stereoscope. Gone was his frustration at being denied Ida's body in that triangular room. In its place was delight at what felt like an initiation. Now, he felt he knew them in their quiddity. He'd been reading Martin Buber lately, and wondered if this is what he'd meant by the shift from I–It relationships to I–Thou.

He inhaled the scents of their impromptu night shift – hot chocolate, toasted tobacco and the earth smell of ground coffee – and felt loved. He noticed he was less frightened, less desperate about what the next day would bring. He wanted to live, but his own death was no longer the worst thing in the world. More than his own death, he feared an accident befalling Ida and Merry as they sped on two wheels through the night. He wished he'd asked them to phone him at Benson with news of their safe arrival in the Smoke.

This new love was like mountain air, and made sleep impossible. The exertions of the last however many hours fell from him. He packed his bags and walked the three miles to Marlow. If this was to be his last day on earth, he had never felt more alive. As he hopped on to the milk train to Benson, the train guard asked him what he was so happy about. Glyn was at first surprised by the question, but then realised that he was grinning from ear to ear.

Olympian

―

GLYN SAT IN A RATTLING GREENHOUSE in the sky, ten thousand feet above the Baltic littoral. He clenched his jaw so tightly that his teeth ached. His insulated, front-zipper boots hovered over the sky. Between his knees was the mounted camera with its brand new thirty-six-inch lens. The camera was the size and shape of a sailor's signal lamp, with two hand-grips for aim and a thumb-trigger shutter for taking photographs. The plane banked, and Glyn watched the yellow needles of his repeater compass swing. Compass and altimeter were the only two dials left, since the aircraft's instrument panels had been junked for weight-loss in an attempt to make the Blenheim just a few miles per hour faster. The communication lights had gone the same way. Last time he flew in a Blenheim, the navigator's dashboard boasted an array of flashing coloured lights, but now it was a ransacked box of Rowntree's Fruit Pastilles, with only the yellow and green ones left.

He looked out the starboard side at burnt-out bomb damage down below. A few hours earlier, that still-smoking crater would have been a radar mast or coastal gun battery. Instead of being elated to know his flight path had been cleared of present dangers, he was ashamed that bombs had been dropped for him alone – or, at least, for reasons as much personal as military. Those German conscripts or civil-defence volunteers who had manned that quondam gun battery or radar station were maimed or killed because three Oxford philosophers wished to spare themselves the guilt of having sent a fourth on a suicide mission. His ears burnt with shame beneath his Bakelite headphones. An accusatory grey finger of smoke rose towards him from the bomb crater. Were the four of them any better than those tetchy Olympian immortals whose internecine squabbles and love triangles induced them to hurl bolts of lightning at innocent mortals down on earth? His zippered boots hovering in mid-air only made him feel even more that he was trespassing in the realm of those Mount Olympus superhuman beings with their subhuman morality.

He saw a dart of flame on the ground, followed by the sound of ack-ack. The aeroplane rocked. His Perspex bubble was engulfed in black smoke. Then they were in clear sky again as the Blenheim flew through the ack-ack. Down below, he saw the flash of another coastal gun blazing away at them. The pilot tipped the wings and the Blenheim carved up into a cloud bank. Once safely hidden in the clouds, the blind aeroplane levelled, before banking east again.

Glyn tapped the repeater compass and watched the yellow needle swing east by north-east. He knew the trajectory of the bomb damage must have made their destination clear. Somewhere down below, his German counterpart would be running a slide rule over this morning's trail of destruction, plotting the bombers' course, and now their own, before tapping on a teleprinter: *Destination Peenemünde.*

When they flew out of the clouds, he recognised the Bay of Greifswald. There was Koos Island, and there, at last, he saw the Peenemünde peninsula, faithfully adhering to the section of map glued to a stolen cover studied in the Dog and Badger's attic room.

He flicked a communication switch in the airborne greenhouse to flash a light up in the cockpit. Moments later, Glyn heard the pilot's voice in his headphones, but whatever he was saying was incomprehensible. The faulty headphones only amplified the engine throb, so that it sounded as if the twin engines were themselves attempting to shape vowels. Glyn guessed the pilot must be trying to warn him that he was about to drop in altitude to get within the camera's focal range of the target. He double-checked his harness. The next second, the Blenheim fell. The drop was shocking. It was as though they had discovered a trap door in the sky and were falling through what used to be air but was now antimatter. The altimeter dial was spinning dizzily. He waited for it settle. Below him, Peenemünde lurched into detail. He put his eye to the camera's viewfinder and set his gloved thumbs on its shutter triggers.

Immediately, Glyn saw what looked like the giant joist of a blitzed warehouse, but it was gone from view before he could snap it. Could that have been the fabled rocket launcher? Was that what they had come so far to see? The pilot looped around for another pass at the structure. Glyn resettled his thumb on the camera trigger. When the giant joist or splayed girder reappeared in the viewfinder, it still looked nothing like a rocket launcher, but Glyn clicked the shutter at one and two second intervals, hoping the photographs, when studied by Merry, would tell a different story. The Blenheim slowly circled in a buzzard's lazy corkscrew, allowing Glyn to photograph, besides the structure, a clearing in the forest, a service road, an encampment, what might be a factory, what might be an army base, what might be a hangar, what might be none.

Once he had shot all his film, Glyn pressed his rubber mouthpiece hard against his face and told the pilot that it was time to go. But, to his frustration, the pilot circled round for another pass. The pilot was doing the very last thing he should be doing. In fury, Glyn shouted the same message over again. Now came clouds of ack-ack. Black ack-ack burst right outside the windows of his little greenhouse, crackling like a log fire. In sudden darkness, Glyn unloaded the film canister and thrust it into his jacket. He unbuckled his harness and crawled across the Perspex floor of the transparent cone. The Blenheim burst free of the smoke into clear air to reveal the magnesium-bright Baltic down below his hands and knees.

He hauled himself up into the cockpit, dropped his mouthpiece, pointed upwards and shouted: 'Go! Go! Go!'

The pilot, his face hidden by vulcanised rubber, blinked his bunched-up eyes inscrutably, but then pulled the yoke column towards himself. The Blenheim strained upwards with a whine like other planes make when they've been hit. Black smoke guffed and puffed about them.

On the starboard side of the cockpit, Glyn stumbled back against the navigator's take-off-and-landing seat. He folded it down, strapped himself into its harness and sat facing the pilot, willing the Baltic to become the North Sea and the North Sea to become England.

His arms felt heavy as he zipped the photo canister more

tightly inside his flight jacket. He hadn't slept the night before. He listened to the regular rhythmic drone of the twin engines, looking at the three or four winking lights on the instrument panel, the last Rowntree's Fruit Pastilles in the box. His eyelids were heavy. He closed his eyes and fell into a deep sleep.

The pilot was shaking Glyn's knee to wake him. His mask was off and he was grinning from ear to ear and pointing with a fat glove down at the ground.

'Essex Marshes! Essex Marshes!'

He tipped the wings so that Glyn could see for himself. Down below, a car was driving on the left. Glyn wept hot stinging tears of relief. He took off a glove and thumbed his eyes. He looked back at the fuselage, its sheet-metal walls hung with flare gun, life jackets, fire axe, fire extinguisher, parachute stowage and stretcher. None of this paraphernalia would be needed now. Not today. England was below. Once they landed at RAF Benson, he would pass the baton of his photographic canister to the First Phase crew, who would print the photos and send them by courier to MI14 for Merry's expert Third Phase analysis, and that was when she may find—

Four rivets of light punctured the fuselage. Four bangs. The side of the aircraft blew away, taking with it the flare gun, fire axe and stretcher. In their place, he saw a Messerschmitt describe a looping arc. The Blenheim's tail fin overtook them. Its wheel-well doors sailed by. The aircraft disintegrated in all directions, as if they were in a giant centrifuge. The sky sucked Glyn against the straps of his harness. He was outdoors. Now, there was nothing between his zippered boots and the air. Murderous fields and hedgerows hurtled towards him.

Department-Store Vigil

THE LATE AFTERNOON SUN CAST their shadows ahead of them as they walked through the West End towards Oxford Circus. They were both thinking that, round about now, Glyn might be photographing the long evening shadows cast by a rocket-launch ramp, or by a rocket being wheeled to its hangar.

They walked through an empty side street, whose name neither could recall, where they had to step around a wooden barrier and into the road to avoid a bomb crater that had taken away twenty feet of pavement. The empty street still glowed from a recent shower of rain. Their shadows stretched before them heroically, their coats as long as if they were gunslingers.

On the top floor of Peter Robinson, pushing through the rattling turnstile, Merry echoed the words of a roulette-wheel croupier: '*Rien ne va plus.*'

Betsy Todd was just crossing the floor, clipboard in hand. She stopped and fixed them both a look. 'Decided to put in an appearance, have you, ladies? Come to grace us with your presence?'

'Frightfully sorry to be late,' said Merry, sunnily, 'only there's a new pastry chef at Quaglino's and his profiteroles must not be rushed. Now, is the war still on, Todd? Or did we miss it?'

'A message from Colonel Austin awaits Your Ladyship.'

Merry unsealed an envelope to find a message from Austin. Bomber Command claimed to have knocked out most of the targets on Glyn's flight path.

'We have made Glyn's sortie safer,' she said.

'No longer a suicide mission,' said Ida, 'but still risky.'

'We did all we could. Oh dear, that is such a funeral-parlour phrase. I'm sorry. I didn't mean it like that.'

Ida went over to the gun-metal-grey teleprinter, which stood on what used to be the fabric counter, long and broad enough for huge bolts of cloth, but now only pink ribbons of ticker tape littered its surface. Ida sifted through the coiled pink rinds of that morning's ticker traffic, lifting up tape after tape, just in case she had missed an earlier message.

There came a clacking sound as the teleprinter ejected half a yard of printed tape, which folded itself down to the table and then to the floor. Ida pounced on it, but still did not find what she was looking for.

As Merry ate the last square of American PX chocolate, she marvelled at how much had happened since her first square in the Dog and Badger. She had ridden pillion – a first! – on Ida's low-slung military motorcycle to Cheyne Place, on the river at Chelsea, where Austin's wife Jean had come down in her dressing gown to receive the covers.

Their package delivered, they had ridden across London at first light and flopped into bed in Denman Alley. While they slept, Dowding had authorised a bombing raid. So, while Glyn made his way to RAF Benson in Oxfordshire, sticks fell on radar stations and gun batteries in north-eastern Germany to clear his flight path. Hardly had the dust settled from this morning raid than Glyn's Blenheim had lifted off from RAF Benson.

The teleprinter again nickered into life. Ida read the pink spool of teletype as it emerged. She tore off the tape.

'Glyn's alive, Merry!' she cried. 'He crash-landed near the US base at Boxted.'

Ida ran into the carrel room, where Austin sometimes took secret calls, and phoned USAAF Boxted. When she emerged again, Merry was standing, waiting for her, outside.

'I spoke to the actual ambulance man who found him,' said Ida, eyes shining with joy. 'He's from Wichita Falls – can you believe that? He thought there were no survivors, but he followed the debris trail for a hundred yards, anyway, and found Glyn still sitting in his seat! Out cold and strapped in! He reckons what saved him was how quick the Blenheim disintegrated. Seems it just fell to pieces before the Messerschmitt could loop back around to finish them off.'

'God bless the Great British Blenheim!'

'Boxted have dispatched a motorcycle courier with the photographs,' said Ida. 'He'll be here in an hour or so. Most likely I'll pass him, going the other way.'

'You'll do what?'

'I'm going to Boxted.'

'Now?'

'Oh, Merry, I must!'

'No, Ida. No. Your blackout lights are useless. You can't see anything. Last night's ride was terrifying.'

'We made it here, didn't we?'

'We rode our luck! Don't go, Ida. Wait till tomorrow, I beg you.'

'I want to be there when he wakes up.'

'Why? What if he's already woken up before you get there? Will that be a wasted journey? I need you here. We've both just endured one long, torturous vigil for Glyn. Don't put me through another one for you. Is that what you want me to do? To fret and pace this empty office for a whole night at the prospect of losing you?'

'Sweetness, I will ride slowly and steadily and carefully.'

'No, you won't – you'll ride like a lathered-up mare in oestrus.' She walked to the window, twitching her shoulders and tossing her head in a most un-Merry-like way. She inexpertly lit a cigarette from the PX soft pack. 'I've been thinking lately, if only I could have persuaded Ken to skip the early show, stay with us for a drink in Soho, then he'd still be alive. He almost did. He was teetering on coming in. Please, let me persuade you, now.'

'Well, I'm not teetering, I'm going. But fear not, old heart. It's only seventy miles of road. That's what? Twenty minutes?'

'Ida!'

She had never heard Merry shout before. And it was a shout that set the closest metal ceiling lamp ringing.

'Have mercy!'

'Forgive me, Merry.'

'Stay with me,' she cried. 'Help me decipher the photos when they come.'

'You know you don't need me for that. Listen, Merry, I survived riding a motorcycle while the Abwehr took potshots at me. Trust me to ride to Essex and back on a near-empty road.'

Ida tried to kiss her, but Merry turned away, waving her off.

'All our nerves are fit to burst, Merry. When I come back, will you take me to Kirklockham? You said you would, remember? Meet your folks?'

Merry stood at the window's blackout boards, smoking noisily and drumming her fingernails on the brick sill, not looking at Ida, and pretending not to be able even to hear her when she said: 'Well, I'll see you. Goodnight, Merry.'

Ocular Proof

MERRY WOKE TO THE SOUND of footsteps. She had fallen asleep at her desk. The commissionaire was walking towards her, holding an envelope.

'This was delivered by a Yank motorcycle courier from 589th Army Postal Unit, attached to the US Eighth Air Force, miss. He impressed upon me its urgency. Several times, miss. More than was necessary. Like I was a ruddy idiot. Had half a mind to give him a right-hander, but resisted the urge.'

'Thank you, Charles.'

'Didn't want to cause an international incident.'

'Quite right, too.'

'Let me not be the man who sundered the Anglo-American alliance and left us at the mercy of the Hun, I thought. So I just bit my lip.'

'You did the right thing.'

In the Ladies', Merry filled the sink with cold water and submerged her face. With the small white folded square of her cotton handkerchief, she patted her face and neck dry, then crossed the empty late-night office, her heels echoing on the wooden floorboards, towards the L-shaped desk.

Squaring the stiff USAAF Boxted envelope containing the Peenemünde covers in front of her, she set out her stereoscope, her china-white pen and the jewellery box containing her loupe. But she put off opening the Boxted envelope for fear it may contain nothing worth the lives that had been risked to bring it to her desk in this empty office in this black night. She felt sick with dread. What if this envelope held no evidence of a rocket launch pad? What if Glyn's sortie had found no sign of any rockets anywhere? What if her hunch was wrong and she had jeopardised all those lives purely to satisfy an intellectual vanity that raised her own surmise on to the high altar of world-historical significance? If the photos in this packet showed no proof of rockets, the Air Ministry would never listen to another word from MI14, Austin would be a busted flush and their whole operation might be rolled up and subsumed under Medmenham and the command of a Carton or a Keating or some other cretin, and heaven help them all.

She opened the green metal thermos and drank the tepid dregs of Eighth Air Force coffee. Then she could put it off no longer. She opened the packet and found only six photographs. Since half of them were near duplicates, having been snapped a second or two apart, there were essentially three photographs in total. Her heart sank. Did this mean that, out of the whole roll of film, these were the only six that were not blurry snaps of Glyn's left boot? Or was this a good sign? Did it mean that Boxted's First Phase PIs were supremely confident that the covers had the precise information London wanted?

She arranged the first stereo pair on her desk and set her four-legged stereoscope over the twelve-by-twelve-inch prints. Lowering her head to its twin lenses, she took a breath, like a diver, and watched two dimensions become three.

Peenemünde had changed a lot since last she viewed it at Wembley, back in the phoney war, way back before Ida went to France. Since then, the area had undergone quite the construction boom. Those zigzag shadows were the ridges of factory roofs. That giant cake-tin silhouette was an oil silo, and definitely not a nanny goat circling on her tether. So far, so good. But there was nothing that said 'launch site', nothing that said 'V-weapons', no rocketry.

She placed the second pair of covers under the stereo, bowed her head to its lenses and waited for the pop. Those chamfered shadows in neat rows were army tents, those fruit peelings razor wire. That rectangle in a narrow tube was a juggernaut in a country lane – perhaps the very one that ran over the little boy delivering the morning papers in the dark, the boy whose death led to his classmates petitioning the mayor about daylight-saving hours. So, this was definitely a military base – but what good was that to her? What she needed was rockets. Where was that old ski-jump structure she'd seen in 1940, for heaven's sake? Had it been disassembled, packed up and carted off, like the fairground ride it always was?

She took out the last pair. The near-duplicate snaps showed a field between two conifer plantations with some scaffolding. A sports field with bleachers, perhaps. She aligned the photographs and placed her eyes to the stereoscope. When the stereo pair popped into 3D, she found herself down among the struts of a long ramp, perhaps one hundred feet long. A glistening monorail gleamed along its centre, like a snail's slime trail. She traced that trail to the base of the ramp, where it turned black and ran like a snake in the grass for perhaps forty feet. Her heart began thumping at the sight of this blackened grass.

She set aside her spectroscope and fetched out the loupe, placing it where the trail turned black at the foot of the monorail ramp. The loupe's extra resolving power revealed this black snake to be a long streak of scorched earth. Here were the scorch marks of rocket thrusters. Here was the first ever positive identification of a rocket launcher. She had tracked the V-weapons to their lair.

She whimpered with relief and sat back in her chair. Tears filled her eyes. She felt reprieved from the charge of having recklessly endangered lives. She might even have helped save some. From this site, pilotless rockets were to be aimed at London, but now it could be bombed. She drew out another of the USAAF Daws Hill cigarettes and lit it. The smell of toasted tobacco filled the room.

She heard a clicking sound. Through the turnstile came Austin, his high forehead catching the light as he passed under each green pewter hanging lamp.

They did a reversal of their usual mute show: him raising his eyebrows and her slowly nodding.

'It's here,' she said. 'It's here.'

She gave Austin her chair. Still in his coat, he bowed his head to the stereoscope.

'It's there all right,' he said. 'Dear God, it makes the blood run cold to think that the obliteration of London should come from these backwoods.'

'The yokel's revenge.'

'And how.'

'Is there absolutely no defence against rockets, Austin?'

'Only to destroy the launch site.'

'But you can't put the genie back in the bottle. Once we destroy the Peenemünde site, the Luftwaffe will simply shift their base of operations. Start manufacturing the V1s, V2s and V3s in some mountain cave that can't be bombed and can't be stopped.'

'Yes, but that will take time, and time is the great prize. You've won London a few months of respite. You may not have saved London for good, but you've saved it for now – and that is of incalculable value. Incalculable.'

'Not if it means that the Luftwaffe only put off till Michaelmas what they planned for Trinity.'

'No, Merry, it means the world. Literally, the whole world. For, the longer we stay in the war, the more likely our victory. That is what you, Ida and Glyn have together achieved. Let that sink in.'

'Yes, Austin.'

'I'll take these photos to the War Office now. Go home, Merry. Get some sleep. You are due a lot of leave, it seems to me. Why don't you go into the country? Take Ida to visit your country seat. Kirkleatham?'

'Kirklockham. Yes, that's just what I will do.'

'Unless it's become an RAF base. Just don't let me see hide nor hair of you for a month.'

They shook hands.

'Good night, Austin.'

'Good night, Danes.'

Merry watched him go, then packed up her stereoscope and her loupe and shut them in the desk drawer. As she raised her weary arms to the coat hook, she swayed and saw spots in her eyes. Her flared black coat had never seemed so heavy.

She walked across the empty office towards the exit, turned and looked back at the L-shaped desk, then clicked out the row of lights, one by one, until MI14 disappeared.

Charles the commissionaire was asleep at his station. Not wanting to wake him with its loud rattle, she climbed over the turnstile in the way she'd seen juvenile delinquents jibbing into the White City dog track.

Out in the street, Oxford Circus was as black as it must have been in Saxon times. But she knew the way home with her eyes closed, as the cabbies said, and, at the corner of Tottenham Court Road, luminous kerb paint helped her pick her way along for a block and a half.

As she turned into Wells Street, that old feeling returned which she used to experience when walking along the Beresford Road to Wembley: that enlarged sense of being personally enmeshed in intercontinental connections. Nor was this mere whimsy. Should Heinkels and Dorniers come howling over London in the next few days, that might well be in retaliation for the bombing raid against Peenemünde's rocket site, which Austin was now urging upon Dowding at the War Office night shift. Her sense of being intimately connected with faraway places was all too concrete.

She stumbled in the dark, her leg buckled and she twisted her right ankle. Sprained, she thought, but not broken. She balanced on her good leg and raised her other behind her like a flamingo to inspect the damage done. Her ankle was already a swollen jelly. 'That'll learn you to think big picture when walking home across bomb debris in the blackout,' she muttered to herself. 'Concentrate. Get home first, then fall apart.' She found she was able to put just enough weight on the ankle to hobble onwards.

She recalled sure-footed Kenrick Johnson walking her home in the dark, with his dancer's balance and his neat steps, his patent-leather dress shoes as shiny as luminous kerb stones. That night, she could tell that he was making a conscious effort to slow his usual pace, which made her feel as if she had sprouted a dowager hump and pince-nez, even though she was only five years older than he. She wished she had Ken's steadying arm now.

The pavement ahead of her ended abruptly in a large and deep bomb crater. Another step and she would have fallen in. Where was the wooden barrier or cordon tape? She peered over the lip of the abyss. She saw the timber barrier lying a few yards down, possibly sideswiped by a passing truck, or just thrown into the crater for a laugh. She hitched her skirt up over her knees and climbed backwards down a yard of churned earth. The pain this caused her ankle made her gasp. She reached the barrier, put her shoulder under its cross bar and wrapped an arm around one of its posts. Inch by inch, she hauled the timber barrier out of the crater. Once she had regained street level, she leant on the barrier until the pain subsided. Then she set it crosswise on the pavement. The next people who came along would step around the barrier into the road, as she did now, and not tumble headlong into the abyss.

She decided she had better cross the street to where there was pavement, but heard cars approaching in both directions. Their blackout lights pinstriped the street. The nearside car passed so close that she knew it couldn't have seen her. Now would be a good time, she told herself, to put on those ultraviolet gloves that Ida had given her.

Merry thrust both hands deep in her pockets. Her fingertips had just found the folded gloves when another vehicle came speeding out of nowhere, in too high a gear, its engine rising in both volume and pitch. Her heels were on the crater's lip. She had nowhere to step. She half-turned her body. The car struck her and knocked her backwards into the pit.

She lay at the foot of the bomb crater, in pain everywhere. She heard a car door open, heard a man say, 'Thought I hit something, but there's nothing here.'

She opened her mouth to shout, 'I'm down here!' – but blood poured out of her mouth and overflowed into her nose and over her cheekbones and into her ears. She heard the door slam and the car drive away.

If she could only turn her head, she was sure she could tip all this blood away. But her neck wouldn't budge. She needed her hands to scoop the blood away. She wriggled her shoulders, trying to free her arms from her coat. With a great moan of despair, she discovered the hands in her pockets to be as motionless as the gloves.

Blood filled her airways. She choked and spluttered and cried a bitter, furious gargling groan, for tomorrow she would have been in Kirklockham, and far from all this sorrow.

If a Tree Falls in the Forest

'IT IS AN AXIOM LONG ACCEPTED by philosophers that if a tree falls in the forest and no one is there to hear it, then it does not make a sound.'

'Not this one,' Ida said.

'You believe that if a tree falls in a forest and no one hears it, the tree still makes a sound?'

'Yes.'

The sign on the door of the Jowett Society read: *Do we perceive material things or just sense data? – A discussion between Professor A. J. Ayer and Ida Marshall.*

'All right, then,' said Freddie Ayer, her old adversary. 'Let me take a sounding to establish just how deeply sunk in error you are. May I ask, first of all, why you believe the tree still makes a sound even if there is no one there to hear it?'

'The falling tree will be heard by the insects that live in its bark.'

'Aren't most insects deaf?'

'All except bugs and butterflies, ants, moths and flies, katydids, grasshoppers, cicadas and crickets.'

'I bow before your greater store of entomological arcana.'

'Are the facts of life on earth more arcane than the silent world of your imagination?'

Ida found herself identifying with the neglected falling tree. She knew what it was like to fall in a forest and have no one hear. If it had been Dieter Wetzel who came out of the cave alive, nobody would have ever found her. She might have lain there for twenty thousand years, like the Cro-Magnon woman, but with no two parts of her as intact as that femur. In the forest, she had learnt of the imminent fall of France, but nobody in England would listen to her warning. People could hear if they wanted to, they just chose not to for reasons of conformity to fashionable nonsense – be it the fashionable nonsense of the military orthodoxy, which repudiated her Ardennes knowledge in favour of the Dyle Plan, or be it Freddie's fashionable intellectual solipsism. How easily scepticism about the existence of an outside world came to products of the English boarding school, who were so seldom allowed a peek over the school walls!

Merry fell in the dark with no one to hear, or no one save the hit-and-run driver, who must have heard a thud on his fender. Both Merry and Ida had been trees that fell in the forest – but must they go quietly?

'But what if there are no insects in this tree?' Freddie asked.

'I believe you said it's a forest, right?'

'Yes, my dear.'

'In which case, the falling tree will be surrounded by

other trees – trees that do host bugs, ants, butterflies, moths and mosquitoes.'

'Suppose all the trees around the falling tree are dead,' said Freddie. He smiled at the audience, who seemed to share his sense that the American was running out of caveats and exceptions to the rule, and would soon find herself trapped in a logical cleft stick.

'Ah, but dead wood attracts more insects than live wood,' said Ida.

This drew appreciative laughter from the audience, but only in anticipation of the fact that her inventions must from now on become ever more rococo the more she was boxed in, until she finally ran out of excuses. Their appreciative laughter was only for how well she was playing out the end game, how gallantly she fought her lost cause. But Ida herself did not feel that way.

'What you've conjured up, Professor Ayer,' she said, 'is nothing but a giant bug hotel, lousy with insects and swarming with insectivorous woodpeckers, warblers, chickadees, cuckoos and sparrows – not to mention bats, with their ultrasonic hearing. And, if bats can hear a moth's wing beat, they'll hear a falling tree.'

Ayer began to grow impatient. Time to close out.

'Let us assume that the trees are not just dead, but sterile,' he said, 'that they've been poisoned with some sort of insecticide, so there is no life of any kind in any of the trees around the tree that falls. Now, I ask you once again, if the tree falls and no one hears it, does it make a sound?'

For all Ida's passionate revolt against Freddie Ayer's line of argument, her brains did not, for once, get washed away by her own hot blood. Now, at last, she found herself able to be more Merry. Even though she did not know how to rebut Ayer's last objection, she did not panic, but inclined her head in the way that Merry used to do, a quizzical look on her face, and smiled. And then into her mind came the memory of the otter's brown eyes staring at her on the banks of the Meuse. The brown eyes had seemed to be waiting for her to find them, just like Merry's had been waiting after Ida had lost her place in the Wilfred Owen sonnet, and just like the following rebuttal had been waiting for her to find it, as she remembered the otter's underground holt:

'When the falling tree hits the forest floor, vibrations of its fall will be detected by the animals that live underground – otters, voles, shrews and foxes, and of course all the ants and bugs that live in the soil itself.'

'The soil does not support life of any kind,' said Ayer, with an imperious sweep of his arm.

'Please will you repeat what you just said?' said Ida.

'The soil does not support life of any kind,' he repeated testily.

Ida slowly folded her hands in her lap. Then she turned to Freddie and said, 'Then how did the forest grow?'

There was a long silence, followed by loud and hard applause. He was hoist by his own petard. She had won. She stood up, funnelled her hands around her mouth and shouted: 'Tiiiimbbbeeeerrrr!'

Which wasn't very Merry. But Merry would have enjoyed it. Because it was, after all, very Ida.

Fair Stood the Wind for France

ON THE TOP FLOOR of Peter Robinson, Austin placed another box of old tat on her desk.

'Here, you will find intelligence crucial to the invasion of north-west France. We have been tasked with building up a detailed picture of possible landing sites. Let's do one of our famous lucky dips.' He pulled a dog-eared black-and-white snap from the cardboard box and held it up to her. 'Now, apart from Darby and Joan snoozing in their deckchairs,' he asked, 'what do you see here?'

'Shingle,' she said.

'Can you be more exact?'

'Chert.'

'Significance?'

'From how deep the deckchair has sunk into the chert,' said Ida, 'can one perhaps calculate how deep a marine carrying full pack will sink? Amphibious landing craft too, maybe?'

'Go on.'

'And, from that, make a further calculation as to how long it might take them to struggle up the beach?'

'Excellent. And please notice how the exact grade of chert shows up clear as day in the foreground by the deck-chairs. You can even work out the diameter of the pebbles. This is important because small chert pebbles will snap tank tracks, but large ones a tank can roll over easy as pie. All this is precisely the sort of nitty-gritty completely invisible from a spy-in-the-sky. I'd much rather have a local news clipping from *La Presse de la Manche* about a shrimper run aground on a sandbank than a hundred undercover agents skulking around Normandy. It's all very well moving pins about a map, but who will do the hard thinking about how exactly a dozen commandos are supposed to climb from a rubber dingy straight on to a cliff?'

'Sounds like a lot of work.'

'I've seconded someone to assist you.'

'No, thank you.' Her gaze fell on the half of the L-shaped desk where Merry used to sit. 'I don't want anyone to take her place. I'd prefer to work on my own.'

'Why don't you just give them a chance?'

Over the clacking of typewriters, the ringing of phones and the nickering of teletype, Ida heard the turnstile's ratcheting twirl. She looked up. In RAF blue, and leaning on a walking stick, Glyn came limping towards them.

A Bouquet of Luminous Yellow Roses

THE EARLY MORNING SKY was heavy with grey-black clouds. The white-jacketed milkman's crate of bottles clinked as he carried them down what was left of the street. A grocer sluiced the pavement in front of his shop with a bucket. An air-raid warden shooed schoolchildren out of a windowless newsagent's, before resuming his search for the source of a small geyser of steam that was softly spraying the air, lending the morning a gauzy look. The last child to climb out of the newsagent's window frame was a stocky girl in a knitted orange cardigan. She paused with one leg in, one leg out of the shop, transfixed by a curious scene over by the bomb site.

A woman in an American army coat held a bouquet of luminous yellow roses. She stood in silence on the edge of the bomb crater. Her lips were moving as if she were saying a prayer or talking to the air. She tossed the yellow roses into the black earth of the charred crater, where the iron sky kindled their glow.

Acknowledgements

Rowan Cope, Clare Alexander, Lucy Whitaker, Leonie Gombrich, Sabine Durrant, Penelope Price, Georgina Difford and Vesselina Newman.

Conversations with my late friend Mary Midgley about wartime Oxford philosophy proved crucial, as did the following excellent reads: *Metaphysical Animals: How Four Women Brought Philosophy Back to Life*, Clare Mac Cumhaill and Rachael Wiseman; *A Terribly Serious Adventure: Philosophy at Oxford 1900–60*, Nikhil Krishnan; *The Women Are Up to Something*, Benjamin J. B. Lipscomb; *J. L. Austin: Philosopher and D-Day Intelligence Officer*, M. W. Rowe; *The Eye of Intelligence*, Ursula Powys-Lybbe; *Air Spy: The Story of Photo Intelligence in World War II*, Constance Babington-Smith; *Spies in the Sky: The Secret Battle for Aerial Intelligence During World War II*, Taylor Downing; *Women of Intelligence: Winning the Second World War with Air Photos*, Christine Halsall; *London War Notes*, Mollie Panter-Downes.